Crouching Buzzard, Leaping Loon

*Also by Donna Andrews
in Large Print:*

Revenge of the Wrought-Iron Flamingos

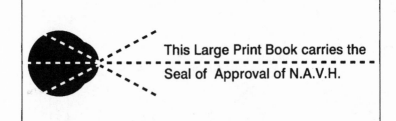

This Large Print Book carries the
Seal of Approval of N.A.V.H.

Crouching Buzzard, Leaping Loon

Donna Andrews

Thorndike Press • Waterville, Maine

Published in 2003 by arrangement with St. Martin's Press,
LLC.

Thorndike Press® Large Print Mystery Series.

The tree indicium is a trademark of Thorndike Press.

The text of this Large Print edition is unabridged.
Other aspects of the book may vary from the original edition.

Set in 16 pt. Plantin by Elena Picard.

Printed in the United States on permanent paper.

Library of Congress Cataloging-in-Publication Data

Andrews, Donna.
    Crouching buzzard, leaping loon / Donna Andrews.
        p. cm.
    ISBN 0-7862-5488-2 (lg. print : hc : alk. paper)
    1. Receptionists — Fiction. 2. Women detectives —
Fiction. 3. Psychotherapists — Fiction. 4. Computer
games — Programming — Fiction. 5. Large type books.
I. Title.
PS3551.N4165C7 2003b
    813'.54—dc21   2003045257

Thanks. . . .

To all the usual suspects and a few first-time offenders.

Stuart and Elka, my brother and sister-in-law, helped inspire this book by telling me about the day they walked into their therapy office to find themselves sharing space with an Internet startup company. For allowing me to poke gentle fun at their profession and helping me invent the Affirmation Bear, all my thanks.

Thanks also to Pat Tracy, who convinced me to study Kenpo; Jim Harbour, my teacher; and Al Tracy, his teacher (and Pat's husband). If they'd been in charge of Rob's martial arts training, Meg would have had a much easier time foiling the villain in this book.

I continue to be astonished and grateful for the patience of my friends, none of whom have ever thrown anything at me when they heard the familiar words, "Ooh, in the next book, I could have Meg. . . ." For brainstorming with me, straightening out my mangled facts, and reading manuscripts, usually on very short notice, many thanks to Elizabeth Sheley, Lauren Rabb, Mary Bird, David Niemi, Kathy Deligianis, Paul Thomas, Suzanne Frisbee, and Maria Lima.

I should note that the strange and unruly staff of Mutant Wizards are, of course, not based on any real programmers I have known. Especially not any of the ones who could figure out my password if they didn't like the way I portrayed them. For that matter, no specific therapists, police officers, family members, or other real beings were used in the making of this work of fiction, with the exception of Meg's dad and Spike, the small evil one. And they're used to being in my books.

Finally, thanks to all the online friends who keep me sane during those long hours at the keyboard, and to all the readers who make it seem worthwhile by continuing to tell me how much they enjoy visiting Meg's world.

As the Founder/CEO of NAVH, the only national health agency solely devoted to those who, although not totally blind, have an eye disease which could lead to serious visual impairment, I am pleased to recognize Thorndike Press as one of the leading publishers in the large print field.

Founded in 1954 in San Francisco to prepare large print textbooks for partially seeing children, NAVH became the pioneer and standard setting agency in the preparation of large type.

Today, those publishers who meet our standards carry the prestigious "Seal of Approval" indicating high quality large print. We are delighted that Thorndike Press is one of the publishers whose titles meet these standards. We are also pleased to recognize the significant contribution Thorndike Press is making in this important and growing field.

Lorraine H. Marchi, L.H.D.
Founder/CEO
NAVH

Chapter 1

"Mutant Wizards," I said. "Could you hold, please?"

I switched the phone to my left ear, holding it with my awkwardly bandaged left hand, and stabbed at a button to answer another line.

"Eat Your Way Skinny," I said. "Could you hold, please?"

As I reached to punch the first line's button and deal with the Wizards' caller, I heard a gurgling noise. I looked up to see that the automatic mail cart had arrived while I was juggling phones. A man lay on top, his head thrown back, one arm flung out while the other clutched the knife handle rising from his chest. He gurgled again. Red drops fell from his outstretched hand onto the carpet.

"Very funny, Ted," I said, reaching out to press the button that would send the mail cart on its way again. "You can come back later to clean up the stage blood."

I could hear him snickering as the cart beeped and lurched away, following an invisible ultraviolet dye path that would lead it out of the reception room and into the main office area. I'd gotten used to seeing a set of metal shelves, six feet long and four high, creeping down the corridor under its own steam, but I was losing patience with the staff's insatiable appetite for playing pranks with the mail cart.

Ted leaned upside down over the side, waggled the rubber knife suggestively, and made faces at me until the cart turned to the left and disappeared.

I scanned the floor to see if he'd shed any more valuables this time — after his first tour through the reception area, I'd found eighty-five cents in change and his ATM card, and a coworker had already turned in a set of keys that were probably his. No, apparently his pockets were now empty. I wondered how long before he came looking for his stuff — I wasn't about to chase him down.

Then I glanced at the young temp I was teaching to run the switchboard. Uh-oh. Her eyes were very wide, and she was clutching her purse in front of her with both hands.

"What happened to him?" she asked.

"Ignore Ted; he's the office practical joker," I said. "He's harmless."

I could tell she didn't believe me.

"What about that?" she asked, pointing over my shoulder.

I followed her finger.

"Oh, that's just George, the office buzzard," I said. "He's harmless, too."

When he saw me looking at him, George shuffled from foot to foot, bobbed his head, and hunched his shoulders. I suspected this behavior was the buzzardly equivalent of a cat rubbing itself against your ankle when it hears the can opener. At any rate, George had started doing it on my second or third day here, when he realized I was the one delivering his meals. I'd actually begun to find this endearing — doubtless a sign I'd been at Mutant Wizards too long. The temp edged away, as if expecting George to pounce.

"Don't worry," I said. "He can't fly or anything. He's got only one wing. One of the staff rescued him from some dogs and brought him back for a company mascot."

I vowed once again to try convincing my brother that a buzzard was an unsuitable mascot for his computer game company. Or at least that the mascot shouldn't live in the reception area, where visitors had to see him. And smell him.

"He stinks," the temp said.

"You get used to it."

"You've got four lines lit up," the temp said, pointing to the switchboard, and then jumped as a loud snarling noise erupted from beneath the counter of the reception desk. I knew it was only Spike, the nine-pound canine-shaped demon for whom I was dog-sitting, testing the wire mesh on the front of his crate, but the sound seemed to unnerve the temp.

"Why don't you take over now?" I suggested. "I can stick around until you get the hang of it, and then —"

"I'm sorry," she said, backing toward the door. "I probably should have told the agency not to send me out at all today. I'm really not feeling very well. Maybe I should —"

"Meg!" my brother, Rob, shouted, bursting into the reception room. "Take a look!"

He proceeded to fling himself about the room, performing a series of intricate shuffling movements with his legs while flailing his arms around, hunching his shoulders up and down, and uttering strange, harsh shrieks at irregular intervals.

Normally, the appearance of my tall, blond, and gorgeous brother might have provided some additional incentive for a temp to stay. At least a temp this young. Under the circumstances, though, I wasn't surprised that the temp fled long before he ended up, perched on his left toes with his right leg thrust awkwardly out to the side and both arms stretched over his head.

"Ta-da!" he said, teetering slightly.

I sighed and punched a ringing phone line.

"Meg?" Rob said, sounding less triumphant. "Was my kata okay?"

"Much better," I said as I transferred the call. "I just wish you wouldn't practice in the reception room."

"Oh, sorry," he said, breaking the pose. "Who was that running out, anyway?"

"Today's temporary switchboard operator," I said. "She decided not to stay."

"I'm sorry," he said. "I guess I did it again."

I shrugged. It was partly my fault, after all. I was the one who'd invented the fictitious Crouching Buzzard kata — named, of course, for our mascot, George — and taught it to Rob in a moment of impatience. Or perhaps frustration at his unique

13

combination of rabid enthusiasm and utter incompetence.

And to think that when Rob first became obsessed with the martial arts, I'd encouraged him, naively believing it would help build his character.

"Give him backbone," one of my uncles had said, and everyone else around the Langslow family dinner table had nodded in agreement.

Rob had brains enough to graduate from the University of Virginia Law School. Not at the top of his class, of course, which would have required sustained effort. But still, brains enough to graduate and to pass the bar exam on the first try, even though instead of studying he'd spent his preparation classes inventing a role-playing game called Lawyers from Hell.

He then turned Lawyers from Hell into a computer game, with the help of some computer-savvy friends, and failing to sell it to an existing computer-game maker, he'd decided to start his own company.

As usual, his family and friends tripped over each other to help. My parents lent him the initial capital. I lent him some money myself when he hit a cash flow problem and was too embarrassed to go back to Mother and Dad. Michael

Waterston, my boyfriend, who taught drama at Caerphilly College, introduced him to a computer science professor and a business professor who were restless and looking for real-life projects. The desire to stay close to these useful mentors was the main reason Mutant Wizards ended up in the small, rural college town of Caerphilly, instead of some high-tech Mecca like San Jose or Northern Virginia's Dulles-Reston corridor.

And now, less than a year later, Rob was president of a multimillion-dollar company, inventor of the hottest new computer game of the decade, and founder of Caerphilly's small but thriving high-tech industry.

Not bad for someone who knew next to nothing about either computers or business, as Rob would readily admit to anyone who asked — including *Forbes* magazine, *Computer Gaming World*, and especially the pretty coed who profiled him in the Caerphilly student paper.

At the moment, the young giant of the interactive multimedia entertainment industry was looking at George and frowning. George ignored him, of course, as he ignored everyone too squeamish to feed him. Although I noticed that when

15

Rob was doing his phony kata, George had paid more attention than he usually did to humans. Maybe I'd accidentally invented something that resembled buzzard mating rituals. At least George wasn't upset. I'd found out, on moving day, that when George got upset, he lost his lunch. Keeping George calm and happy had become one of my primary goals in life.

"He's looking a little seedy," Rob said finally.

"Only a little?" I said. "That's rather an improvement."

"Seedier than usual," Rob clarified. "Sort of . . . dirty. Do you suppose he needs a bath?"

"Absolutely not," I said, firmly. "That would destroy the natural oils on his feathers. Upset the chemical balance of his system. Play havoc with his innate defenses against infection."

"Oh, right," Rob said.

Actually, I had no idea what washing would do to a buzzard. All I knew is that if George needed washing, I'd be the one stuck doing it. And I suspected it would upset him. No way.

"Then what about birdbaths?" Rob said.

"For small birds," I said. "Songbirds. And they only splash gently."

"That's right," Rob said, his face brightening. "They clean themselves with sand."

"Exactly."

"We can get him a sandbox, then," Rob said. "You can rearrange the chairs to make some room for it. What do you think?"

He was wearing the expression he usually wore these days when he suggested something around the office. The expression that clearly showed he expected his hearers to exclaim, "What an incredible idea!" and then run off to carry it out. At least that was what his staff usually did. I was opening my mouth to speak when —

"Rob! There you are!"

We both looked up to see Mutant Wizards' chief financial officer at the entrance to the reception area.

"We've got a conference call in three minutes."

Rob ambled off, and I dealt with the stacked-up calls. A sandbox. I'd been on the verge of coming clean. Confessing to Rob that Crouching Buzzard was a practical joke, not an abstruse kata.

Instead, as I whittled down the backlog of phone calls for Mutant Wizards and for the motley collection of therapists with whom we shared office space, I began in-

venting a new kata, one even more fiend-
ishly difficult and amusing to watch.

Stop that, I told myself, when I realized
what I was thinking. I wasn't here to invent
imaginary katas. Or to mind the switchboard. I was supposed to find out what was
wrong at Mutant Wizards.

It all started two weeks ago, when Dad
and Michael brought me back from the
emergency room with my left hand hidden
in a mass of bandages the size of my head.

"Wow, what happened?" asked Rob,
through a mouthful of Frosted Flakes.
He'd come over to Michael's apartment to
feed and walk Spike while the rest of us
were at the hospital, and had stayed to
empty the pantry.

"Long story," I said, and disappeared
into the bathroom for a little privacy. Michael went to the kitchen to fix me some
iced tea, while Dad, a semiretired general
practitioner, began telling Rob in excruci-
ating detail exactly what was wrong with
my hand and what the doctors at Caerphilly Community Hospital had done to
repair it, along with a largely favorable cri-
tique of their professional expertise. I
sighed, and Michael reached over to pat
my good hand.

Yes, I know I said he was in the kitchen

18

and I was in the bathroom. The kitchen of the Cave, as we called Michael's one-room basement apartment, consisted of a microwave and a hot plate perched atop a mini refrigerator. The bathroom was separated from the kitchen by a curtain I'd hung five minutes after walking in the door on my first visit. The seven-foot ceiling felt claustrophobic to me, so I could only imagine how it affected Michael at six feet four inches. The fact that several of Michael's colleagues envied him for snagging these princely quarters showed how tight living space was in Caerphilly.

"Actually, I meant how did she injure it?" Rob said. I could tell by his voice that he was turning a little green. Rob fainted at the thought of blood. "What happened, Meg?"

"Like I said, long story."

"My fault," Michael said. "She was trying do her blacksmithing in that tiny studio I found for her, and it was just too small. She hit her elbow on a wall while hammering something, and hammered her other hand instead."

"Too bad," Rob said.

You have no idea, I thought, staring into the cracked mirror, fingering the bruises and lacerations that covered my face. Michael had forgotten to mention that, along with my hand, I'd also banged the hell out of a structural wall and brought part of the ceiling down on my own head. The studio might have worked for a painter, but it was just too small for a blacksmith. Still, I'd tried to make it work. Tried desperately, because after nearly a year of looking for somewhere for the two of us to live and me to work, the tiny basement apartment and the even tinier converted garden-shed studio were the best we'd found. Apart from being painful and keeping me out of work for weeks, my injury meant that I still hadn't found a place to work in Caerphilly, and we'd have to go back to square one, with me living several hours away in suburban northern Virginia, seeing Michael only when one or the other of us could get away from work for long enough.

Although obviously I wouldn't be working for a little while, I thought, staring at the bandage.

"How long till she can do her blacksmithing again?" Rob had asked, as if reading my mind.

"At least two months," Dad said.

"That's great!" Rob exclaimed.

"Rob!" Dad and Michael said it in unison, and I stuck my head through the bathroom curtains to glare at him.

"What I meant was, it's too bad about the hand, but I have a great idea about what she can do in the meantime," Rob said hastily. "Remember how I was saying that I think there's something wrong at Mutant Wizards? Maybe Meg could come and pretend to work there and figure out what's going on."

"That's brilliant, Rob!" Dad exclaimed.

"Except for one tiny detail," I said. "What on earth could I possibly do at a computer company?"

"You can organize us!" Rob said, flinging his arms out with enthusiasm. "You said yourself that you can't imagine how we'll ever get moved into our new offices and that we should hire a competent office manager. You're perfect for it!"

I wondered if he really was worried about the company, or if that was just an excuse to get me to come and organize them.

"I was rather thinking Meg could come back to California for the last few weeks of my shoot," Michael said. "You'll have plenty of time to rest while I'm filming, and then we can spend time together in the evenings."

Nice try, but I knew better. Oh, not that

he didn't mean it. But I'd seen what Michael's life was like when he was filming these TV guest shots. He'd be up at dawn for makeup call. I'd twiddle my one working thumb during the twelve to fourteen hours he was shooting. And then, over dinner, when he wasn't mumbling lines under his breath, he'd be fretting about whether playing a lecherous, power-mad sorcerer on a cheesy syndicated TV show was really how a serious actor — not to mention a professor of drama — should spend his summer break.

Maybe not. But he enjoyed it so much that I didn't have the heart to say so. And besides, it paid well.

And while the few decent houses we'd found for sale in Caerphilly over the past year were well beyond the means of Professor Waterston and Meg the blacksmith, they might not be unreachable for Mephisto the sorcerer. Especially if they signed him for several more episodes.

And if you added in what my Mutant Wizards stock might be worth if the company continued successful, home ownership might eventually be within our means. Which, I realized, gave me more than an idle interest in why Rob thought there was something wrong at his company.

I glanced up to see that all three were looking at me expectantly.

"So, what's your decision?" Michael asked.

I should know better than to make major decisions while taking Percocet.

Chapter 2

I frowned at the ibuprofen bottle perched on the reception desk. Mutant Wizards had been so much easier to tolerate with Percocet. Still, having a clear mind had some advantages. I answered all the blinking lines in two minutes flat, cleared out the calls on hold, and was phoning in a cry for help to the temp agency when I heard the suite door open.

I looked up and froze with my lips halfway into a smile.

A pale young woman wearing a LAW-YERS FROM HELL T-shirt sidled into the reception area. She smiled in my general direction, but her eyes slid right over me and feverishly scanned the opening that led back to the main part of the offices.

"Hi," she said, absently fingering an ear decorated with at least a dozen varied rings and studs. "I wonder if you could help me."

24

"Probably not," I said. "And anyway, why would I want to?"

I'm not usually that rude to visitors. But this wasn't your usual visitor.

"Huh?" she gasped, finally looking at me.

"I was here last Monday when you came around, pretending you were from the plant-care service," I said. "And also on Wednesday, when you claimed you were bringing your boyfriend his lunch. And I'm the one who caught you trying to crawl in through a window last Friday."

"You must have me confused with someone else," she began.

"Just give up, will you? Buy a copy of Lawyers from Hell II on December first, when it goes on sale. No one's going to give you a sneak preview before then, no matter how long you hang around here harassing people in the parking lot. I wasn't here when that CD-ROM found its way into your purse, but I heard about that, too."

I'm not sure I'd have gotten rid of her, even after being so blunt — I'd been working at Mutant Wizards only for two weeks, but I'd already seen how persistent the rabid Lawyers from Hell fans could be. But help arrived: Katy, a 170-pound Irish wolfhound, strolled into the reception area and gave a gruff, bass bark.

Anyone who worked here would have known that the bark was Katyese for "Hi! Don't you want to feed me? It's been at least five minutes since I ate, and I might starve to death any second. So feed me! Please?"

The fan looked nervous, though. Not surprising; Katy was large, even for a wolfhound, and she had a disconcerting habit of not wagging her tail when she was trying to look pitiful. Or perhaps the fan was intimidated by the frantic growling that emerged from beneath the reception desk. If she could have seen Spike, the source of the growling, she'd probably have laughed — ironic, since Spike, though only a nine-pound fur ball, was much more liable to cause grievous bodily harm than mild-mannered Katy. Fortunately, Spike was confined to a dog crate, on the theory that eventually he'd calm down enough to participate fully in the Mutant Wizards' Bring Your Dog to Work policy. I wasn't betting on it.

Just then, the suite door opened, and a tall figure in a blue police uniform jingled his way into the reception area.

"Can I help you, ma'am?" he said.

The persistent fan turned and fled. If she'd been paying attention, she might have noticed that the uniform fit rather badly. Or wondered if many real police officers wore black leather Reeboks and hung PEZ dispensers from their belts in addition to handcuffs and nightsticks.

"Ma'am? Ma'am?" he called, following her into the hall. "Hey, lady, come back, please!"

The fan pressed the elevator button and then, when she saw he was following, bolted into the open door to the stairwell. Which was how most people came and went anyway, since the World War II-vintage elevators rarely arrived in less than ten minutes.

"Jeez, Meg, I'm sorry," he said, taking off his hat and wiping sweat from his forehead. I recognized the tall, gangly figure now. Frankie, one of the junior programmers. I was still struggling to attach names to faces for most of the thirty or so programmers and graphic artists on staff. Frankie I'd tagged the first day as "the eager one," because he was always underfoot, trying to help with anything anyone was doing. Anything, that is, except the apparently boring programming chores that actually constituted his job.

"Don't worry about it, Frankie," I said.

"It was that rabid fan again."

"The one who tried to get herself delivered in a Gateway box?"

"That's the one," I said. "So why are you dressed up like Caerphilly's finest?"

"The art department is going to use me as a model for some new characters," Frankie said. "What do you think?"

He twirled for me to admire his outfit.

"I'm amazed," I said. I was, actually. The uniform so emphasized Frankie's gangliness that he looked remarkably like a stork. And his habit of balancing on one leg and wrapping the other around it only enhanced the resemblance.

I must have kept a straight face, though. Frankie beamed with delight.

"Just make sure you're leading the pack if I have to push the panic button," I said.

"Panic button?" he said, blinking vacantly.

"We went through this last week," I said. "This button under the desk that the receptionist can push discreetly if he or she feels threatened, remember? And it rings the bell back in the offices —"

"And we all run out to the reception area and rescue the receptionist from the intruder."

"Very good."

"Unless you're filling in for the receptionist, in which case we'd probably need to rescue the intruder," Frankie said, accompanying his words with a flailing gesture that was probably supposed to be some kind of karate move. Either that, or he was swatting gnats.

"Yes," I said, gritting my teeth. "That button."

"Right," Frankie said. "No problem. I'd better go; the art guys are waiting."

A model? I mused, as Frankie stalked off. True, Lawyers from Hell was populated with hundreds of characters — defendants, jurors, judges, bailiffs, arresting officers, witnesses, reporters, and, of course, lawyers. But they were represented on screen by cartoon characters, maybe an inch tall at the most. And while the graphic artists had done a wonderful job of giving them distinctive personalities, I had a hard time imagining the process required models.

Maybe it was just a practical joke to get Frankie to show up at the office in a police uniform, I thought, as I gave Katy a doggie treat and thumped her gently on the head with my bandage. That sounded more likely, here at Mutant Wizards.

I glanced up to see what Liz, Mutant

Wizards' real live lawyer, thought of Frankie's outfit. Way up, since that's where she was at the moment. The office was mostly a jungle of cubes with five-foot partitions. Even the few enclosed rooms — the reception area, the executives' offices, the lunchroom, and the central library — generally had partitions instead of real walls. Sturdier partitions that were eight feet high instead of five, but partitions, just the same. The only permanent rooms in the whole place were the computer lab, which had floor-to-ceiling glass walls, and the bathrooms, which had old-fashioned solid walls, thank goodness. And the therapists' offices, of course, which were off on a small side corridor that would have given them a lot more privacy if it hadn't led to the bathrooms.

On the plus side, the minimal number of real walls meant that every part of the office got a lot of natural light, which not only cut the electric bill but also helped morale — the long hours the staff worked would otherwise have kept many of them from seeing sunlight for days on end. On the minus side, it made for a pretty noisy environment, and anyone who wanted to chat privately with one of his creditors or make an appointment with her gynecologist usually ended up dragging a cell phone into the john.

It also meant that when Liz was hitting the books, boning up for a complicated legal brief, as she had been for the last several days, I could usually see her, sitting atop a set of library steps, leafing through books from the topmost shelves, to which the legal reference works had been exiled. The lower shelves, of course, were packed with books on programming and military history, not to mention gaming magazines and obscure and incomprehensible comics and graphic novels.

I could see that she had looked up from her book and her eyes were following something down the corridor Frankie would have taken. She glanced over at me with one eyebrow raised, as if to say, "What on earth did you let into the office?" I shrugged, and she rolled her eyes, shook her head, and returned to her book with a smile.

I turned back to the switchboard, also smiling. Liz was one of the few other females at Mutant Wizards. Also one of the few other normal people. And at the risk of being accused of female chauvinism, I confess that I didn't think this was a coincidence.

"I am a strong, self-reliant woman who makes her own decisions," a voice said at my elbow. I frowned. Not that I didn't approve of the sentiment, but it didn't sound quite normal when uttered in a voice that sounded like a kiddie-show host on helium. Spike didn't like it either, I deduced from the growl at my feet.

"Good morning, Dr. Brown," I said, glancing first at the bubblegum pink plush teddy bear and only as an afterthought at the more nondescript woman holding it.

"How do you like my new invention?" she asked. "I call it an Affirmation Bear. Every time you press his tummy, he delivers another positive, affirming statement to his human friend."

She demonstrated.

"I take care of my body by practicing wellness and exercising regularly," the bear squeaked. Spike began barking hysterically at the sound.

"Fascinating," I said. And meant it, actually; though what really fascinated me was trying to figure out what strange pranks the programmers would play if — no, make that "when" — they got their hands on the Affirmation Bear. And was she just here to show me the bear, or was she about to lodge another complaint?

Dr. Brown was one of the six therapists who had a preexisting sublease on part of the office suite into which Mutant Wizards had just moved. Liz, the lawyer, had negotiated valiantly to have them kicked out or bought out, with no luck. Thanks to the surrounding county's militant antigrowth policy, the office space market in Caerphilly was only slightly better than the housing market, and the therapists had no intention of giving up their quarters.

They had whined and complained their way through the build-out, but back then only Liz, Rob, and the real estate broker had to listen to them. Last Monday's moving day was a disaster. Liz had given the therapists ample warning and arranged to move as much stuff as possible over the weekend, to limit disruption during working hours. Maybe that helped a little. But moving day was the first time techies and therapists had to coexist in the same space. It was loathe at first sight.

Last Monday was also when I'd realized that I'd suddenly acquired responsibility for keeping the peace between the two groups. They'd quickly gotten used to running to me with their complaints and outrageous requests, like squabbling children running to their mother. I was already sick and tired of it.

But it's temporary, I told myself, forcing a smile onto my face as I looked at the garish pink bear. I can leave as soon as I figure out what's wrong, or reassure Rob that nothing's wrong. Or, more likely, as soon as my hand gets better. How can Rob expect me to get to the bottom of some kind of wrongdoing if I have to spend all day minding the switchboard, keeping the shrinks and the geeks from killing each other, and listening to people's talking toys?

"Chill, Spike," I said. "It's only a bear."

"Here, would you like to try it?" Dr. Brown asked, thrusting the bear into my hands. "Just tickle his tummy to make him talk."

I tickled. Nothing happened.

"You have to tickle a little harder."

I finally got the bear to talk. It took a bit more than tickling; I'd have called it a gut punch.

"I am a calm, rational person who never resorts to physical violence to solve my problems," the bear reprimanded me. Spike settled for growling this time.

"Why don't you keep that one and try it out for a few days?" Dr. Brown suggested.

I glanced behind her and realized that she was dragging around a box larger than the one Dad's new monster television had come in. And it was chock-full of Affirmation Bears — all, alas, in the same ghastly shade of pink.

"Toodle-oo!" she said as she left the reception area, trailing the box behind her.

My spirits rose — was it possible that she was going to wander around the office, passing out flamingo-colored teddy bears to anyone she encountered? That would certainly shorten the time it took for the guys around the office to turn Affirmation Bear into Withering Insult Bear, Dirty Limerick Bear, Monty Python Quote Bear, or whatever else struck their fancy.

I whacked the bear in the tummy again.

"I always try to see the best in every situation," the bear advised, and fell off the desk.

As I leaned down to pick him up, I saw a slender black paw reach out to bat at him. I leaned down farther and peered into the space where the drawer would have been if Rob hadn't removed it earlier that morning to make room for the latest addition to our menagerie: a very small but very pregnant black cat.

"If you want him, you can have him," I

told her. She hissed softly and withdrew as far back into the drawer space as she could. I sighed. Cats usually warm to me much faster.

Then again, maybe it wasn't me. Maybe it was everything else. Especially the number of dogs wandering in and out, not to mention having Spike caged only a few feet away beneath the other end of the desk.

While answering yet another line, I suddenly started. Someone was hovering at my shoulder. It was Roger, my least favorite programmer. He'd been hovering near me a lot, since my arrival — to the point that I'd begun to suspect he was working up his nerve to ask me out. Of course, to manage that, he'd have to figure out how to talk to me, instead of addressing random cryptic remarks to the ceiling of a room we happened to be sharing. I was only half joking when I'd tagged him "the Stalker." I made a mental note to bring in a picture of Michael and me together, so I could make sure Roger saw me gazing fondly at it. I pretended to be so absorbed in the switchboard traffic that I didn't see Roger, and eventually he wandered off.

The mail cart chugged through again,

with Ted still draped on top. The switch-board routine worked so well on Roger that I repeated it with Ted, pretending the calls absorbed my attention so completely that I could barely be bothered to punch the switch to set the cart in motion.

Spike barked hysterically until the cart disappeared. I wondered, briefly, what Ted was doing to set him off. But just then my pager went off.

I found the right button to silence its beeping and, after several tries, managed to read the message.

COPIER 2 OUT OF PAPER.

"That's it," I said. "Will someone please explain why they think it's easier to go back to their desks and page me about the copier, when the damned paper is just sitting there on the shelf, waiting to be loaded?"

"Because they're idiots?" suggested a baritone voice behind me. I turned to see Jack Ransom, one of the team leaders. I'd have nicknamed Jack "the Hunk" if it didn't feel disloyal to Michael, so I settled for "the Sane One." He didn't have a lot of competition for either title.

He had propped his tall, rangy frame against the partition just inside the opening that led to the main part of the office and was watching me with folded arms and a wry smile. I couldn't help smiling back, although something about the way he was looking at me suggested that yes, it probably was a good idea to buy a nice frame for that picture of Michael and me last New Year's Eve, and place it prominently on my desk.

"I thought they were supposed to be brilliant and original programmers," I said.

"Idiots savants, then," he said. "Want me to see about the paper?"

"You're an angel," I said. And then, worried that my enthusiasm would make him jump to a wrong conclusion, I concentrated on frowning at the pager while he strode off.

The pager had served its purpose when we were moving, and no one knew whether they could find me at the old offices or the new or maybe down in the parking lot, putting the fear of God into the movers.

But now that we were settled in and they always knew where to find me . . . Yes, it was time for a discussion with Rob. About abuse of the pager.

And also abuse of my cell phone, which had started ringing. I reached over and punched the button to answer it.

"This had better be good," I said.

"Do I sense that you're having a less than pleasant morning?" Michael asked.

"Sorry. Yeah, you could say that," I said, sinking back into my chair. "No worse than usual, really. Where are you calling from?"

"One of the parking lots natives of Los Angeles playfully call freeways. The 110, I think. Or did I already turn onto the 101? I'll have plenty of time to figure it out before the next turn; we're only going about three miles an hour."

"Sounds stressful."

"Mostly just boring," he said with a chuckle. "I think it would get stressful if I knew I had to do it for longer than a couple more weeks. So now that I know how your day's going, give me the details."

With brief interruptions to field phone calls, I told Michael about my morning, trying to sound light and amusing instead of frazzled and whiny. Apparently it worked.

"No wonder you keep refusing to come out to Los Angeles," he said. "I don't have anywhere near that much fun on the set."

I hoped he was serious. I knew that in the episode they were filming this week, Michael's character had to seduce an Amazon princess. That was the one thing I didn't like about the TV gig — apart from its location across the country, of course. Why couldn't they have cast Michael as the prim, puritanical monk character? Or any other role that didn't involve romancing so many female guest stars? I fingered the fading but still visible lacerations on my face and sighed. Another reason I'd decided to remain in Caerphilly for the time being. At my best, I knew my looks couldn't compete with the parade of twenty-something starlets who populated the show's sound stage, and while Michael seemed to appreciate my other qualities, I still thought I'd be better off avoiding a side-by-side comparison with them until I'd healed a bit.

I looked up to see that the mail cart was again chugging around the corner into the reception area, with Ted still on board.

"Oh, Lord," I said.

"What's wrong?" Michael asked.

"Here comes the mail cart again. Are you sure you didn't bribe Ted to do this? So anywhere would seem better than staying here?"

He chuckled.

"No, but it's a thought," he said. "Who is Ted, and how do I reach him to bribe him?"

If I were Rob, I thought, I'd crack down on Ted — speak to him about cutting out all these practical jokes. Not because of how disruptive they were; Ted would counter that by accusing the complainer of having no sense of humor. But clearly, if he spent this much time on practical jokes, Ted couldn't possibly be putting in a full day on his job. And we were on a tight deadline to release Lawyers from Hell II, weren't we?

Of course, if I asked Rob to crack down on Ted, he'd probably tell me to take care of it. Me or Liz, and part of my assignment as temporary office manager was to take over a lot of the nonlegal responsibilities Rob had dumped on Liz.

So maybe I'd put off speaking to Rob until I had time to deal with Ted myself. Or maybe I shouldn't even bother speaking to Rob. Just pretend I already had Rob's authority and put the fear of God into Ted. I rather liked the idea.

The mail cart had stopped at my elbow, but I planned to ignore it until I had time to tackle Ted. I focused on Michael.

"I should go now," he was saying. "But one more thing —"

I heard a scratching noise by my feet. I glanced down and saw that the cat had emerged from her hiding place and was batting at something hanging down from the mail cart. It was an off-white computer cord, the thin kind that attaches a mouse to the computer.

Why was Ted riding around trailing mouse cords?

My eyes followed the cord up to Ted's throat. The mouse cord was wrapped around it, tightly, and the mouse lay neatly in the middle of his chest.

I glanced at his face and then pulled my eyes away quickly, wishing I hadn't. He wasn't just playing dead. He really was dead.

I sat there, watching the cat bat at the trailing end of the mouse cord for a few moments, until I realized that several lines on the switchboard were blinking. And George was getting restless.

"Dream on," I told George.

"What?" Michael said. I'd forgotten I was still holding the cell phone.

"Oh, Michael, I'm sorry; I have to go now; I think he's really dead this time," I said, and hung up.

By now, all the switchboard lines were blinking. No free lines. No problem, I thought; I'll use the panic button.

No, I thought, as common sense began

42

to return. The only people who would answer the panic button were any employees still quivering from my earlier rant about not abandoning the switchboard operator in an emergency. Probably the last people I wanted around in a real emergency.

So I began waving frantically, hoping Liz would look up from her law book soon and come to my aid.

My cell phone rang. It was Michael. Of course; I could use the cell phone to call out.

"Meg, what do you mean? Who's really dead?"

"Ted, the practical joker," I said. "Listen, right now I really need to call the police."

Chapter 3

"Meg, can't I — ?"

"No. Stay out," I said. I was standing in the opening that separated the reception area from the rest of the office, arms folded, keeping people from leaving the premises or traipsing through the crime scene before the police arrived.

Part of the crime scene, anyway. For all I knew, Ted could have been killed anywhere in the office. And any time during the last several hours. The few people I'd been able to ask had, like me, been ignoring him so successfully that we had absolutely no idea when we last noticed signs of life. But since there was no way I could cordon off the entire office, I settled for the reception area. Abandon hope, all ye who even think of entering here before I say so.

"But I need to get some lunch," Frankie the Eager whined. I frowned more sternly while wondering if Frankie could possibly be old enough to have graduated from high school. Make that junior high. Did child labor laws apply to programmers?

"Later," I said. "After the police get here. When the police say you can."

"Aw, c'mon," he began.

"Never mind," said his much shorter companion, whom I recognized as Rico, one of the graphic designers. Actually, I recognized his RHODE ISLAND SCHOOL OF DESIGN T-shirt; without that distinctive wardrobe item, Rico would be yet another vaguely familiar new face. I still hadn't quite determined whether Rico owned only the one T-shirt or whether his alumnus zeal had inspired him to buy a wardrobe of them, though observation of distinctive pizza stains pointed to the former.

"But I'm hungry!" Frankie whined.

Rico said something to him in a low voice.

"Okay," Frankie said. "I guess I can eat later."

They turned and disappeared. Planning to sneak out, of course. At the back door, they'd find Liz. Fat chance getting past her. Dad, who happened to be in the office providing technical advice to the programmers working on a proposed new Doctors from Hell game, was guarding the side door to the hall. Having achieved what some mystery buffs only dream about — getting close to a real, live murder — he'd normally be wild with excitement and thus useless as a watchdog. But since I'd refused to let him examine Ted's body, he was sulking, and had apparently decided that if he couldn't have any fun, neither could anyone else. I did hope the police showed up before anyone figured out how to escape by rappelling down the side of the building.

I heard a noise behind me — someone opening the front door. I turned and shouted.

"Stop right there! I said no one comes in, and I meant it!"

The door stopped about two inches open.

"You didn't tell us this was a hostage situation," murmured an unfamiliar voice out in the hall.

"It's not," I heard my brother, Rob, say. "That's just my sister, Meg, keeping people away from the crime scene. Meg? It's Rob. I have the police. Can we come in?"

"Of course," I said. "You should have identified yourselves; I thought you were just more stupid sightseers."

"You can stay outside, Mr. Langslow," the unfamiliar voice said. "We'll take it from here."

I heard murmured conversation from the hall, and then the door opened, cautiously, and a head appeared.

"Ms. Langslow? I'm Chief Burke."

Chief Burke was a balding, middle-aged African-American man whose laugh lines suggested that his face more often wore a smile than the current anxious frown.

"Please come in, Chief," I said. "I'm just trying to keep all the rubberneckers out."

"We appreciate that," he said, stepping a little farther into the reception room. "Could you — ? Oops!"

I heard a thud, followed by the squeaking voice of the Affirmation Bear.

"Whenever something makes me angry, I stop, take a deep breath, and try to see the humorous side of the situation."

"That's God-damned easy for you to say," the chief growled. And then he added, "Who the hell said that, anyway?"

"I'm sorry," I said. "I guess you tripped over the bear."

By this time, he had fished the bear out from under him and was frowning at it. "It talks?"

"Poke his stomach," I said.

He did, tentatively.

"Harder," I said. "Vent your frustration over being tripped."

The chief punched, harder, and I suspected, from his form, that he had boxed during his youth.

"Don't keep anger and hurt feelings bottled up inside," the bear advised. "Find positive ways of expressing negative feelings."

"Mouthy little thing," the chief said, heaving himself up with the help of a worried-looking officer in uniform. "Sure hope the grandkids don't want one of them for Christmas. So — good Lord."

He'd noticed George.

"Office mascot," I said quickly.

"O-kay," the chief said. "Thought for a moment maybe you'd waited a little too long to call us."

We both laughed — nervously, and maybe a little more than the joke deserved. I found myself wondering if they saw many murders here in Caerphilly.

"I'm going to have to clear people out of the crime scene while we investigate," he said.

"I figured as much," I said. "Can we shoo everybody down to the parking lot?"

"Well, by crime scene, all I meant was this room here, where he was killed."

"Yes, but he wasn't killed here. He was killed on the mail cart."

"Which is here in the reception area."

"Yes, now it is; but he certainly wasn't killed here. I've been sitting here at the switchboard all morning. I think I'd have noticed something as bizarre as one of my coworkers getting strangled with a mouse cord."

"Um . . . right," the chief said, glancing at George. "So someone moved the body?"

"Not really. He was on the mail cart."

"You're not suggesting some lunatic wheeled the mail cart in here without even noticing there was a dead body on it?"

I explained about the automated mail cart, Ted's obsession with it, and his annoying antics of the morning.

"Let me get this straight, then," the chief said. "We have no idea where he was killed, because he was riding the mail cart all over creation, and no idea when, because everyone was ignoring him all morning."

"You got it."

"You're not going to make this easy, are you?" he said. I was startled, until I realized he was looking up, not at me. "Okay," he said, turning back in my direction. "I guess we have to move all these good people out into the parking lot after all. You got an accurate list of who's supposed to be here?"

"On the reception desk," I said. "There's a copy of the phone list. I already marked the employees who aren't here today, earlier this morning, so I wouldn't put through calls to them; and the sign-in sheet shows the visitors."

Half a dozen police officers fanned through the suite to herd everybody out. Just then Liz appeared in the reception area.

"Chief Burke?" she said, extending her hand. "I'm Elizabeth Mitchell, the firm's general counsel."

The firm. I noticed that, as usual, she avoided uttering the words "Mutant Wizards." According to Rob, about every six weeks she'd send another earnest memo suggesting half a dozen logical reasons for changing the company's name. I could have told her this was useless — the only reason Rob had named his company Mutant Wizards was that he thought it sounded cool. If she wanted to change the name, she should forget logical reasons and try to think of an even cooler name.

"Pleased to meet you," the chief said. He

looked a little wary. Maybe he expected her to raise some objection to his investigation. Or maybe he just found her a little intimidating — many people did. Not physically — she was only about five feet four. But I'd seen some pretty tough characters, like the guys from the moving company, back down when she went toe to toe with them.

She was dressed, as usual, in monochrome — a slim, tailored black skirt, an off-white silk blouse, a scarf in tones of gray, black hose, and sensible black pumps. Only her face and hands kept her from looking like a black-and-white movie; and come to think of it, they didn't look real — just badly colorized. But she oozed chic, and I could easily have hated her, except for one thing — she always had some tiny flaw in her outfit. The sort of thing only another woman would notice. One day she'd been wearing two similar but not identical shoes. Another day one of her earrings had been bent at an odd angle so it looked as if a tiny hand was giving the world the bird. Last Friday, all day, she'd walked around with a spent staple stuck to the back of her calf, inside the pantyhose.

I wondered if this were deliberate, like the flaws oriental rug makers always included in their works. Since it wasn't the sort of thing I could ask without mortally embarrassing her, I'd probably never know.

And had she broken the curse today? No, I finally spotted the flaw. Poking up out of her collar was a tag, giving the size, fabric content, and manufacturer of her blouse. It was, I noticed, from an inexpensive catalog I sometimes ordered from. On her, the blouse looked chic, sophisticated, and expensive, just as it would in the catalog. On me, clothes from the same source always looked as if I'd chosen them with only a vague idea what size and cut would suit me, and kept them largely to avoid the trouble of a trip to the post office to return them.

She and the chief had begun chatting in what I recognized as the polite, small southern-town version of declaring one's turf and sparring for advantage. I left them to it and took out my cell phone to call Michael.

"Meg!" he exclaimed. "Thank God! Hang on a second." And then I heard him shout, "Can we take five?"

"Michael, you're on the set; I'll call back," I said.

"No, it's fine; they need to glue the mermaid queen's tentacles back on anyway. What's going on?"

I gave him the Cliff's Notes edition of what had happened, as I watched the chief and Liz talking — with the uniformed officer scribbling notes at the chief's elbow. Apparently, Liz was telling what she'd seen during the day. I saw her pointing up to her perch in the library, gesturing as if describing the mail cart. Then she made a face and stuck out her tongue at the chief. Since he only nodded calmly, I deduced she was describing something Ted had done while riding around on the cart, not actually opening hostilities with the local authorities.

"So, anyway," I said to Michael, "we've got the police crawling all over the office looking for I'm not sure what, and a dead body here in the reception room. I'd feel a lot better if they took Ted away before Dad has a chance to barge in and annoy the chief by trying to horn in on his investigation. You know how he is."

Michael chuckled. He had, indeed, seen plenty of examples of Dad's burning desire to get involved in real-life crime. As a sleuth, of course, not an actual perp.

"Just don't let your dad suck you in," Michael advised. "Chief Burke is okay. I doubt he's investigated that many homicides, but he's a realist. I'm sure if he has any trouble finding the killer, he won't hesitate to call in the state authorities or the FBI or whoever small-town police chiefs call when they need backup."

"No problem," I said. "All I ever wanted to do was figure out if there's something fishy going on here, like Rob wanted."

"You think maybe Ted's murder just answered that question?"

"Definitely," I said. "And with luck, the chief will solve it all while he's wrapping up the murder."

"And then maybe I can talk you into coming out here for the rest of the shoot," Michael suggested. Was he a little too blasé about this? Easy for him, since he hadn't seen Ted's body. Then again, more likely he knew me well enough to realize that the last thing I needed was someone making a fuss about how I was holding up.

"That's sounding better and better," I said. "As soon as I'm sure everything's under control here, I'll book a flight."

"Fantastic!" Michael exclaimed. "Listen, they're ready for me — keep me posted on what's happening and when you're coming out, okay?"

"Will do," I said, and signed off.

While I'd been on the phone, a technician in a lab coat had arrived — a skinny kid so young I'd have mistaken him for an undergraduate. He'd begun doing what I recognized as a forensic examination of the reception area.

"There you are," the chief said when he saw I was off the phone. "As soon as we get the staff cleared out, I want you to show me around the place."

Clearing the staff out wasn't going quite so smoothly as the chief seemed to expect, partly due to the pressure created by corralling a lot of very young programmers and graphic artists in a confined space with a heavy deadline looming over them. I could hear voices coming from the cube jungle, complaining loudly that they couldn't possibly leave their desks now or they wouldn't be ready for this afternoon's "build."

A build, I'd learned in the last two weeks, was an important recurring event in companies that developed software. As far as I could understand, it meant that Jack, as team leader, told everybody to stop messing around with their parts of the program — yes, right now, dammit, not in half an hour — and launched a two-hour semiautomated process that was as temperamental as cooking a soufflé. On a good day, the result would be a new, improved version of Lawyers from Hell II, containing all the cool stuff everybody had added since the previous day's build. All too often, though, the build would be so badly flawed that you couldn't even get the game started, much less play it — at which point, Jack would convene an all-hands meeting, chew people out, and then send them off to fix everything that was broken in time for an evening build. Evening builds were supposed to be rare. In the time I'd been around, we'd had one every day, Saturday and Sunday included.

So while I could understand the programmers' eagerness to keep on with their work, I realized that someone might have to break the news to them that this afternoon's build would probably be canceled, and if they didn't stop arguing with the increasingly red-faced young police officers, they'd probably miss tomorrow afternoon's build, too, unless the chief allowed them to telecommute from the county jail.

Beneath the shrill protests of the enthusiastic youngsters, I could also hear the deceptively calm, reasonable voices of some of the older programmers. By older, I meant that they were in their thirties, like me, and had some vague recollection of what life was like before computers ruled the earth.

I don't know whether this was true of more mature techies in general or just of the crew Mutant Wizards had attracted, but they were, almost without exception, stubborn, independent iconoclasts with a sneaking fondness for anarchy, entropy, and coloring way outside the lines. My kind of people, under normal circumstances. But these were not normal circumstances. I could hear them calmly and rationally questioning the cops' authority to be there, disputing the necessity for clearing the premises, and generally causing trouble.

Chief Burke could hear them, too. Every second he was looking less like somebody's kindly uncle and more like Moses, working up a head of steam to give some idolaters what for. And if he whacked the pink plush bear against his leg any harder, it was probably going to pipe up with another affirmation and really tick him off.

I decided to intervene.

"Hang on a second," I said to the chief. I stepped out into the middle of Cubeland and announced, in what Rob called my drill sergeant voice, "All hands meeting in the parking lot now! I'm not ordering the pizza or the beer until everyone is present and accounted for!"

"That seemed to do the trick," the chief remarked five minutes later, surveying the nearly empty office.

"I'm putting in the pizza order," I said, looking up from my cell phone. "How many officers do you have here, anyway?"

"You don't need to order for us," he said.

"You'll be sorry in an hour," I said. "Do you really want your officers watching everyone else pig out while their own stomachs are rumbling?"

"Nine," he said. "Counting me; plus two, three others who might show up if the dispatcher ever gets hold of them."

"That's more like it," I said.

Just then the forensic technician shrieked and jumped up on the reception desk.

Chapter 4

I was impressed with how quickly the four officers who'd been scattered throughout the premises made it back to the reception room with their guns drawn and ready. But I couldn't figure out which ones made me more nervous: the two whose hands were shaking so badly they could barely hold on to their guns or the two who looked way too excited at having a chance to shoot something.

"What in creation's wrong?" the chief asked.

"I'm sorry," the technician said. "I can't stand rats."

"Rats?" the chief echoed. "Where?"

"Down there," the technician said, "Inside the desk. I'll chase it out."

With that, he began pounding his fist on the side of the desk.

"Stop!" I shouted. "It's not a rat, it's only —"

"Meg," my brother said, ambling into the reception area. "Can you come down and — urk!"

The pregnant cat leaped out of the desk when she heard the door opening, and made a break for freedom through Rob's legs. Rob, startled, tried to get out of her way and ended up lying on his back, looking up at the four armed officers. I saw the cat disappear into the open stairwell door.

"Oh, for heaven's sake," I said. "Do you know how long it took Dad and me to catch the poor thing this morning?"

"Sorry," the technician said, climbing down from the desk. "I really did think it was a rat."

"What are you people running up here, a pet store?" the chief said as his officers holstered their weapons. "You can get up now, Mr. Langslow."

"Meg, could you come down and be ready to pay the pizza guy," Rob said, recovering from his paralysis once the guns had disappeared.

"Put it on the corporate account," I said.

"Oh, do you think this is a deductible expense?" Rob said, looking cheerful. "Cool. Don't worry; I'll take care of it. And I'm sure someone down in the

60

parking lot will see the cat and catch her."

The chief and I watched as Rob went back to the stairs, performing the Crouching Buzzard kata along the way.

"Knows karate, does he?" the chief remarked.

"Well . . . ," I began.

"Meg, what's going on?" Liz said, appearing in the room. "The officer assigned to the back door ran away and left it unguarded. I've got your father watching it now."

"Sorry, Chief," one of the officers said, and hurried away.

"Cheer up," I said to Liz, who looked a little frazzled. "At least with all the police on the premises, you don't have to worry about any of our suspicious characters hanging around."

"Suspicious characters?" the chief said. "Is that another joke, or have you really had people hanging around?"

"Yes, we've had people hanging around," Liz said. "One in particular worries me — an employee who was terminated three weeks ago."

"Terminated?" the chief asked. "As in fired, right?"

"If she meant terminated as in killed, we wouldn't be worrying about him," I said.

"Dismissed from our employment, yes," Liz said, frowning at me. She obviously thought her official, corporate demeanor was called for under the circumstances, instead of the more down-to-earth person she could be off duty. "He had to be escorted from the premises when we released him, and he's called several times to make vague threats to get even with us."

"You think he could be dangerous?" the chief asked.

Liz thought for a moment. "I'm more inclined to think he intends some legal action," she said finally.

"I thought you said he had absolutely no grounds whatsoever for any legal action," I put in.

"No; he doesn't," she said. "But that doesn't mean he won't try to find an attorney to take his case. And it would be annoying to have him running up our legal expenses with a nuisance suit. But at least as long as he's thinking about legal remedies, he's not taking any other, more violent action. Although from what I've found out, I think the concern over his interest in guns is exaggerated."

"Interest in guns?" the chief said, looking interested himself.

"There was a rumor going around the

office that he was a somewhat overzealous gun enthusiast," she said. "He has a gun permit, true; but he's also taken out a hunting license during deer season for the last several years, so I don't think his gun ownership is as ominous as some people think."

"Still, we'd like to check him out," the chief said. "Let us have his name and contact information."

Liz nodded.

"We can get you a copy of his personnel file if you like," I said.

"My desk sergeant mentioned that you reported a trespasser last week," the chief said. "Was he the one?"

"No," I said. "It was one of the fans. The really obnoxious one," I added to Liz.

"The one who tried to pass herself off as a copier repair person?" Liz asked.

"I hadn't heard about that one, but probably."

"Fan?" the chief asked. "What do you mean by fan?"

"A gaming fan," I explained. He still looked blank. Apparently I needed to start further back.

"Mutant Wizards makes games," I said.

"Interactive multimedia entertainment," Liz corrected.

"Computer games," I continued. "Three or four of them, though the only one anyone ever pays much attention to is our one phenomenally successful game called Lawyers from Hell."

"Lawyers from Hell," the chief said with a guffaw. "Damn! You sure got that —"

Liz sighed. The chief started.

"I mean that sure is a peculiar title for a game," he finished, rather awkwardly.

"It's a peculiar game," I said. "My brother invented it. Anyway, the reason you had so much trouble clearing the staff out of here so you could investigate is that we're on a very tight deadline to release a new game."

"A new version," Liz said.

"Right, new version — the aptly though unoriginally titled Lawyers from Hell II. It's going to be bigger, better, more exciting, more complicated, more realistic, more imaginative, more everything than the original Lawyers from Hell. Mutant Wizards has been saying that for months now. But we haven't given out any specific details about *how* it's bigger, better, et cetera. And that's driving the fans nuts."

"Our computer security staff has logged thousands of attempts to break into our system," Liz said. "Fortunately they're highly qualified individuals."

"The main qualification seems to be that they have to be paranoid as rabid wolverines, to the point that they wouldn't trust their own mothers," I added. "And these guys are; they're very good. So the fans have resorted to good old-fashioned corporate espionage methods. They try to sneak in."

"To find out about this game?" the chief asked.

"Exactly," I said. "I guess they hope to get some advance information about the game or maybe even steal a prototype. That's also one of the reasons we have a stupid, old-fashioned switchboard," I added with a glance at that much-loathed object. "To try to screen out as many nuisance calls as possible."

"So you think one of these fans could have committed the murder?"

"I have no idea," I said. "But you were asking about suspicious characters hanging around the office. You want suspicious characters, we've got 'em. Disgruntled ex-employees, demented game fans — oh, and don't forget the biker," I added, looking at Liz.

"Biker?" the chief said.

"This guy we keep seeing hanging

around the parking lot at night," I explained. "He's wearing what looks like a motorcycle gang outfit — you know, greasy jeans, heavy boots, ragged T-shirt, denim vest with some kind of lurid painting on the back."

"And tattoos," Liz said, shuddering.

"Yes, he's covered with tattoos," I said. "And hair — long hair and a bushy beard. And he's about six and a half feet tall and built like a linebacker."

"We'll keep our eyes peeled," the chief said. "Has he accosted anyone? Caused any trouble?"

"I've only seen him standing around at the edge of the parking lot," I said. "But that makes me nervous."

"I haven't heard of any problems," Liz said. "Yet."

"Okay," the chief said. "Now let me take you through this list of visitors — I want to see if any of them need to be investigated."

There were only a dozen visitors on the day's list, and except for the hardware repairman who'd come at eight to fix a rebellious printer, they were all patients who had appointments with one or another of the six therapists.

"I'm afraid you've lost me there," the chief said. "I don't understand why you have these six therapists on staff."

"They're not on staff," I said.

"Miserable squatters," Liz muttered through her teeth.

"They were here when we came," I explained.

"We tried to convince them that staying wasn't a viable option," Liz said. "That their very differing business requirements were going to make coexistence quite difficult: So far they have chosen to stay."

"Can you blame them?" I asked. "I mean, where else are they supposed to go? You know how hard it was for Mutant Wizards to find this space."

"So other than the shared office space, there's no connection," the chief said. "No reason for them to interact with the deceased."

Liz and I looked at each other.

"No logical reason," I said. "But they did interact, thanks to Ted."

The chief sighed. "Why do I think you're going to tell me they had a reason to dislike him?

"You must be getting a good picture of Ted's character," I said. "I don't think his constant practical jokes endeared him to them, but I think it was his bugging their offices that really ticked them off."

"Bugging their offices?"

"We don't know for certain that was him," Liz said.

"Yeah, but do you have any doubt?" I countered.

"He could get in a lot of trouble, doing that," the chief said.

"I'm well aware of that," Liz said. "I'm still dealing with the legal ramifications of that little escapade."

I couldn't help thinking, not for the first time, that Liz did rather seem to enjoy having legal crises to deal with. Was she, perhaps, a bit of an adrenaline junkie? She was certainly a cutthroat negotiator, and I suspected she'd be a pretty sharp litigator if the occasion arose.

"Are the therapists suing you?" the chief asked.

"They threatened to," Liz said. "Fortunately, because of the danger of industrial espionage, we'd arranged for a weekly sweep by a security firm to detect electronic surveillance devices."

"So they found the bug?" the chief asked.

"No," I said. "We found the bug because Ted —"

"Or whoever planted it," Liz corrected.

"Or whoever planted it gave in to the

temptation to broadcast from one of his microphones over the office announcement system," I said. "That shut things down pretty quickly."

"However, the weekly security inspection enables me to demonstrate that the firm took the appropriate action to prevent electronic surveillance and cannot be held responsible for the bugging incident," Liz said.

"That's nice," the chief said. "But I guess the shrinks have to stay on my suspect list for now."

"Meg," came Dad's voice from the office door. "The medical examiner's here!"

I should have known Dad would manage to attach himself to the medical examiner. He had stuck his bald head through the partially opened office and was looking steadily at us with a deceptively innocent look on his face. You'd think he had no interest whatsoever in the corpse that was still reposing on top of the mail cart — unless, like me, you knew what excellent peripheral vision he had.

"Shall I bring him in?"

The chief nodded and made a little shooing motion at Liz and me.

"Let's move out in the hall, shall we, and let the medical gentlemen do their job."

"Fine," Liz said. "Better yet, unless you need me for something, I'd just as soon not hang around in the hall while they work."

"That's fine," the chief said, nodding. "But if you could stay down there in the parking lot . . ."

"Understood," Liz said. I could see her pulling her cell phone out of her purse as she crossed the lobby to the stairs.

Apparently Dad had managed to attach himself to the ME's entourage. At least he stayed behind in the reception area when the chief and I moved out into the hall. I made a mental note to avoid having dinner with Dad. Let him spoil someone else's appetite with all the grisly forensic details.

The chief was still quizzing me about the therapists' patients when the young technician stepped out into the hall.

"Chief," he said. "What do you make of this? We found it when we moved the body."

I recognized the lethal little circle of metal he was holding up on one latex-gloved hand. It was a *shuriken*.

Chapter 5

"A what?" the chief asked.

"A *shuriken*," I repeated, and spelled it out this time.

The technician was opening up a baggie in which to store his find. Okay, it was probably some kind of official evidence collection container, but it looked like a baggie to me.

"*Shuriken*," the chief said, nodding. "That's those things martial arts people are always throwing around."

"Not throwing around very much, unless they're either quite advanced or morbidly fascinated with self-mutilation," I said. "You could slice your fingers off on that thing and hardly even notice till they're on the floor."

"If it's sharpened," the chief said.

As if on cue, the technician slid the *shuriken* into the baggie. It sliced right through the bottom and thunked to a halt in the carpet, about three inches from the chief's left boot.

"It's sharpened," I said.

The chief looked at the technician, eyes narrowed. The technician avoided his boss's stare as he fished another baggie out of the pocket of his lab jacket, pried the *shuriken* out of the carpet, and placed it, more carefully, in the baggie.

"Interesting," the chief said.

"Very interesting," I said. "You don't usually see them that well made; most of the ones you could buy ready-made, at least around here, are cheap, flimsy pieces of junk that wouldn't hold an edge like that."

"You can buy those things?" the technician asked.

"At any martial arts supply store. They're illegal in a lot of states, but Virginia's not one of them. Still, since Ted appears to have been strangled, does it have anything to do with anything?"

"You let us figure that out," the chief said. "So . . . all you folks do around here is make games?"

Did this have something to do with the *shuriken,* or was he deliberately changing the subject?

"That's right," I said.

"The kind where you shoot a bunch of space aliens and all that?"

"No, Lawyers from Hell isn't a live-action combat game; more of a combination role-playing and simulation game."

"You don't say," the chief said, looking over his glasses at me.

"I should go into a little more detail?"

"You should go into a lot more detail if you want me to understand it."

"Want us to explain it, Meg?" I heard Frankie say with characteristic enthusiasm.

I glanced over to see several heads peering out of the stairwell doorway. I gathered that the police had forbidden anyone to step out into the hall, since none of them could possibly see much from the doorway — with the possible exception of Frankie, who by standing on one leg and raising the other behind him for balance, had managed to cantilever his entire body out into the hallway without breaking the letter of the law.

"Sure," I said. "Why not?"

Why not became quite apparent after Frankie had been talking a few minutes. I was sure another programmer would find Frankie's explanation fascinating — the heads peering out of the stairwell seemed

73

to, at any rate — but the chief's eyes were glazing over. Hell, my eyes were glazing over, and I already knew how to play. Why couldn't Frankie just say that Lawyers from Hell lets you pretend to be a lawyer and defend or prosecute the accused in a growing library of simulated trials?

"Frankie?"

I wasn't the only one relieved to see Jack Ransom stepping out of the stairwell.

"Go see Luis, would you?" Jack said.

"But I'm explaining Lawyers from Hell to the chief," Frankie said.

"That's okay," the chief said, quickly. "I think I understand it now."

"I'll take care of it," Jack said.

Frankie retreated to the stairway, looking crushed. Jack and the chief sized each other up.

"Ever played any computer games?" Jack asked.

"No," the chief said. "Seen my grand-daughter play one where this little cartoon character on the screen kills trolls and dragons."

Jack nodded.

"Same thing," he said. "Instead of trolls and dragons, we've got lawyers, but it's pretty much the same."

"My granddaughter spends hours on

that fool thing," the chief said. "She'd play all night if we didn't make her stop."

"That's typical," Jack said.

"And people do this for fun," the chief said, musing.

"Millions of them, yes," Jack agreed.

"Takes all kinds," he said, shaking his head. "Why don't they just go to law school if they're that interested in trials?"

Jack shrugged.

"That takes three years and a pile of money," I said. "You can buy the basic Lawyers from Hell game for thirty-nine ninety-five and learn how to play it in an evening. In three months, if you really work at it, you can become the game equivalent of Clarence Darrow."

"I still don't see how it's fun," the chief said.

Obviously the chief was not a potential customer.

"So what does it look like, anyway?" he asked.

"We can show you," Jack said. "If we can go to one of the computers, that is."

"Please," the chief said, holding open the side door and nodding to the officer loitering inside.

Jack and I followed, and out of the corner of my eye I saw Frankie scuttle out of the stairway to trail after us. I led the chief to the nearest cube and leaned over the computer to start Lawyers from Hell. Every computer in the office had the game on it, of course — some of them had multiple versions, including experimental prototypes of proposed new features. When the welcome screen came on, I punched the key combination that would run the demo — a little awkwardly, since I had the mouse in my right hand and had to use one of the fingertips that protruded slightly beyond the bandage on my left hand. Then I stepped aside so the chief could see it.

"This is what it looks like in the trial phase," I said.

He watched for a few minutes. One eyebrow went up, and his eyes widened. Frankie's head and shoulders popped into sight over the partition that separated this cube from the next. From the height he'd achieved, I suspected he was kneeling on someone's desktop.

"Pretty strange," the chief said.

I leaned over so I could see the screen and winced.

"Oops," I said. "I typed that wrong; I'm still awkward with this hand. That's not the real version. It's an unauthorized version someone cooked up. Nude Lawyers from Hell."

"Oh, great," Jack muttered.

Frankie snickered.

"Yeah, they're nude, all right," the chief said.

Tiny, naked cartoon figures filled the screen. A portly, naked, anatomically correct defense attorney was jumping up and down, waving his arms. The twelve nude jurors variously slept, yawned, or sat with crossed arms in mute condemnation of his speaking ability. They were also anatomically correct, at least as far as one could see over the top of the jury box. The nude judge — mercifully, only his bare shoulders showed above the judge's bench — frowned and toyed with his gavel in a way that boded ill for the defense attorney the next time the cartoon prosecutor made an objection.

"Let's try that again," Jack said, stepping over to the keyboard.

"Sorry," I said. "Everyone's been studying that, trying to figure out how they did it and how to stop it. This is the real version."

Jack started the legitimate Lawyers from Hell demo. The chief watched impassively as the same courtroom scene played out, this time with the characters decently clad.

"Other one's more interesting," he commented.

"If you like looking at naked cartoon characters."

"Funnier, anyway."

"Apparently everyone in the world thinks so, too," I said. "The guys have figured out that there's a program called X-ray that you can download from the Internet and install on your machine, and it removes all the clothes from your Lawyers from Hell characters. They're still trying to figure out how to prevent it."

"You mean they can't figure out how to get the little cartoon clothes back on?"

"No, that's easy," I said. "If you delete the X-ray program, the clothes come back. What they can't figure out is how to prevent the X-ray program from working in the first place."

"If you can undo it, what's the big deal?" he said.

"The big deal is that we have irate parents all over the country, screaming at us that Lawyers from Hell is corrupting their little darlings," I said. "They've been threatening a boycott if we can't prevent nudity in our software."

"Good Lord," the chief said. "I still

don't see what the big deal is. I can't imagine anyone would get that much of a kick, watching naked cartoon characters. Unless maybe they hadn't ever seen the real thing."

A distinct possibility, I thought, for many of the fans. And maybe some of our younger programmers, too.

"It's a big deal because it's an inside job," Frankie piped up from his vantage point atop the partition.

"Inside job?" the chief echoed. "You mean someone who works here did the nude version?"

Jack opened his mouth and then shut it again and settled for looking daggers at Frankie. I'd noticed that the nude version was a touchy subject with Jack. Maybe he was getting some heat for not having un-covered the culprit. He clearly wasn't happy to see Frankie airing our corporate dirty laundry in front of the chief.

"Someone who works here, possibly; or maybe someone who used to work here," Frankie answered, ignoring Jack's frown. "But we've been around so short a time, there haven't been a lot of people leaving. So it's almost sure to be someone who's still here."

"But what makes them think it's an inside job?" I said. "I mean, I thought all it did was replace one set of graphics with another."

"That's what everyone thought at first," Frankie said. "But I've spent a lot of hours playing the nude version —"

"And you're actually willing to admit it," I said. "That takes guts."

"For my job," Frankie said with injured dignity. "To help find a fix. And if you play it long enough, you figure out that it's not just the graphics that are changed. The program plays differently. The characters do . . . different things."

"I still say you're imagining that," Jack said.

"What kind of things?" the chief asked.

"Play it and see," he said, snickering. "But the program behaves differently, anyway, and you know what that means!"

"No," the chief said. "Tell me."

"They have the source code!" Frankie exclaimed, throwing his hands up like a magician displaying the finale of a particularly showy trick. He then disappeared, with a thud, behind the partition — from which I suspected he had been perched on one knee and had managed to knock himself off balance.

The chief waited a few seconds and then

looked at me for a translation.

"Imagine that Lawyers from Hell is a food," I suggested. "Some special dessert. And no one can make it but us. Unless, of course, they know all the ingredients, including the top secret sauce, and every detail of the recipe, in which case, not only can they make it just as well as we can, but even we can't tell the difference."

"Yeah, that sort of explains it," Frankie said, appearing over the partition top again.

Sort of explains it? I thought it was a pretty damned brilliant analogy, myself.

"So this naked lawyer thing is an inside job," the chief said. "You think it might have something to do with Corrigan's death?"

Frank, Jack, and I looked at each other. Frankie shrugged. Jack shook his head.

"Good question," I said. Obviously the chief thought it might, or he wouldn't be wasting time on it.

"There's a rumor going around that when they figure out who did the naked version, they're going to can him," Frankie said.

"Well, that's interesting," the chief said.

"If they figure it out," I said.

"It'll come out, sooner or later," Jack

said, shaking his head.

"Maybe," I said. "But I don't think whoever did it is going to step forward with a rumor like that going around."

"So you think maybe the nude programmer killed to keep Ted from revealing his secret?" Frankie exclaimed. "Whoa!"

"Keep it to yourself, will you?" the chief said. "Was there something you wanted?"

"It's really hot outside, and we were just wondering if you knew how much longer we all have to stay down there in —"

"No," the chief said. "When I know, I'll tell you. Now scoot."

Frankie nodded and left. Jack took this as a signal to make his own exit.

"He won't, you know," I said. "Keep it to himself, I mean."

"No, I don't expect he will," the chief agreed. "What do you think?"

"I think he's already blabbing down in the parking lot."

"I meant what do you think about this nude program having something to do with the murder?"

"Since we don't know who programmed Nude Lawyers from Hell or what, if any, connection there is between it and Ted — who knows?"

"Someone thinks he's going to get

fired — that could be a reason to kill in this job market."

"Yeah, except that anyone who really knows Rob knows better," I said.

"Knows better how?"

"I doubt if Rob wants to fire whoever programmed the nude version," I said. "He thinks it's a hoot. He could sit there for hours watching it and giggling."

"Might change his mind if it starts hurting his company," the chief said.

"Maybe," I said. "Then again, Rob's not too practical."

"So let 'em all blab about the naked cartoon characters having something to do with the murder," the chief said. "If it's true, maybe our killer will get scared and do something stupid. If it's not true, maybe he'll think he's gotten away with it and get careless."

He stared at the screen on which the Lawyers from Hell demo was still running. After about a minute, he shook his head and roused himself.

"How the hell do you stop this fool thing, anyway?"

I reached over and pressed the escape key to exit the demo.

"Thanks," he said. "Why don't you come down with me to the parking lot?"

I suspected that meant he was through picking my brains for now and wanted to deposit me safely with all the other suspects, witnesses, and seemingly innocent bystanders.

Down in the parking lot, chaos reigned.

August isn't a month when you want to spend much time outdoors in Virginia. The temperature and humidity were both hovering in the high nineties, and would probably stay that way until the daily thunderstorm hit in the late afternoon. Walking out the door was like entering a steam bath when you already had a high fever. I could feel my feet sinking slightly into the liquefying asphalt, not to mention the first breath of almost liquid air starting to leach away my wits and my temper.

An ambulance was parked in the handicapped space right beside the building entrance, but nobody seemed to be paying any attention to it. I could see a dozen programmers or therapists talking on their cell phones, most with their heads cocked toward their phones, backs to the crowd and their free hands over their unoccupied ears. Several others were playing Frisbee with the eight or nine dogs who'd come to work today. Or trying to play. The dogs were mostly lying in the shade, panting, and watching the crazy humans leaping about on the hot asphalt.

The rest of the staff was attacking the pizza and beer.

I noted, with a sigh, that a vegetable rebellion was brewing among some of the younger programmers clustered at one side of the parking lot.

They were all standing about, eating slices of pizza, but they didn't look happy. Some were chewing, stoically, as if half expecting to be poisoned at any moment. Others were prodding their slices with cautious fingers, perhaps hoping to find that the broccoli and green peppers on top were actually a strange new species of sausage. Others had picked up the green pepper strips between thumb and forefinger and were holding them up at eye level, inspecting them with the same expression of outrage and disgust that I'd be wearing if I'd found an earthworm perched on my sausage and mushroom with extra cheese.

"You'd think they'd never seen vegetables before," I muttered. And for that matter, I suspected some of them hadn't since whenever they'd last lived at home with their mothers cooking for them. That was the reason I always added broccoli and green peppers to the toppings of any pizza I ordered for the office. I suspected the broccoli and green peppers Rob ate on pizza might be the only green vegetables he saw from one week to the next since he'd moved to Caerphilly.

If he ate them at all; I saw several guys picking off anything green and feeding it to Katy the wolfhound, who didn't seem to share their disgust for the vegetable kingdom. No wonder she was such a healthy, growing girl. And since the Mutant Wizards staff always seemed to imitate whatever Rob did, I expected both their melodramatic disgust at the vegetables and their method of disposing of them were modeled on Rob's antics.

Elsewhere in the parking lot, other staff members were eating their vegetables obediently enough, no doubt because they had concentrated their rebellious energies on reenacting *The Great Escape*. Every few minutes the police would intercept one making a break for the street or the office door. Or a few would approach an officer — presumably, from the officers' expressions, to make some annoying, unreasonable, and oft-repeated request.

I spotted Spike's crate under a tree just outside the door and bent down to check on him. The ungrateful little monster lifted his lip in a snarl before curling up with his back to me.

"Fine, be that way," I said. "I guess you don't need a walk, then."

"He's had a walk."

I looked up to see Jack hovering over me.

"You actually took Spike for a walk and escaped unscathed?" I said. "I'm impressed."

"Not exactly unscathed," he said. "But I'm not bleeding anymore."

"Sorry," I said, wincing. "He's had his shots, in case you were worried."

A sudden hush fell over the parking lot, and I stood up to see what was happening. Dad was standing outside the building entrance, holding one of the doors open for the two men wheeling out the gurney.

I scanned the crowd, trying to observe people's reactions. Not that I expected the killer to jump up and confess or anything; I just found it interesting to see how differently people reacted. Some people stood, heads slightly bowed, as if watching a formal funeral procession. Some stood, frankly staring. Quite a few pretended to be absorbed in conversations or reading papers, but you could tell they were watching by the angle of their heads.

The chief spoke briefly with Dad and the ME, both of whom pointed several times at their throats. Explaining exactly how Ted was strangled, perhaps.

It was as if someone had pressed the universe's pause button — everything stayed on hold for the few minutes it took the EMTs to load the gurney into the ambulance, Dad and the ME to climb aboard, and the ambulance to pick its way out of the parking lot. And then, as the ambulance gathered speed and disappeared, the noise level returned to normal.

I glanced over to see what the chief was up to. He was still surveying the scene. So was I, for that matter. I don't know what he was looking for, but I was trying to spot the news media when they showed up, so I could make sure they talked to the right person. Like Liz. Or the CFO. Or even me. Anyone, in fact, but Rob.

"How's it going?" I heard the chief ask the nearest officer.

"What is this, anyway, some kind of cult?" the officer said. "More than half of these people have the same address."

"Let's see that," the chief said. "Five thousand South River . . .

"Why does that sound familiar?"

"It's the Whispering Pines Cabins," I

said. "Given the housing shortage, it was about the only place a lot of the guys could find to live."

"Glory be," the chief muttered under his breath.

I could understand his reaction. Before Caerphilly's housing crisis, the Pines had been a hot sheets motel. Its transformation into an overpriced residential hotel had been accomplished without any detectable renovation or redecoration. The more discriminating residents usually chose to provide their own bedding, though a card on the back of each room's door still displayed the price of requesting clean sheets at times other than the maid's daily visits.

The door also carried notices sternly instructing motel guests that they were required to open the door immediately if requested to do so by the police, and forbidding them to entertain unregistered male visitors. Since most of the current guests were young men in their late teens or early twenties, living four or more to a room, this last part of the notice was largely disregarded, and the place had taken on much of the rustic charm of a fraternity house.

Another frazzled officer hurried up to

the chief. "Don't these people understand that we have a murder here?" he exclaimed. "They keep demanding that we let them back into the building or bring their computers out here."

As if on cue, several members of the staff spotted me and rushed over.

"Meg, how much longer are they going to keep us here?"

"Meg, can't you talk to them? We have deadlines!"

"Meg, make them listen —"

"Meg, this is crazy; we can't —"

"Meg, why are they — ?"

"Quiet!" I shouted, and when they all shut up, or at least changed from shouting to muttering, I continued.

"I realize how important meeting your deadlines is," I said. "But stop and think a minute. We've had a murder here! A fellow human being — one of our own staff — has been brutally murdered! You can't expect things to just start back up in five minutes as if nothing had happened."

"Well, yeah, okay," one of them said. "But it's been two hours."

To give them credit, several of his colleagues gave him a dirty look.

"Why won't they tell us anything?" another asked. "If they're going to keep us out here, at least they could tell us what's going on."

"They won't even tell us how he was killed," one complained. "I mean, maybe we would have some useful information if they did."

"I told you," Frankie said. "He was strangled with a mouse cord! I saw it before Meg chased me out."

"How do we know you're not just blowing smoke?"

"Or pulling our legs?"

"Gentlemen!" the chief said. "And ladies," he added, though I was the only female within earshot — the few others on staff were scattered about the parking lot, apparently doing useful things. Or at least quiet things that did not involve badgering the police.

"I don't think there's any harm telling you how he was killed," the chief said. "As the gentleman said, he was strangled with a mouse cord."

This set off a muttered chorus of exclamations. One voice rose above the rest.

"Wow!" one of the graphic artists exclaimed. "Just like Meg showed us!"

Chapter 6

"Just like Meg showed us?" the chief repeated, glaring at me. "You've been showing these jokers how to strangle each other with mouse cords? Any particular reason why you failed to mention this?"

"Oh, God," I muttered. "Purse fu."

"Beg pardon?" the chief said.

"I was demonstrating a martial arts technique one day," I explained. "My teacher showed me some self-defense moves using a belt. Which works great if you have a belt, and enough time to take it off before you're actually attacked. But I happened to remark that I almost never wear a belt, and neither do many women, and would the same techniques work with a purse strap."

"And they work great," Rob exclaimed. "Meg foiled a mugger with them once!"

"Anyway, the subject came up around the office one day last week," I said. "And Rob asked me to demonstrate. And my purse was locked in my desk drawer, so I used what was handy."

"A mouse cord," the chief said, nodding.

"Actually, it was a Kensington security cable," Jack said.

"You show him," Rob said to me. "I'll pretend to attack you!"

I instantly went into an alert, defensive mode, the way I usually did when Rob offered to pretend to attack me. I was getting way too familiar with the kind of damage Rob could do when he was pretending to attack. Not that he meant any harm, any more than Katy the wolfhound did when she bounded up to greet me in the morning. But both of them were very young, even for their age; and they didn't know their own strength.

"My hand is still bothering me," I reminded Rob.

"You don't have to do it hard," Rob said. "Just show how it works, like you did last week."

"I don't have my purse," I said, keeping my eyes on Rob, in case he did something stupider than usual.

"Borrow a belt from someone," Rob suggested.

"Are you sure — ?" the chief began.

"Here," Jack said, handing me his belt. I

gripped it with both hands, which wasn't easy to do, given that the left was still bandaged. I settled for wrapping it around the fingertips of my left hand, which wouldn't work on a real assailant, but would do well enough for a demonstration.

"So pretend I'm a mugger," Rob said to the chief. "And I'm going to come up and take a swing at Meg."

Which he did. A very healthy swing. As usual, he'd forgotten that you were supposed to move more slowly when demonstrating. Out of the corner of my eye, I could see several of the cops start.

I was holding the belt with both hands, leaving about a foot and a half of the strap between them. When Rob swung, I snapped up my arms, bringing the belt taut in the path of Rob's arm.

"And then she —," Rob began, but I'd decided if he was going to swing at full speed and strength, I wasn't going to hold back on my response. With a quick twist of my right hand, I wrapped the belt around his arm. Then I stepped to the left and pulled down at the same time, trying to take as much of his weight as possible with my good right hand. Rob stumbled and put out his arm to cushion his fall, and by the time he hit the grass, I was standing behind and over him. His right arm was still caught in the belt, and I'd wrapped the rest of the strap around his throat.

"Isn't that cool!" he exclaimed, sounding slightly choked. Apparently I'd overcompensated for the hand. I loosened the belt and sighed. That was one of Rob's better and more guilt-inducing characteristics: he enjoyed showing off his friends' and relatives' skills and accomplishments as much as his own.

And I had to admit, if he were just a little bit more predictable, he'd make the perfect *uki*. If you translate it literally from the Japanese, *uki* means "receiver." If you ask me, it ought to mean either "punching bag" or "fall guy." In the martial arts world, the *uki* was the person whose job it was to pretend to attack the teacher so the teacher could demonstrate how easily you could foil your attacker and do unto him something at least as nasty and painful as he was planning to do unto you. *Ukis* spent a great deal of time horizontal, contemplating their bruises.

I made a fairly rotten *uki* — I had a tough time not losing my temper and playing too hard. But no matter how many times you flipped, tripped, kicked, punched, or knocked the wind out of Rob, he'd get right back up, smiling. He might get up a little more slowly by the twentieth or thirtieth time, but he never seemed to resent being thrown, or to lose his optimistic belief that next time he'd get the drop on you instead of the other way around.

He also knew how to fall down — largely through being an utter klutz. A vastly underrated skill, falling down. Most people tense up and try to resist a fall, which is the worst possible thing to do. You break and sprain things much more easily that way. Which is why some martial arts teachers spend a lot of time teaching their students how to fall properly — something life had already done for Rob. Tripping and falling was such a normal part of his everyday experience that he almost always landed with the boneless relaxation the rest of us had to work years to cultivate.

From his seat on the grass, he was prattling happily about the wonderful advantage the belt gave me, despite the differences in our weight and size.

"Not bad," Jack said as I handed him back his belt.

"Rob's not hard to impress," I said with a shrug.

"I am," he said with a slow smile that set off all kinds of alarm bells in my head. Yes, definitely time to bring in the New Year's photo.

Jack looked down at my hand and frowned. "You're bleeding," he exclaimed.

"Oh, sorry," I said. "I hope I didn't get too much of it on your belt."

"Never mind the belt," he said. "You need a bandage."

"That's one thing I have plenty of already," I said. I loosened the butterfly clip that held the end of the gauze down, unwound a couple of loops, and wrapped them around my knuckles. Time to get Dad to redo my bandage, I noted. I could live with toner, ink, and coffee stains, not to mention Spike's teeth marks, but these days visible bloodstains tend to make people nervous.

"Ms. Langslow," the chief said.

"Yes?"

He glanced down at my hand and frowned. "Should you be doing this with an injured hand?" he asked.

"Probably not," I said.

"What did you do to it, anyway?" he asked.

"Smashed it with a hammer. By accident," I added, rather unnecessarily.

"You did have it looked at by a doctor, I hope," he said.

"Yes, by several of them at Caerphilly Community Hospital the day I did it, and my dad every weekday since," I said, not trying to hide my impatience at having yet another person fretting about whether I was taking proper care of myself. And then I had to stifle a chuckle when I realized that the chief wasn't worrying about me — he was sizing me up as a suspect.

"So tell me about this strangling lesson you were giving your coworkers last week," he said.

"It was just a demonstration," I said. "Pretty much what I did just now, only with a computer security cable, instead of a belt. And I managed not to hurt myself that time; last week I had a bigger bandage that cushioned the knuckles."

"Chief," an officer said. "Danny wants to talk to you."

"I'll be right up," the chief said, and headed for the door, motioning me to come with him. "Who was there when you did this?"

"I don't really remember," I said.

"Try, then," he said. "It could be important."

"You mean you think whoever strangled Ted learned it from my demonstration," I said as we walked in and began climbing

98

the stairs. "Which could be true, but there's no need for me to remember who was at my demonstration. Half the idiots in the office were running around showing each other for the next three days."

"So pretty much everyone in the office knew about this belt fu thing?"

"Even the therapists probably know about it by now," I said. "So I feel bad that I may have showed the murderer how to commit the crime, but that isn't going to narrow your suspect field down any."

"Damn," the chief said with a sigh. "Not getting any easier," he told the ceiling.

He strolled into the reception room, and I tagged along. The mail cart was still there, I noticed, though Ted's body was gone. I wondered if the police would be taking the mail cart as evidence.

An officer — Danny, I presumed — hurried over when he saw the chief.

"Found this," the officer said. He handed the chief a piece of paper in a plastic baggie.

Whatever he'd found, the chief seemed to consider it very interesting. He read it — probably several times, from the length of time he stared at the paper — and then nodded with a grim look on his face.

"You got someone named George working here?" he asked, still looking at the paper.

"No," I said.

He looked over his glasses at me. "You're positive?"

"If you don't believe me, check the phone list," I said. "Or the personnel files."

"No George? At all?"

"He's the only George around," I said, indicating the dozing bird.

"He's George?"

"Can't be," the officer said. "Got to be someone with an office."

"What do you mean?" I asked.

The chief frowned and then held out the baggie. Inside was a note that said, "Put $5000 in small, unmarked bills in George's office, under the papers, or I'll tell everyone about the naked pictures."

"That's easy," I said. "You're in George's office."

The chief looked at George the buzzard. And then at the nest of newspapers surrounding him.

"You've got to be kidding."

"No, but I suspect Ted was."

"You think the deceased wrote this?" the chief asked. "Why?"

"I think it's obvious," I said. "It fits his

sense of humor. He'd leave this around where someone would find it, and then watch to see if they'd go scrabbling around under George's papers."

"You don't think this could be a real blackmail note, then?"

I considered it.

"It's possible, I suppose," I said. "I didn't know Ted that well, of course. But from what I did know of him . . . yeah, it's possible. But I still think it's more likely it was his idea of a practical joke. The man was an incurable practical joker."

"Looks to me like someone figured out a cure," the chief said, nodding toward the vacant mail cart. "You picked this up in an office?" he continued, turning to the officer.

"Yes, sir!" the officer said.

"Why don't you go down and see if you can find whoever belongs to that office and bring him on up here."

"Or her," the officer added.

"Or her," the chief said genially. "You run along down to the parking lot and find him or her. Of course," he said, turning to me, "statistically speaking, around this place, the odds are the owner of the office is going to be a him."

"About nineteen to one," I agreed. "For

some reason, we have a hard time getting women even to interview here, much less take jobs."

"But it's nice to see the troops are paying attention in all those expensive classes I send them to."

I nodded absently. I had a bad feeling about this. I wasn't the least bit surprised when the eager young officer returned escorting Rob.

"Hey, what's up?" Rob said.

"You recognize this?" the chief asked, showing him the baggie.

Rob peered at the paper inside the baggie and nodded. "Yeah, I found it in my in-basket last week," he said.

"And did you comply with the blackmailer's instructions?"

"Blackmailer?" Rob echoed. "You think this is a real blackmail note? Cool!"

"What did you think it was?"

"I figured it was someone's idea of a joke," Rob said. "Or maybe someone was putting together the evidence for a new trial."

"A new trial?" the chief asked.

"A new fictitious trial for the Lawyers from Hell game," I clarified.

"Yeah, exactly," Rob said. "We have this subscription service for registered users, you see; they get to download two new cases a month from our Web site."

"I see," the chief said, looking disappointed. Why did I think he'd have liked it better if Rob's past were filled with prosecutions for blackmail and indecent exposure and other lurid crimes? "So you never followed the blackmailer's instructions?"

"No," Rob said. "I didn't realize it was a genuine blackmail note. Do you really think someone was trying to blackmail me?"

"You say it was found in your in-basket."

"A whole lot of stuff ends up in my in-basket by mistake," Rob said.

"Including the occasional bit of actual work," I said.

"Yeah, probably," Rob agreed. "Most people know better than to leave stuff there. I mean, if they really want me to see something, they usually just stop me in the halls and show me."

"So when was the last time you cleaned out your in-basket?" the chief asked.

"July third," Rob said promptly.

"That was six weeks ago," the chief said. "You're positive?"

"Absolutely," Rob said, nodding.

"You cleaned out your in-basket the day before the Fourth of July?" I said. "What was it, some kind of declaration of independence from paper?"

"Actually I didn't deliberately clean it out," Rob said. "A bunch of us were fooling around with firecrackers in my office, and we set it on fire."

"Your office?" the chief asked.

"Mainly just my desk," Rob said. "But it burned up all the papers on my desk. Melted the in-basket, too. Had to get a new in-basket."

"So this paper couldn't possibly have been on your desk before July third, but it could have arrived there any time since."

Rob nodded.

"What nude pictures do you think this note refers to?"

Rob shrugged.

"You've never, for example, posed for nude pictures?"

"Not since I was in college," Rob said, as if it were ancient history, instead of less than a decade ago.

"You posed for nude pictures in college?" the chief said.

"I used to pose for life drawing classes to earn extra money," Rob explained. "I expect there are a bunch of paintings of me."

"Nude?"

"Some of them, yeah," he said.

"Could someone be threatening to make them public?"

"They already are public, some of them," Rob said. "There's one in the UVA art department student museum that's not too bad."

This was the first I'd heard of Rob's adventures in the art world, but I wasn't surprised. Rob took after Mother's side of the family, who tended to be drop-dead gorgeous and make Lady Godiva look like a shrinking violet. Apparently I took after Dad's side of the family. Since Dad was adopted, we didn't have any pictures of his blood relatives, but if we had, I was sure they'd show my female ancestors attempting to tiptoe out of range before the cameras immortalized their shapely but far from slender forms.

"So you don't see these paintings as grounds for blackmail," the chief asked.

"No," Rob said. "Unless the students who painted them decided that they've gotten much better and don't want anyone to see their student work, but then someone would be blackmailing them, not me — right?"

"What about the nude version of your game?"

"Amazing," Rob said, shaking his head

and snickering, the way he usually did when Nude Lawyers from Hell was mentioned.

"Do you think that could be the naked pictures referred to in the blackmail note?"

"Those?" Rob exclaimed. "But . . . they're cartoons! Who cares about naked cartoons? And besides, the note threatens to tell everyone about the naked pictures — what kind of a threat is that? Everyone already knows about Nude Lawyers from Hell. It's all over the Internet."

"Maybe it wasn't when that note first arrived in your in-basket," the chief suggested.

"No, the nude game's been out for months. First showed up around April Fools' Day."

"What if the blackmail note wasn't even intended for Rob?" I put in. "What if the blackmailer found out who created Nude Lawyers from Hell and was threatening to tell?"

"Maybe the blackmailer did find out," the chief said. "Maybe he found out that you were the one responsible for creating the nude version of your own game."

"Me?" Rob exclaimed.

"You're the one who knew the game the best," the chief said. A natural mistake; I hadn't explained to him who did the actual work around here and who sat around throwing out bright ideas and saying, "Cool! Amazing! That's exactly what I had in mind!" when one of the programmers finished the work and showed him the results.

"And then there's your knowledge of karate," the chief continued. "Mighty interesting, considering the indications we have that someone with a knowledge of the martial arts might have something to do with the murder."

Even Rob snickered at that, which probably didn't help him in the chief's eyes.

"You mean because of purse fu and the *shuriken?*" I said.

"And the crushing blow to the victim's larynx, which was used to stun him so the killer could strangle him," the chief said.

"Crushing blow?" I echoed, and then remembered the chief's conversation with Dad and the ME, when they'd both kept gesturing at their throats. The doctor's daughter part of my brain mused that it must have been quite a strong blow, if the results showed up during the fairly superficial examination they'd have done on the scene. The rest of my brain asked if we could please think about something else now.

"The kind of blow you could do with one of those karate chops," the chief went on. He leaned back on his heels with his thumbs tucked in his belt, looking quite pleased with himself.

"Oh, for crying out loud," I said. "You don't really believe —"

"I think we should go down to the station where we can talk without all these interruptions," the chief said, frowning at me.

They led Rob down to a waiting patrol car, with me trailing after, pointing out things the chief was overlooking, especially the many other people who might have had it in for Ted. Although, since most of those people were standing around, mouths open, watching the chief haul their fearless leader off to jail, I refrained from naming names.

"And what about all the suspicious characters we told you about?" I said. "The crazy fan, the angry ex-employee, and the sinister biker."

"We're not going to forget about them," the chief said. "We'll continue to explore every avenue."

But as I watched the patrol car drive off, I didn't believe it.

"Damn the man," I muttered. I felt

strangely betrayed. I'd told him everything I could think of about Ted and Mutant Wizards. I'd let him pump me for information. And just when I'd started to feel comfortable and think he was a sensible and intelligent person who stood a good chance of solving the murder, he had to go and settle on Rob as his prime suspect.

Maybe Dad had the right idea after all. Maybe I did need to do my own investigating. At least if the police were misguided enough to focus on Rob as a suspect.

I'd worry about that later. Meanwhile, the first order of business was to keep Rob from saying anything stupid or incriminating to the police. Anything more than he'd already said.

I groped in my purse for my cell phone and the notebook-that-tells-me-when-to-breathe, as I called my combination to-do and address book, looked up a number, and dialed frantically. I breathed a sigh of relief when a familiar voice answered.

"Liz! Thank goodness I got you! Where are you?"

"The police told us we could all go home, so I was just getting into my car. What's wrong now?" she said, sounding tired. Sounding, in fact, as if she were trying very hard not to reveal her irritation, and failing miserably.

"I think they're planning to arrest Rob for the murder," I said. "At any rate, they're taking him down to the police station. He needs a lawyer. Could you —"

"I'm a corporate attorney, remember? I do contracts and stuff. I'd be worse than useless; I don't know anything about criminal law. Half the programmers around here know more about criminal law than I do, thanks to the damned game."

"Yes, I know, but —"

"For that matter, Rob's a lawyer, and he invented the damned game, which means he's forgotten more about criminal law than I'll ever have any reason to learn. So —"

"Yes, and who was it who said that a lawyer who represents himself has a fool for a client?"

A pause. Then a sigh. "I don't know. I could look it up for you."

"I'd rather you went down to the police station to keep Rob from doing anything really stupid until we round up a good criminal lawyer to help him. I could try, but they'd only keep me cooling my heels outside. They'll have to let you in because you're a lawyer. Besides, he wouldn't pay the slightest attention to what I told him, but he might listen to you."

She sighed again. "Okay," she said. "Can do. Sorry I vented on you; it's been a long day."

"I know, and I'm not making it any shorter."

"I'm off, then; get that criminal lawyer down there as soon as you can."

"Any ideas who it should be?"

"Afraid I don't know the local talent yet. Which is stupid; I should have had someone lined up. I mean, sooner or later, I should have known that a key employee would need a defense attorney; it happens occasionally even in the most normal firms —"

"And it was even more likely to happen in a whacked-out place like this?"

"Well," she began.

"Don't worry," I said. "I know who to ask. Go put a lid on Rob in the meantime."

I hung up, and this time I called a number I knew so well I could dial it in my sleep.

Chapter 7

I was in luck; Michael answered on the third ring.

"Hey, great timing; we just finished the ritual sacrifice scene and broke for lunch," he said. "I have an idea that will take your mind off all the horrible stuff that's been going on. Want to have a virtual date?"

"A what?"

"I got the idea from Walker — he does it all the time when he's on location or something. We figure out a restaurant chain that has a branch here and in Caerphilly."

"Probably either Pizza Hut or McDonald's," I said.

"Or maybe not a chain," he said without missing a beat, "maybe we just both go to the restaurant of our choice, and we can call each other on our cell phones and talk to each other while we order and wait for our food and eat. Ta-da — a virtual date."

"And this is Walker's idea of a date? Do

you think this could be at least part of the reason Walker's girlfriends keep dumping him after a couple of weeks?"

"Actually, I hear they find the virtual dates rather sweet; it's the real ones that kill things. I have it on good authority that he likes to read them his fan mail."

"Ick."

"In bed."

"Double ick," I said. "I know he's been your buddy since you were both on the soap opera together and you feel grateful that he helped you get the role on his show, but given Walker's track record, let's do a rain check on the virtual date thing. Anyway, I need to ask you something."

"Ask away, angel."

"If you were in Caerphilly — ?"

"Now if I were in Caerphilly, you could forget all about the virtual date thing, absolutely. We'd start with dinner at Luigi's — an early dinner, because —"

"Hold that thought," I said. "We can discuss it later; things are a little hectic right now. If you were getting arrested in Caerphilly and needed a good criminal attorney — ?"

"Oh, God — what have you done now?"

"What have I done?" I repeated. "What have *I* done? I like that!"

"I meant the collective you — as in you, your father, your brother, and the whole motley staff of Mutant Wizards, for whose mere existence I feel at least partly responsible. What have you all been doing, and who has gotten himself or herself arrested for what crime?"

"Nice recovery, but I'm not buying it," I said. "Just tell me who you'd call if your suspicions were correct and I'd gone off the straight and narrow in your absence. I think the police are going to arrest Rob, and I don't want him talking any more without a lawyer."

He came up right away with the names of two attorneys he thought would be the best prospects and made me promise to call if I had news.

"And I didn't mean that I thought you'd committed a crime," he said. "Only that you have this absolutely charming tendency to wade in to protect your family and friends when you think they're in trouble —"

"And sometimes the local authorities don't like me interfering," I said. "Yes, I know."

"For that matter, whoever really killed this Ted guy might not like you interfering," he said. "Be careful, will you?"

"Don't worry," I said. "I'm a big girl; I can take care of myself." And then, seeing out of the corner of my eye that someone was hovering at my elbow, I added, "Gotta run; I'll call you later."

"Can I help you?" I said, turning. It was Dr. Gruber, one of the therapists — although I'd learned by now that she preferred not to be called Dr. Gruber, and I still couldn't quite bring myself to address this severe and stately woman as Lorelei. Or perhaps I couldn't warm to her because I didn't like the way she, at six feet, loomed over me. I was only two inches shorter, but I wasn't all that used to being shorter than another woman, and I wasn't at all sure I liked it.

"Not a good sign," Dr. Lorelei said, shaking her head.

"I beg your pardon?"

"Sounds as if he's trying to control your behavior from afar," she said. "Not a good sign."

"He's not trying to control my behavior," I said. "He's worried about me."

"Sometimes it takes that form," she said, nodding. "Tell me, have you considered using this enforced separation as a time to reexamine your relationship with this . . . actor person? To establish appropriate boundaries?"

I blinked, somewhat taken aback. If you asked me, it was Dr. Lorelei and some of the other therapists who needed to work on the appropriate boundaries thing. Since the first day I'd met them — only two weeks ago, though it seemed rather longer — they all seemed to think me badly in need of their services. And not just therapy, but the particular species of therapy each one of them practiced. For instance, the woman who did weight management counseling, calling her business Eat Your Way Skinny, and her arch rival, a size-acceptance guru, began feuding over me the minute they saw me. Which I couldn't help resenting; I thought I'd already reached not only a pretty acceptable weight but also a decently philosophical attitude about the fact that I would never be a willowy blonde like my mother.

And now here was Dr. Lorelei trying to shoehorn me into her couples' therapy practice.

"I'll think about it," I said. I'd found that was as close as I could get to "leave me the hell alone" without triggering a discussion on why I always reacted with such hostility to their efforts to help me. "Was there something you needed?"

"Will the offices be open tomorrow?"

she demanded. "We'd all like to be able to notify our patients if the offices will be closed tomorrow. Or if the police will be present; it could be extremely traumatic for some of our patients to see the police on the premises."

"As far as I know we'll be open tomorrow," I said. "But I can't guarantee police-free premises, under the circumstances, so maybe you should advise any clients who might be on the lam to skip this week's appointment."

I left her with her mouth hanging open and went in search of a phone book.

Roger had begun trailing after me, looking as if he were about to say something, but then Roger was capable of looking that way for hours with no audible results. I ignored him, and he continued to follow me, an irritating and faintly threatening presence. I couldn't quite tell why I found him threatening — he was only about five-ten, the same as I, or would be if he stood up straight. Perhaps it was the combination of his stooped posture, stocky form, and shaggy hair — it was rather like having a hulking bear shambling along at my heels, and a bear I wasn't entirely sure was tame.

I shook him off, finally, when I dropped

by the shoe-repair shop across the street and used their phone book to look up numbers for the lawyers Michael recommended. Then I went back to a reasonably empty corner of the parking lot and pulled out my cell phone. The first lawyer wasn't in. The second one agreed to race down to the police station.

The parking lot had emptied out considerably by the time I finished. I was relieved to see that most of the other dog owners had already taken their charges home — to air-conditioning, I hoped. A dozen of the programmers still seemed to be harassing the officers guarding the entry to the office. No sense upsetting the local authorities more than necessary, I thought, so I strode over to tell them all to get lost until tomorrow.

"But what about our build?" moaned Keisha, a petite African American who was one of Mutant Wizards's few female programmers. "Do you realize what it's going to do to our schedule if we miss today's build?"

"Schedule's totally f— I mean, it's totally messed up already," Frankie muttered.

"No, we'll manage," Jack said, arriving on the outskirts of the group. "We've got that spare server over at the Pines, remember? We can do the next build there."

"Yeah," Frankie said, "but what good will that do if they won't let us in to get our files?"

"Don't worry," Jack said, "Luis took care of that." All eyes turned to Luis, but only briefly, since they realized almost immediately that Luis wouldn't be giving them any explanations. Luis, a slender twenty-something Hispanic, was one of the few staff members for whom I hadn't found a nickname — he was so quiet that I tended to forget he existed when he wasn't actually around. When he saw us looking at him, he blushed and stooped slightly as if trying to make his already slight form too small to be seen.

"As soon as we heard the police were coming, Luis realized that they'd probably kick us out and shut us down," Jack went on. "So he tarred up the contents of our server and e-mailed them to his home e-mail account."

"Way to go, Luis!" Frankie exclaimed, and they headed off in a cheerful, chattering herd.

"Anything I can do for you?" Jack said, lingering behind.

"Nothing I can think of, beyond what

you just did," I said. "No, I tell a lie — here, take Spike, and ask Frankie to keep him until Rob gets back. If Frankie balks, tell him I need to be free to dash out at any time during the night to bail Rob out."

"Can do," Jack said, picking up Spike's crate.

Offloading Spike cheered me up a little. The only thing more depressing than spending the evening alone in the dark, cramped Cave was having to share it with Spike.

I finally got into my car, still ignoring Roger the Stalker, who stood at the edge of the parking lot, hands in pockets, watching me drive off. I revised my assessment of Roger. He wasn't just a little strange; he was seriously creepy. Maybe it would be a good idea to have the chief check him out. Or better yet, one of our resident shrinks.

I turned on the radio before starting the car, and I punched the button for the college station to see if our murder had made the news. As usual, I hit the middle of a commercial, and a particularly annoying commercial at that, for a local auto-repair shop. I'd have switched stations, but I needed my good hand on the wheel, so I tuned out the Fabulous Singing Muffler Sisters and was fretting uselessly about what might be going on down at the police station — and should I drop by the police station? — when a familiar voice broke into my reveries.

"One more important thing you should remember," I heard Lorelei proclaim. I whirled and checked the backseat, thinking for a moment I had taken a stowaway aboard.

"And this is a very important thing to remember about all relationships," she continued. I realized the voice was coming from the radio.

"They're not static."

"Yeah, but you are," I growled back.

I fumed for a few more minutes as Dr. Lorelei imparted more generic advice on managing one's relationship. Possibly good advice, if you weren't too irritated to pay attention. The woman — she sounded very young — who had apparently called in to ask Dr. Lorelei a question fell all over herself with gratitude, so maybe it was good advice. But I couldn't help feeling irrationally annoyed that after I'd managed to cut Dr. Lorelei off in the parking lot, she'd found a way of following me home.

Though as I learned at the end of her show, it was only luck and my normal preference for quiet thinking time on the drive home that had saved me from hearing her before. The college radio station aired *Lorelei Listens*, her advice show, on Monday, Wednesday, and Friday afternoons at this same time, with a repeat at 1 a.m. Prerecorded, then — of course, it had to be, since the half-hour show would have been just about to start when she'd badgered me in the parking lot.

Perhaps I should complain to the programming director. I began phrasing a witty letter accusing the station of air pollution. But no need — Lorelei's days on the college station were already numbered. September 1 would bring the debut of a new nationally syndicated version of *Lorelei Listens* on the rival commercial radio station.

I wondered if the college radio station would be replacing her with another psychologist who hadn't yet broken into the big leagues. Perhaps she had recommended one of her colleagues around the office? Not that any of them seemed hot prospects to me. Certainly not Lorelei's partner. Apparently couples therapy, like mixed doubles, had to be done in coeducational pairs. I wasn't surprised that Lorelei had chosen to join forces with a mousy-looking male therapist so self-effacing that he never seemed to speak except to echo something Lorelei had just said.

But at least they didn't squabble, like the dueling weight therapists. Or Dr. Brown, inventor of the Affirmation Bear, whose improbable specialty was anger management, and who carried on a running feud with the burly, red-faced psychologist who seemed intent on browbeating the world into studying assertiveness.

My cell phone rang. Normally I try to avoid using it while I'm driving, but I was only one block from the apartment, and when I recognized Michael's number, I managed to pause at a stop sign and answer it. And pin it between my ear and my shoulder, which meant I looked like Quasimodo but I could still drive.

"Are you off work?" Michael asked.

"Finally," I said. "And here I was hoping to get off a little early, what with the murder and all."

"So that's the real reason ya bumped him off," Michael said, in his best Cagney imitation.

"They'll never prove a thing. Hang on, I'm turning into the driveway — I don't want to sideswipe the landlord's bike again."

I parked the car and returned to our conversation as I descended the steep stairs into the Cave.

"So what else is new?" Michael asked as I checked the mailbox.

"Oh, God, no," I muttered.

"What's wrong?" he said. "If you need to hang up and call the police —"

"Nothing's wrong," I said. "Mother sent another package."

"Another decorating book?"

"Odds are," I said, stuffing the package under my left arm so I could open the front door with my good right hand.

"She's not still into faux finishes, is she?" Michael asked, anxiously. "I really was worried that I'd come home last weekend to find she'd faux marbled the whole place."

"No, I convinced her that no amount of faux marbling would make the Cave look like anything other than a dank, underground hole."

"That's a relief."

"I did have a little trouble talking her out of the underwater grotto idea."

"Underwater grotto?"

"Faux coral walls decorated with tasteful murals of seaweed and colorful marine life."

"But you did talk her out of it, right?" he asked. "She doesn't still think it's a good idea?"

"She may, for all I know. But after I told her what I thought about it, she hasn't spoken to me for nearly a week. I suppose the book's intended as a peace offering."

"What's it about?"

"Hang on, I think I need my teeth to finish opening this," I said.

"You'll break them if you aren't careful," he said.

I didn't argue, partly because I was tired of arguing about the subject, and partly because I had a mouth full of packaging tape.

"It's called *Living Graciously in a Single Room*," I announced when I'd spat out the tape.

"At least she's getting practical," he said, chuckling. "Seriously, have you learned anything new since the last time we talked?"

"Only that Dr. Lorelei thinks we should use our enforced separation to reevaluate our relationship," I said. I kicked off my shoes and collapsed on the couch with Mother's book, so I could leaf through it as we talked.

"Lorelei Gruber? The radio shrink? How

the hell did you run into her?"

"She's one of the therapists we're sharing space with," I said. "You know her?"

"In a way, though I doubt she remembers me fondly. I was one of the people who blew the whistle on her."

"Blew the whistle," I repeated with glee. "What was she doing?"

"Ever heard that show of hers? The inaccurately named *Lorelei Listens*?"

"Just caught the tail end of it a few minutes ago," I said. "I can't exactly say I'm rushing to note the broadcast times on my calendar."

"That's good, because with any luck they'll be pulling the plug on her eventually. For using actors to call in with pre-rehearsed questions, instead of real callers."

"How did you figure that out?"

"I recognized the voices of a lot of her callers as students of mine," Michael said. "A couple of the other drama professors and I filed a complaint last fall. It dragged on forever, but someone told me that she was going off the air at the end of the summer."

"Off the college station, anyway," I said. "She's going into national syndication."

"Oh, good grief," he said. "I wonder if whoever signed her knows about her credibility problems. Probably wouldn't care if they did. She'll probably move up to a TV talk show before we know it."

"Michael, this is great," I said.

"You obviously weren't listening to that show of hers."

"No, I mean it's great, because we can use this to help Rob. One of the main reasons Chief Burke is so interested in Rob is that he thinks Ted was blackmailing him."

"Because of the note, right."

"So what if Ted were also trying to blackmail Dr. Lorelei? She obviously has a lot to be blackmailed about — which means she could have a really good motive for murder, not to mention the same means and opportunity Rob had."

"Hmmm," he said. "Maybe. How big was Ted?"

I thought. "A couple of inches taller than me," I said. "Six feet — maybe as much as six-one."

"Physically fit?"

"About average," I said. "On the skinny side, but no one would call him lean and muscular. Still, he could hold his own in the hallway Frisbee matches. Why?"

"Given her size, it's not impossible, but

still — strangling sounds more like something a guy would do than a woman. Especially if the victim is a little above average height and not physically impaired in any way. Wouldn't it take a lot of strength?"

"The chief mentioned something about the killer stunning him with a karate chop to the larynx before strangling him."

"And he knows for certain it was a karate chop . . . how?"

I laughed. "Good point," I said. "For all we know, the killer could have whacked him with some common desk object, like a phone receiver or a bookend or a three-hole punch. But I'm not entirely sure we want to discourage the chief if he thinks some martial arts expert was the killer."

"You're always quoting your teacher about how really good martial artists avoid violence. Why let the chief keep on looking for a martial arts expert?"

"Because right now, he thinks Rob is a martial arts expert," I said. "As soon as he finds out Rob is a complete klutz, maybe he'll release him and investigate someone else. Yeah, I know it's ridiculous," I continued, a little more loudly, so he could hear me over his hoots of laughter, "but he saw Rob doing the Crouching Buzzard kata in the hallway, and now he's arrested him, because of the coincidence of the buzzard kata, purse fu, the *shuriken,* and the blackmail note. Which means it's all my fault he's arrested. Well, partly my fault; I didn't have anything to do with the *shuriken* and the blackmail note."

"Oh, brother," Michael said, and I suspected he was wiping tears from his eyes. "And you know Rob isn't in any hurry to let the chief know that he's not a martial arts master. Right now, he's probably enjoying being prime suspect."

"I'm sure he is," I said. "But sooner or later, he'll panic when he realizes the chief is serious. So I'd like to make sure the chief looks at some other people."

"And you're going to pick on anyone who's a martial arts expert."

"Maybe not," I said. "Apart from me — and I'm certainly no expert, even when I have both hands in good working order — Jack Ransom's the only other person I can think of who seems to have done any real martial arts training. And I don't know that he's an expert; he just doesn't seem quite so clueless as everyone else around there. Maybe I'll see if I can get the chief to pick on the other Bruce Lee wannabes."

"You have others, besides Rob?"

"Tons of them," I said. "Mostly because of Rob. It's monkey see, monkey do around here; as soon as they see Rob's interested in something, they all jump on the bandwagon. Ever since Rob took up karate, they've all been trying to join studios, wearing gis, and waving around *nunchaku* and *shurikens*. That's probably where the *shuriken* the police found came from, anyway. It was probably just lying on the mail cart, nothing to do with the murder."

"Why do I not find that reassuring?" Michael mused. "That you're spending your days in a place with lethal weapons just lying around on the mail cart? I don't suppose I could convince you to come out here after all?"

"I thought you liked the idea of me staying here, keeping my eye open for a house."

"Oh? Have you had a lot of free time today for house-hunting? For that matter, have you had a lot of free time for anything since the minute you walked into that crazy place?"

"It's bound to get better, now that we're in the new office," I said. "At least it will once all the fallout from Ted's murder is over with. And then I might actually have time to read *Living Graciously in a Single*

Room. Which isn't going to be as helpful as you'd think."

"Why not?"

"Most of these single rooms are giant lofts with panoramic views of the Manhattan skyline or the San Francisco Bay. So much for Mother turning practical."

"At least she's trying."

"Trying too hard, if you ask me," I growled. I flipped the book closed and added it to the two-foot-high stack of decorating books that we were using as an end table. If Mother didn't stop sending books soon, we'd have to start building a second end table. Or perhaps a room divider. I was beginning to dread checking the mail and finding yet another large, flat parcel, I thought — and that jogged my memory.

"Hang on a second," I said. "I just remembered something I need to do first thing tomorrow; I want to jot it in my notebook."

"Things to do today," Michael intoned. "Number one, find a new receptionist. Number two, find Ted's killer."

"No way," I said. "I just want to remember to call the company that supplies the mail cart. The police impounded the one we had, so I need to get them to bring over another one."

"So finding Ted's killer moves to number three."

"No way," I said.

"I thought that's the whole reason you were there," he said. "To find out what's wrong in the company."

"And fat lot of good I've been at that," I said.

"You haven't figured out anything that could account for Rob's worrying?"

"All I know is that if there's a problem here, it isn't financial," I said. "And I can't even take full credit for that; Mother did as much as I did."

"Your mother?"

"I know everyone thinks she's a financial bantamweight, especially anyone who's seen her in action as a shopper, but she's actually pretty financially savvy."

"Yes, especially when it comes to telling other people what they should do with their money."

"Precisely," I said. "So after I'd looked over the books, I reminded her that any financial malfeasance at Mutant Wizards would ultimately reduce the dividends she received as a stockholder and got her to do the same thing."

"And she didn't find anything?"

"A lot of potential money-saving ideas.

She recommended against installing the mail cart, incidentally. Wish I'd had more success talking Rob out of it. And the lousy discount coffee is her fault; we'll be changing that as soon as I can manage it."

"But no financial irregularities."

"No, more's the pity," I said. "Finding and firing a crooked accountant would be a quick, painless fix."

"And now you have another mystery to solve," Michael said.

"I'll leave that to Chief Burke," I said. "Like I said, all I want to do is give him enough reasons to keep investigating, instead of just latching on to Rob as the guilty party."

"Yeah, right," Michael said.

Chapter 8

Of course, if I was going to inspire the chief to expand his investigation beyond Rob, first I had to find the chief. Two hours into Tuesday, and he still hadn't returned to our office. Or returned any of my calls. Meanwhile I was stuck at the switchboard again.

"We're so sorry," the lady from the temp agency said, when I called to report that the promised receptionist had not shown up. "It's just that — well, you had a murder there yesterday."

"Yes, I know," I said. "If your employees are worried about their safety, please reassure them that there's still a strong police presence here."

Of course, the last time I looked, the police presence was in one of the conference rooms playing Nude Lawyers from Hell and giggling, but the lady from the temp agency didn't need to know that.

"Oh, I'm sure it's perfectly safe," the

woman replied. "But — well, the only person we had available this morning was Muriel, and she's rather timid — she said the idea of trying to work in a place where they'd just had a murder made her blood run cold."

"How long do you think it will take you to find a warm-blooded receptionist?"

"We're working on it," the woman said. There was a pause. "Muriel did say that she might reconsider if we offered her double pay for hazardous duty."

"We want a receptionist, not an extortionist," I answered. "See if you can't find someone who'd love to get a first-hand look at a real crime scene. I'd be happy to give her a guided tour."

So I was punching the buttons on the console just a little harder than necessary and answering the phone in the very brittle, polite voice that any reasonable person would recognize as a red flag.

Of course, why would any reasonable person call Mutant Wizards? I thought as I punched another blinking button.

"And what did that poor switchboard ever do to you?"

I glanced up to see Jack leaning against the wall by my desk.

"Nothing," I said, smiling in spite of myself. "But I can't throttle the dozens of friends and relatives who keep calling to ask what's going on. The staff are another matter. If one more of them asks me what's going on . . ."

"I'm trying to keep them busy," he said. "I realize you don't know any more than the rest of us do."

"Not quite true," I said. "I can make some deductions, based on reports from friends and relatives. The Caerphilly police are interrogating everyone who knows Rob. Probing them for any information they can get about his financial status, spending habits, college grades, sexual history and orientation, juvenile transgressions — everything."

"Maybe they're doing that to everybody," Jack said, frowning.

"Caerphilly doesn't have that many police officers. There's only so much they can do. Of course, they did check on me; I gather it's not just in Dad's mystery books that the police are suspicious of the person who finds the body."

"Yeah, but with your injured hand . . ."

"And what if I were faking an injury?" I asked. "At least they did check with the hospital to make sure I was really injured. They looked at the X rays of my hand —

Dad found that out from a radiologist he knows."

"You're more like your Dad than you like to admit," Jack said with a chuckle. "You sound almost pleased to have been a suspect, however briefly."

"That's not it," I said. "I just want to believe that they know what they're doing. And maybe enough of a feminist that I don't want to be overlooked just because I'm a woman. If it weren't for my hand, I could have strangled him just as easily as any man here. More easily than most, in fact. I'm pretty strong."

"So the chief took you seriously and you're happy."

"I'd be happier if Rob weren't the only one being investigated."

"You're sure?"

"Except Ted, of course," I said. "They do seem to be paying a little attention to Ted."

"But not a lot," Jack said. "Or they'd be spending a lot more time talking to my team."

"At least they're not interfering with your team's work."

"What work?" he said, shaking his head. "Everyone just wants to stand around talking about the murder. I think what happened didn't really sink in for some of them till today."

Jack returned to Cubeville. I noticed, when he left, that the place where he'd been leaning was showing signs of wear already, after only a week. Not so much from Jack leaning there, although he'd been doing that alarmingly often, but from everyone else imitating him. His other favorite leaning spots were also getting heavy use. Though why the wannabes bothered I didn't know. When Jack propped himself against a wall, tucked his chin in, and gazed at you from under his brow, he looked cool. And, yes, sexy. When the wannabes did it, they just looked as if they were imitating George. And large sections of the walls were starting to acquire that well-worn patina you usually see on the bottom foot or so of protruding corners in houses with large quantities of cats.

I went back to fielding calls. Including another call from Rob.

At least Rob wasn't hanging about waiting for me to reveal the murderer. He was home — if you could call the Pines home. And to judge by his tone of voice when he called, which he did about every five minutes or so, he was in a remarkably cheerful mood for someone around whom the net of a homicide investigation was slowly but inexorably closing.

Probably because he was the center of a whirlwind of attention. Apparently, Mother had put the word out on the Hollingworth grapevine that her baby boy was in dire legal peril, and every attorney in the family had called him once or twice already. The criminal attorneys, of course, wanted to drop everything and fly to Rob's aid, while the prosecutors offered sage advice about how best to deal with their colleagues in Caerphilly. The far more numerous civil attorneys, frustrated at being denied a major role in the ongoing drama, all offered to come down and take Rob out to dinner. I foresaw good times ahead for Caerphilly's more expensive eateries.

I wondered how long the local defense attorney I'd found would put up with the family interference. But I'd let Rob worry about that. Coping with the avalanche of attention seemed to occupy Rob's time rather fully, but it looked as if Mutant Wizards was carrying on just fine. In fact, did Jack look a little relieved not to have Rob underfoot?

Ah well. As long as Rob was happy. And he was happy. Deliriously, relentlessly happy, which struck me as odd; usually the only time he was this happy was when he thought he'd fallen in love again. Strange that he would react this way to falling under suspicion.

Or maybe not so strange, I realized, the fifth or sixth time he called to have me hunt down Liz. It dawned on me that he probably didn't realize that Liz's appearance at the police station had been motivated by her sense of corporate responsibility combined with my arm-twisting. He seemed to think she had rushed to his side for personal reasons. Well, he could do much worse. And often had. It had been a long time since Rob had fallen for anyone sane and likeable.

I wondered what Dad was up to now. Probably still looking for evidence somewhere. When I arrived, he'd already been doing his best Sherlock Holmes imitation. Mainly examining every floor, wall, and desktop in the place from a distance of about four or five inches, with or without his trusty magnifying glass. He was probably still doing the same thing, someplace. When Sherlock Holmes went through this routine, he would usually produce a clue at some point. So far all Dad had managed was a couple of sneezing fits. At least he wasn't wearing his deerstalker hat. Though since he wasn't expecting to encounter a murder when he came up to Caerphilly, he had probably left the hat at home. And had probably called last night to ask Mother to mail it to him. With luck, the chief would have arrested the killer before the hat arrived.

Dad also assumed what he called my "secret mission" to find out anything fishy going on at Mutant Wizards gave me a head start over the police in finding the killer. He didn't seem to understand that to date, my so-called sleuthing efforts had been completely useless.

"Now, now," he said. "You're too modest. Just let me know if you think it's time to gather all the suspects so you can reveal the solution."

I was about to explain how unlikely it was that I would be revealing the solution anytime this century when the switchboard blinked again. Another reporter. We'd been getting quite a few calls from reporters — who seemed to think, from the questions they asked me, that anyone whose job included answering the phone must automatically be an idiot.

"No, I will not give you Mr. Langslow's home number," I was telling the latest Woodward-and-Bernstein wannabe when I noticed that Roger was once again lurking beside the reception desk. "I can take a message, and if you rephrase that last remark a little more politely, I just might remember to give it to him. What was that? Thank you — the feeling is mutual."

I hung up, closed my eyes, and counted to ten. When I opened them again, Roger the Stalker was leaning against the wall by my desk. He wasn't a relaxed leaner. The way he hunched his shoulders forward made it look as if he had been ordered to lean and found touching the wall vaguely distasteful.

"Yes?" I said. "Anything I can do for you?"

He frowned as if this were a trick question.

"While you're thinking, do you want to make yourself useful?"

He shrugged. Was that a yes or a no?

"It's almost time to feed George; you want to take care of that?"

He glanced at George, pried himself awkwardly off the wall, and left.

Good riddance.

Of course, that meant I still had to feed George myself, eventually.

Later, I thought, answering another line.

"Meg! What's going on?" shrieked a voice. I winced as I recognized the caller —

Dahlia Waterston, Michael's mother. "What in the world are you doing with my poor baby?"

"Michael's fine," I said. "He's out in California, remember? In fact, I just talked to him a few minutes ago, and he says the filming's going very well."

"Of course Michael's fine," she said. "I meant Spike."

"Spike's fine, too," I said. "He had a nice breakfast and a long walk, and he's sitting right here at my feet."

"I knew it — you're still bringing him into that death trap!"

"It's not a death trap. It's a perfectly ordinary office," I said, and then winced at how inaccurate that was. "Anyway, you can relax. We haven't had any dogs killed. Just humans. Just one human, actually. So you don't have to worry."

She didn't seem to be worried about my presence in the office, of course. I put her on hold, answered another call, and then returned.

"Sorry," I said. "Busy day."

"I want to talk to him," she said.

"Talk to whom?"

"Spike. I want to talk to Spike. Put the phone near his face so he can hear me."

Okay. I leaned down and put the phone to the wire at the front of Spike's crate.

"It's for you," I said.

He opened one eye, saw that I wasn't holding out food, and closed it again.

I could hear Mrs. Waterston's voice chirping out endearments. He ignored her, too. I gave it a couple of minutes and then took the receiver back.

"Is that okay?" I said.

"He's not speaking to me," she said. "Is he ill?"

"Just asleep."

"Are you sure he's really asleep? What if he's being slowly poisoned by carbon monoxide fumes?"

"We have a bird in the room," I said. "Remember how they used to keep little canaries in the mines, to detect gases before they affected the miners? I'm sure if we had any toxic fumes, it would affect the bird before Spike."

Actually, George was as big as Spike, and I'd bet he was more impervious to toxic fumes than most humans, but it sounded good.

"I still don't understand why he won't speak to me."

"Let me see if I can wake him up a moment."

I put her on hold and fished out a doggie treat. Slowly, because several other lines interrupted me by ringing while I was doing it. I could see Spike perk up when the treat box rattled. Then I reached down with the treat and scraped it against the wire of the crate.

As I suspected, this set him off. I balanced the receiver on my bandage, punched the phone button, and let him bark for thirty seconds or so before lifting the receiver back to my ear again.

"Okay?" I said.

"Hello?" came a voice. Not, alas, Mrs. Waterston's voice. I glanced at the switchboard — damn, I'd punched the wrong line.

"I was trying to reach the accounting department of Mutant Wizards," the voice continued. "Do I have the wrong number?"

"I'm so sorry," I began.

"What was that?" the voice asked. "That barking."

"That? Oh, that was the Vets from Hell development team," I improvised. "What a bunch of cutups — but you know what those game developers are like. Let me connect you with Accounting."

Then, of course, I had to apologize to

Mrs. Waterston for keeping her on hold, and repeat the trick on Spike.

"He sounds healthy," Mrs. Waterston said when I finally let Spike have the treat and put the phone back to my ear.

"If you're really worried, I could send him back," I offered. "Dad's up here doing some consulting on the new game; he'll be going back Friday at the latest — I could send Spike back with him."

"No, no," she said. "I think we need to follow the allergist's instructions to the letter, or it won't be a valid experiment."

"And how are your allergies?" I asked. The allergies were the reason she'd saddled Michael and me — well, for the moment, just me — with taking care of Spike for the summer. Spike had been accused of causing, or at least exacerbating, her allergies, and the allergist wanted to supplement the skin tests with a trial separation from her beloved fur ball, to see if her symptoms improved.

"A little better, I think," she said. "Of course we'll have to see once the ragweed starts."

I sighed. I had a sinking feeling the verdict on Spike as an allergen would be guilty, and Michael and I would be stuck with him permanently.

"Give him a big kiss for me," she said. "And please keep an eye on him; I'm not sure what I'd do if anything happened to him!"

With that, she hung up.

Big kiss, my eye. Spike had finished his treat and was gazing up with an air of wide-eyed innocence that might have fooled someone who didn't already have scars from his teeth on several of her extremities. No way I was going to let her saddle us with Spike permanently. If she decided she was allergic, I was going to have to find another home for him.

Of course, the only person I thought might possibly be gullible enough was Rob. And I doubted if Mrs. Waterston would even consider allowing Spike to relocate to any institution run by the Virginia Department of Corrections. So if I wanted to pawn the little monster off on Rob . . . yet another reason to concentrate on finding out who really killed Ted.

But first I had to figure out a way of getting away from the damned switchboard. I needed a patsy, someone gullible enough to take over the switchboard while I strolled around sleuthing.

Was there anyone here that gullible?

Dad strolled in.

Chapter 9

"How's it going?" Dad asked.

"Great!" I said. "At least, now that you're here. I need your help!"

"You've got it!" he replied. "What can I do?"

"Mind the switchboard for a little while."

His face fell. I could see he was trying to think of an excuse.

"I don't want to ask just anyone," I said, dropping my voice to a conspiratorial whisper. "We need to have someone here who'll notice if a suspicious call comes through."

"What kind of suspicious call?"

"Precisely!" I exclaimed. "If I could define suspicious, anyone could do it."

Showing him how to operate the switchboard took a little longer. Strange that most of the vapid young women the temp agency sent over managed to grasp the rudiments of operating the switchboard far faster than a man who had graduated from medical school near the top of his class. But eventually I decided he was ready to solo, and hurried off. I had a feeling his enthusiasm for serving as a human wiretap would fade rather quickly, and I wanted to get as much done as possible in the time I had.

Given all the interruptions we'd already had this week, I didn't want to bother anyone who seemed to be doing actual work. So I headed for the lunchroom. Sure enough, I found half a dozen of the staff hanging out there. Better still, they were already talking about Ted. I fixed myself a cup of coffee and joined the edges of the group.

Unfortunately, my arrival silenced them.

"Don't let me interrupt you," I said. "Go back to whatever you were saying."

They all looked uncomfortable.

"Unless, of course, you were saying uncomplimentary things about me, in which case, you'd better change the subject."

"Actually, we were saying uncomplimentary things about Ted," Frankie volunteered over the nervous laughter. "Kind of a rotten thing to do, I guess."

"Getting murdered didn't make him a

saint overnight," I said.

"Tell that to the *Caerphilly Clarion*," the usually silent Luis murmured, gesturing with the front page of the rag in question.

"Yeah, listen to this," Frankie said, snagging the paper from Luis:

"He was a gifted programmer," said Mutant Wizards spokeswoman Elizabeth Mitchell. "He has made a significant contribution to our upcoming release, Lawyers from Hell II, and I think I speak for the entire staff in saying that his loss will have a profound effect upon all of us."

"Like maybe we can get some work done without having to dodge water balloons," Keisha grumbled.

"And maybe we'll actually get credit for our own work for a change," Frankie said. He propped himself against the wall, his height allowing him to achieve a Jack-style lean that was reasonably authentic — until he surrendered to the temptation to tuck one foot behind him like an advanced yoga pose.

"Are those the main things everyone had against him — the practical jokes and hogging credit for other people's work?" I asked, a little disappointed. It sounded like the Ted I knew, but neither sounded much like a motive for anyone to murder him.

"If it was just hogging the credit, yeah, that was irritating, but we just blew it off," Frankie said. "I mean, we figured everyone knew who really did the work, and if Ted wanted to pretend he was some kind of supergenius, let him. He wasn't fooling anyone. At least that's what we thought."

"Until year-end bonuses came out," Keisha put in.

Much head-shaking.

"The amounts everyone got were supposed to be confidential, see," Frankie explained. "But in a place like this — word gets around."

"Yes, I imagine it does," I said. "Especially if whoever's supposed to keep the bonus amounts confidential is foolish enough to put them in an unencrypted file on the network."

Several people looked sheepish.

"Rumor has it Ted got way more than he had a right to get," Frankie went on. "And some other people got way less as a result."

"What other people?" I asked.

"I think Jack was the most hurt," Frankie said.

"The jury selection logic was all Jack's invention," Luis put in. "And the cross-examination sequence — in fact, the whole courtroom module would never have gotten done if not for Jack. Everyone knew that."

"And Ted claimed credit?" I asked.

"Yeah," Frankie said. "Ted was always getting up in meetings and grandstanding about how he'd fixed this and he'd thought up that. Nobody realized anyone believed him."

"I'm sure Rob didn't realize —," I began.

"Exactly!" Frankie said. "That was the whole problem. We know Rob thought the accounting people knew what they were doing . . . but they didn't. They fell for Ted's bull — uh, Ted's blarney. If you get a chance, tell Rob that he needs to keep an eye on them this year. Or better yet, decide on the bonuses himself."

A chorus of agreement greeted this statement. I nodded, while wondering to myself how Rob managed to lead such a charmed life. I happened to know that Rob had decided on the bonus amounts himself. He'd dithered about them all through the Thanksgiving weekend, trying to decide how much to give for seniority, how much for team spirit, how much for spectacular individual contributions. Accounting may have figured out how much

Mutant Wizards could afford to give out and done all the final calculations, but the percentages were Rob's doing. Not that I was going to tell the staff that. Still, was it a motive for murder?

"I'll keep it in mind," I said. "People are still pretty resentful eight months later, I see."

"The closer we get to the initial public offering, the more people are going to resent it," put in Rhode Island Rico, the graphic artist. "Bad enough Ted got such a honking big pile of cash to wave around in January . . . but knowing he could get thousands — maybe millions — more than he deserves when the IPO happens . . . man! He didn't steal any credit from me, but it still burns me up, how much more he gets than he deserves. I can imagine how ticked off people like Jack are."

"Yeah, working like they did, only to see a jerk like Ted reap all the benefit," Luis said.

I sighed. I wasn't sure I liked the way this was going. Yes, I was looking for suspects other than my brother. Not that I expected to find Ted's murderer myself — I don't share Dad's conviction that solving murders in real life is as easy as it seems in the mystery books he devours by the dozen every week. But I did want to present the chief with a couple of plausible suspects other than Rob. His growing legal team didn't anticipate any difficulty getting Rob acquitted if the DA tried to charge him with Ted's murder, but in the meantime the trail of the real killer would be growing colder and colder.

But I wanted to point the chief to a plausible alternative subject, and I had a hard time believing Jack Ransom fit the bill. And I didn't think it was just because I liked him. He was one of the few genuinely sane people around the office, which made him, in my mind, one of the least likely suspects.

Or was I too influenced by selfish motives — specifically, my investment in Mutant Wizards? Was that coloring my thinking, making me deliberately shy away from steering the police toward a key employee like Jack at this critical time in the development of the new game? At least he seemed to be key, and fairly high ranking. The only organizational chart I'd ever seen was ten months out of date, and Rob had allowed people to choose their own creative job titles, which meant I had no idea how the firm was really organized. Was a Unix Crusader — the disgruntled ex-staffer — more important than Keisha, the Cyber Goddess? Would Frankie, as Programming Warlock, report to Luis, the Senior Software Guru, or vice versa? I had no idea, apart from observing how they treated each other, of course.

When Frankie suggested something, people shrugged. When Luis suggested something, people listened. When Jack suggested something, people scrambled to do it.

But even Frankie appeared to perform a key role, if the number of people who complained when he played hooky was anything to go by. Which led me to another, more useful thought. Now was certainly a bad time to throw any obstacles in the path of the development team. Unless, of course, you wanted to cause Mutant Wizards the kind of problems that would result from a missed deadline on the new game. Was it possible that someone had killed Ted not for any of his many unpleasant characteristics but merely as a way of sabotaging Mutant Wizards? Who would have a motive to do that? Obviously not Rob or any of the other Mutant Wizards staff I knew and liked, since they all, like Rob, had a major stake in the company's success. It would have to be someone who had it in for the company — another strike against Liz's bête noire, the disgruntled ex-staffer? Assuming, of course, that Ted's death would cause obstacles. No way to know without asking.

"So how badly will Ted's death hurt our deadlines, anyway?" I asked.

Apparently this was the topic du jour. The group erupted into a flurry of incomprehensible technical jargon, until I called time-out.

"In English, please, someone," I pleaded.

"Losing Ted won't hurt us all that much if the police would just bring back his computer so we could get his damned files," Jack Ransom said. Having arrived, apparently, in the middle of the argument, he was leaning against the doorjamb, taking everything in. The several people who had been propped against various walls or articles of furniture leaped to attention. I wasn't sure if they wanted to look alert in his presence or just felt too embarrassed to exhibit their inferior leans in the presence of the master.

"From what we saw the last time Ted showed us what he was doing, he'd effectively finished the module he was working on," Jack went on.

"Finished it all wrong, though," Frankie put in.

"I have no doubt he ignored all the technical standards, as usual," Jack said, pushing away from the doorway and heading for the coffee machine. "And, as usual, someone else will have to clean up behind him. Probably you again, Luis; you've got that down to an art."

"Yeah," Luis said, shaking his head. "By now, I know exactly how his mind works — or doesn't work."

"Good thing whoever bumped him off didn't do it last week," Frankie said. "We'd really be hurting then. But now — gee, it sounds cold, but to be perfectly honest, we can do without Ted better than just about anyone, right now."

With the possible exception, I thought, of Rob. Who knows? Having Rob in jail for a day or two might actually speed up the project. And having Ted permanently absent wouldn't cause a problem — did that make it more likely that the killer was someone closely involved in the project, who would know when it was safe to strike Ted down? Drat.

"Of course, that assumes we can get Ted's files sometime this century," Keisha said, tossing her braids in a characteristic gesture of impatience.

"And assumes that some of us actually

manage to get some programming done today," Jack shot back. The rest of them looked a little guilty, and the impromptu meeting broke up.

"Sorry," I said. "I didn't mean to keep anyone from work."

"You're not," he said with a shrug. "No one can concentrate; I think for a lot of these kids, it's the first time they've ever known anyone who died. Anyone close to their own age, anyway. I'm just trying to give them enough time to talk it over among themselves, but not enough to sit around getting morbid."

"Let me know if I can do anything to help," I said.

"If you could get the police to hurry up and give back Ted's files, that would be a lifesaver," Jack said.

"The files are really that big a problem?"

"Not yet, but they will be pretty soon."

"You don't have a backup?"

He rolled his eyes. "If Ted had backed up regularly, or better yet, stored his stuff on the server, the way he was supposed to, we wouldn't have a problem at all," he said. "Unfortunately, this was Ted. Hell, half the time we needed something, it wouldn't even be on his desktop machine; it'd be on his laptop, and he'd have left that home for the day. If we get the police to give us a copy of his files within a day or so, Luis can clean them up in time. If not . . ."

"I'll do what I can," I said. "Not that there's all that much I can do, but we have a whole lot of lawyer relatives who've been begging us to let them know if they can do anything. Maybe I'll call their bluff."

"Great," he said. "Well, this thing isn't going to program itself."

With that, he left the coffee room.

I heard a noise in the hall — a familiar yet oddly chilling sound. The rhythmic beep of the mail cart making its rounds.

I confess I was a little anxious when I stepped out into the hall to see the mail cart. It wasn't the same mail cart Ted had been killed on, of course; the police had that. I'd called the company that supplied and serviced the mail cart, explained the situation, and asked them to bring over another one, ASAP. And while their initial definition of ASAP wasn't at all what I had in mind, they quickly revised it, after I remarked that I hadn't yet had any reason to tell the media what brand of mail cart had been used in the murder. So I'd been expecting to see a mail cart.

Still, it was more than a little odd to hear

it for the first time, and to see it chugging down the hall again. I was strangely relieved to see nothing on it but mail. No still form — and for that matter, no attempts at decoration. Thank heaven for small favors.

As I watched it chug by, I noticed that several other people had stepped out of their cubes or offices to do the same thing. It was almost as if we'd declared a minute of silence to coincide with the start of the cart's first run of the day. We all watched until it rounded the corner into the next corridor, and then we looked at each other, sheepishly.

"Ironic, isn't it?" Rico said, plucking at the hem of yet another RISD T-shirt. "Him getting killed on that thing."

"I think it's more ironic that he was killed with a mouse cord," another graphic artist said. "Just think, maybe if we'd spent the money for wireless mice, Ted might be alive today."

"No, but look at the irony of it being the mail cart," Rico insisted. "It was like he was obsessed with it. Always playing with it."

"And everyone else around here wasn't?" I asked.

They shrugged their shoulders, sheepishly. If they'd tried to argue, I would have pointed out how much time the art department had spent over the past week decorating the mail cart.

"Yeah, we all played with it," a programmer said. "But Ted was obsessed, definitely. He was the only one trying to reprogram it."

"Reprogram it?" I echoed.

"Yeah. You know how the thing works, right?"

"It follows a line of ultraviolet dye on the carpet."

"More like a series of dots, really. It reads the dots, like Morse code. There's patterns that mean turn left, turn right, stop. Ted got a black light, so he could see the dots, and he spent hours trying to make a dye that the machine could read and then something to wash out the dye. Didn't work, of course."

"Then how did he manage to reroute the machine?" I asked. "I don't think we had a day last week when the damned thing didn't turn up someplace where it wasn't supposed to be. I was trapped in the women's room for half an hour, remember, when he managed to get the thing stalled outside the door."

"Just be glad he wasn't successful at

161

opening the door," one of them said while the others snickered. "He had a couple of Web cams hooked up to the cart that day, you know."

"No, I didn't know," I said. "And it's a good thing I didn't, or he wouldn't have lived as long as he did. So if he didn't figure out how to make and erase dots, how did he manage to reroute the mail cart?"

"He was moving carpet tiles around," Rico said. "You walk around this place and half the carpet tiles are loose. See!"

He walked a few steps, scuffing each tile as he went. The fifth tile he touched moved a few inches out of position when he kicked it.

"He was gluing them back down," a programmer said. "I saw him."

"Yeah, but whatever he was using didn't do the job like the commercial adhesive the carpet installers use," Rico said. "Another week and you wouldn't have been able to walk around here for loose tiles."

Was this useful? I didn't see offhand how Ted's high jinks with the mail cart got me any closer to finding his killer. Still, you never knew.

Now that the cart had disappeared, everyone began drifting back to their cubes and offices. All except Roger the Stalker, who, as usual, had been lurking silently at the edge of the group. I forced a smile. He might be a creep, but who knows, I thought. Even Roger could have some useful information.

"What's new, Roger?" I said.

He blinked and glanced back, as if he thought there might be some other Roger in the hallway.

"We're having pizza," he said finally. "Luigi's. Seven-thirty."

"That's nice," I said.

He nodded and drifted back into Cubeville.

Apparently the guys were planning a little outing and had forgotten to tell me. Or maybe hadn't intended to invite me — perhaps they thought I'd force-feed them more vegetables. In any case, this could be useful. Gathering information would be much easier when no one expected them to hurry back to work. And when they were full of pizza and beer.

See, I told myself. Even creepy Roger can serve a useful purpose, now and then.

Two useful purposes, in fact; seeing him reminded me that I still needed to feed George.

I was heading back to the lunchroom when I ran into Liz.

Chapter 10

"You look a little tired," I said. Actually, she looked as if she'd gotten even less sleep than I had. I decided it would not be a kindness to tell her about the giant run in her pantyhose. "How's it going?"

She shook her head. "Slow," she said. "As if I needed yesterday's interruptions. Or all the media stuff."

"You do a good job with that," I said.

She shrugged. "I suppose," she said. "I just try to do whatever needs to be done to take care of the problem."

"You're doing great."

"They don't like me a lot," she said. "I don't give them much."

"They probably like you a lot more today," I said. "I've been biting their heads off all morning."

"Good show," she said. "But we shouldn't have to be doing this, either of us. Why couldn't Ted have managed to get himself killed somewhere where it wouldn't be my problem? Our problem, really."

"What is it that's keeping you so busy, anyway?" I asked.

"Preparing a brief," she said. "And I'm not likely to get an extension just because we've had a murder here. If what your dad says is true, and you're trying to find Ted's murderer, maybe you should look at the guy who's suing us. If you ask me, he's got a great motive."

"Someone's suing Mutant Wizards?"

"Someone's *always* suing Mutant Wizards," she said. "Anyone who's ever invented any kind of board game, role-playing game, or computer game that even mentions lawyers thinks we stole their idea."

"Or pretends to think it," I suggested.

"Precisely," she said. "Not surprising, I suppose, given how successful the game has been. Still, it's enough to destroy your faith in human nature, if you have any left."

"So you don't think this guy will win?"

"I don't think any of them will win, ultimately; but that doesn't mean they can't keep us tied up in court for years, wasting my time and the firm's money. We really ought to hire outside counsel, sooner rather than later. A firm that specializes in intellectual property disputes. I may ask you to help me talk Rob into it."

"It's bad enough that we need outside help?"

"I can barely handle the volume of paperwork as it is," she said. "When they start releasing some of the brand extensions — Doctors from Hell, Cops from Hell, things like that — there are a lot more games on those subjects than there ever were about lawyers. The number of vultures trying to get a piece of the action will increase geometrically. Yeah, we're going to need outside help."

"Let me know when you want help tackling Rob," I said. "So that's what's been keeping you so busy in the library?"

"What else?" she said.

"I don't know," I said, smiling. "I figured maybe you just liked sitting up there where you could keep your eye on everyone, make sure no one got up to anything."

"Yeah, right," she said with a chuckle. "And some job I did yesterday. I wonder how many times Ted's body chugged around the office right under my nose, and I didn't even realize he was dead."

"Not just *your* nose, don't forget. I didn't notice either."

"Some watchdogs we are. Speaking of that, though — remember the guy I told you to watch for?"

"Eugene something-or-other, the disgruntled ex-employee?"

"Eugene Mason, yes."

"I haven't seen him," I said. "Not that things have been quiet enough to spend much time looking for him."

"Keep your eyes open, then. I can't imagine that he has anything to do with Ted's death, or that he'd do anything rash at all, but you never know."

"Especially if he had some kind of a thing about guns," I said. "Wasn't that what you were telling the chief?"

"I told the chief that I thought concern over his interest in guns was exaggerated," she said. "Which I still think is true."

"But it's bound to interest the chief, knowing someone with a grudge has access to weapons."

"For heaven's sake, there's nothing wrong with knowing how to fire a gun and even owning one," she said. "I learned to fire a gun myself when I was at Stanford Law and the only place I could afford to live was a pretty bad part of East Palo Alto. Self-defense."

I nodded.

"I didn't want the police to overreact," she went on. "Of course, I didn't want them to ignore him, either, which is what they seem to be doing. Perhaps it would have been wiser to exaggerate our anxiety, not downplay it."

"You did what you thought was best at the time," I said. "Don't beat yourself up. I'll nudge the police about the disgruntled Mr. Mason."

"Thanks," she said. "By the way — this detecting you're doing — are you sure that's wise? You don't want to risk a charge of interfering with an investigation, do you?"

I sighed. "Dad likes to think of me as a real-life Nancy Drew," I said. "I admit, I've been trying to find something I can give Chief Burke to convince him that Rob shouldn't be his prime suspect. But beyond that . . . I'll let the police do their job."

Maybe I was downplaying the amount of snooping I had been doing — or might end up doing. But it wasn't really that misleading. I had every intention of staying out of Chief Burke's way and letting the police do their job. As soon as they started doing it properly. Leaving Rob alone would be a good start.

"Keep me posted on what you discover," she said. "Since anything you find out is bound to affect the firm, one way or another."

"Of course," I said.

She nodded and headed for the nearest of the two doors to the library. A minute later, I saw her head pop up over the top of the shelves. She looked around, scanning the office, and then focused down, presumably on yet another law book.

Although I wasn't sure I shared Liz's suspicion of the disgruntled Mr. Mason, since I couldn't see any indication that he'd been hanging around the office on the day of the murder, I decided to drop by Personnel and see if I could talk my way into getting a look at his file. As it happened, I didn't even need to talk. Darlene, our one-person Personnel department, was out, and the file she'd hunted down for the chief yesterday was still in her in-basket. Later, I'd complain about her carelessness. For now, I snagged the file, grabbed a couple of health insurance forms to put on top so no one would see what I was carrying, and made my escape with it. I'd leave it in Rob's out-basket later. Darlene wouldn't find that suspicious, and Rob would never notice.

Walking back up the hall, I glanced up and waved at Liz, and then I ran into Jack again.

"Saw you talking to Liz," he said. "She celebrating Ted's demise yet?"

"Of course not," I snapped.

"Wouldn't blame her if she did," he said, falling into step beside me. "The guy made her life miserable, every way he could."

"Such as?"

"Looking for alternate suspects to get Rob off the hook?" he asked.

I shrugged.

"Well, we're all suspects, if you like, Liz as much as anyone," he said. "There's this guy who's filed suit against Mutant Wizards, claiming we stole his game idea."

"She mentioned him," I said. "You think he has any kind of a case?"

"You mean you don't believe Rob really invented it?"

"Of course I know Rob invented it," I said. "I had to play it often enough while he was doing it. But it's not such an outlandish idea that someone else couldn't have come up with a similar one — and that could be trouble."

"Yeah," Jack said. "Well I don't know how similar the ideas are — not very, if you ask me. But it's been keeping Liz pretty busy."

"How does Ted come into this?"

"You know how Ted was," Jack said. "Liked to yank everyone's chain."

"And just how did he yank Liz's chain?"

"He went out and bought a copy of the other guy's software and started playing this whole mind game on her," Jack said. "For weeks, every time you went in his office, he was playing it; every time they were both in a meeting, he'd drag the conversation around to the other game. What a great game it was, how worried he was that maybe Rob had been subconsciously influenced by it."

"Not likely," I said. "Would you be surprised if I said that Rob's not exactly a rabid computer game player?"

"Actually, I'd be surprised to hear he'd ever played a computer game before he started inventing Lawyers from Hell," Jack said with a grin.

"And that doesn't bother you?" I asked. "Knowing that he's not exactly the expert all the computer magazines make him out to be?"

"I'll never be a convert to the cult of Rob, like most of the young kids who come to work here," Jack said. "But no, it doesn't bother me. In some ways, it's an advantage, knowing more than the boss does. And to tell you the truth, he does come up with some brilliant ideas, occasionally."

"Probably by accident," I said.

"Usually by accident, yes," Jack agreed.

"Everyone always talks about how great Rob is at thinking outside the box," I said, shaking my head. "I don't suppose they realize that he hasn't the foggiest idea where the box is."

"And I hope he never learns," Jack said.

"So anyway, what does this have to do with how Ted was getting on Liz's nerves?" I asked.

"He started pretending that he agreed with the guy who was threatening to sue us," Jack said. "Walked around shaking his head, saying that he was afraid he'd have to testify for the other side. Stuff like that. Drove her crazy."

"Crazy enough that she'd want to kill him?"

"Liz?" He glanced up at where Liz was sitting in her crow's nest. "Not really. No more than any of the rest of us. I mean, who around here didn't say, 'I could kill him!' sometime or other, but I can't imagine anyone ever really would. Then again, what do I know? Ask some of the shrinks. They're supposed to know that kind of stuff."

"Maybe I will," I said.

"I'd better get back to work," he said.

"Me, too," I said, and turned to head back to the reception room. "See you at the pizza thing."

"Pizza thing?"

I started to turn to give him the scoop on the pizza outing, but just then my pager went off.

"Microwave broken," I read. "Like hell it is."

"Frankie always unplugs it to plug in his popcorn popper," Jack said. "Want me to plug it in again?"

"Thanks, but I need to feed George anyway before I take the switchboard back from Dad."

When I got to the lunchroom, sure enough, I found the supposedly broken microwave merely unplugged. As I leaned over behind the cabinet to reach the outlet, something fell out of my pocket — actually out of the pocket of the sweater I kept around the office for mornings, like this one, when the air-conditioning was out of control.

I reset the time on the microwave. Then

I retrieved a frozen mouse from one of the packages in the freezer, put it on the microwave carousel on a paper towel, and punched the button that was supposed to defrost chicken pieces. George seemed to like his mice at whatever temperature that setting produced. Not that I had any idea what temperature that might be, since I was careful never to touch the mice, before or after nuking them. So I'm squeamish. George's favorite food was pinkies, but as soon as I'd found out that was a euphemism for hairless, three-day-old baby mice, George had been put on a pink-free diet, at least for as long as I was feeding him. Adult mice were bad enough.

While the microwave hummed, I fished behind the cabinet for whatever had fallen out of my pocket.

Ted's keys.

Chapter 11

I stuck the keys back into my pocket and glanced around to see if anyone had noticed. Which was silly, of course. It was just a set of keys. As long as I didn't make a fuss, no one would suspect they weren't my own keys.

Not even whoever had turned them in when Ted had lost them. At least they hadn't mentioned them to the police. Not surprising; he'd lost them early Monday morning, probably during his first round on the mail cart. I'd forgotten them myself until just now.

And of course I was going to turn them over to the police.

Tomorrow. After I found them again.

Today, I was going to make a little side trip over to Ted's house. In the unlikely event anyone — like the police — caught me there, I could always pretend I was searching for his urgently needed files.

By the time the microwave dinged, this

plan had made me so cheerful that I actually hummed as I slid the mouse into George's bowl, shook a little Parmesan cheese over it, which he seemed to like, and headed back down the corridor.

Even running into two of the therapists didn't spoil my mood.

"I'm afraid you're going to have to do something about this," the eating-disorder therapist said.

"You can't expect us to conduct therapy in this kind of atmosphere," the size-acceptance therapist added.

Isn't it nice how a crisis brings people together? I thought. This was the first time I'd ever seen them join forces to pick on someone else.

"It's not exactly ideal for programming, either," I said.

"We've had one disruption after another ever since your group moved in," Eating Disorders went on.

"Frisbee-throwing in the corridors," Size Acceptance said, shaking her head.

"And this juvenile obsession with the martial arts."

"It's worse than Fraternity Row."

"Of course, that's what you get when you have so few women and minority employees to diversify your workforce."

"And now a murder!" Size Acceptance exclaimed. "I assure you, we never had a murder before you people arrived."

"We want to know what you're going to do about this," Eating Disorders demanded.

"I'm not sure what we're going to do about it," I said. "You have to remember that we never had a murder either, before we moved in with you people. We're still assessing the implications of that. Now if you'll excuse me, I have to feed George."

I held the bowl up where they could see its contents. Apparently they had finished complaining — at any rate, they left rather rapidly. I went back to the reception area to reward Dad and George for their patience.

"Really? How do you know that?" Dad was saying on the phone as I walked in.

I put the bowl in the holder attached to George's perch.

"Right here in this office?" Dad said.

"Dad, who are you talking to?" I asked.

"Some reporter," he said, covering the mouthpiece. "An actual murder?" he went on, to the reporter.

"Oh, Lord," I muttered, closing my eyes. "Dad, why are you talking to a reporter?"

"Right here in the reception room where

I'm sitting?" Dad said. "You're kidding."

"I hope you know what you're doing," I muttered.

"No, I certainly didn't know anything about it," Dad said. "Thank you for telling me. If you hear anything else, please call back and let me know."

He hung up, looking very pleased with himself.

"All you really have to do is tell them 'No comment,' you know," I said.

"I did that for the first four," he said. "It was getting boring. Maybe I should tell the next one about how they have me and the other temps washing the blood off the walls."

"Maybe I should take back the switchboard now," I suggested. "The Doctors from Hell team are probably waiting for you."

"They just want to talk about IVs and blood gases," Dad said as he got up from the switchboard. "Don't you want to hear the details of the autopsy?"

"Do I have a choice?"

He chuckled as if he thought I was kidding. "Of course, it was all very ordinary and straightforward," he said, frowning. "No really interesting features at all."

"I will make a point of conveying your

disappointment to the killer, should the occasion arise."

Dad seemed to interpret that as an invitation to fill me in on the details of the autopsy. For an autopsy with no interesting features at all, there were a lot of details, at least the way Dad told it, in between the phone calls I was answering.

"So what do I know now that I didn't before you told me all this?" I asked when Dad had finished. At least I assumed he was finished when he began to reminisce about similar but more interesting past autopsies.

I must have sounded a little testy. Dad thought about it for a second and then summed up the previous half hour of conversation with unusual brevity.

"The blow to the throat required quite a bit of strength — not everyone could have done it. If it was deliberate, it could indicate some special knowledge of anatomy or fighting tactics, but the killer could have just hit the right spot by accident. And once he was temporarily stunned by that, strangling him with the mouse cord didn't require greater than average strength. Or special knowledge."

"So the chief's going to be looking a little harder at anyone who's large, strong, or has special training, but really the autopsy neither conclusively points the finger at anyone nor eliminates anyone," I said. "Keisha and Luis may be long shots, but they're still in the running."

Dad's face lit up. "Is that who you suspect?" he asked in a stage whisper. "And they were in on it together?"

"No," I said, "I named them only because they're about the smallest people on staff."

"Ah," he said, looking glum again.

"The autopsy's not a lot of help," I complained.

"Sometimes science doesn't hold the answers," he proclaimed. "Sometimes only the power of the human mind can ensure that justice is done."

"You've been watching those crime-solving shows again," I said with a sigh. "Why don't you go tell the Doctors from Hell designers about blood gases now?"

He patted me on the shoulder and trotted off.

I was alone in the waiting room, except for one patient waiting meekly in the corner for an appointment with his therapist. At least I assumed he was a patient, since he kept glancing at George out of the corner of his eye and looking anxious if I caught him at it. People who came to see Mutant Wizards for the first time would invariably walk in and exclaim, "Why the hell do you have a buzzard in your waiting room?" And if we kept them waiting, they'd spend the time staring unabashedly at George. Patients, on the other hand, always tried to act as if George didn't exist, or as if there were nothing out of the ordinary about sharing a waiting room with a live buzzard. Perhaps they thought it was some kind of Rorschach test, and if they mentioned it, someone would immediately say, "That's a good question. Why do you think we have a buzzard in our waiting room?"

I suppose I should have drafted Dad to keep minding the switchboard for me as soon as I realized that he wasn't working with the Doctors from Hell team. Shortly after I took the switchboard back, the mail cart cruised through with Dad sitting on top of it. He'd acquired a notebook remarkably similar to the one Chief Burke carried, and was scribbling diligently in it.

The second time he rode by, he'd apparently run out of interesting things to note. He was sitting cross-legged and appeared to be lost in thought.

On his third circuit, he'd begun looking distinctly bored.

The fourth time through, he was lying down on his stomach, gripping the front of the mail cart, looking for all the world like a slow-motion toboggan rider. After that, he lay down on his back.

"What are you doing, anyway?" Jack asked when he happened to be in the reception area as the cart rolled through.

"Detecting," Dad said. "I'm studying the victim's point of view."

"And you're not the least bit superstitious about what happened to the mail cart's last passenger?" Jack asked.

"A sleuth has to take some risks," Dad called as the mail cart rolled out of sight.

"I'd be a little less worried if I hadn't heard him snoring the last time he passed my cube," Jack said.

I sighed. "Here," I said, picking up Spike's crate. "Stick Spike on top of the mail cart with him. If anyone tries anything, Spike is sure to bark."

"Good idea," Jack said.

For the rest of the afternoon, Dad and Spike snoozed comfortably on top of the mail cart, and Jack spread the word among the staff to keep an eye on them, in case anyone tried anything. No one did. Dad awoke, near five o'clock, chagrined at having taken so long a nap, and I took advantage of his embarrassment to dump Spike on him for the evening. I had things to do and didn't want dog walking duties to slow me down.

I found the disgruntled Eugene Mason's personnel file singularly uninformative. According to the paperwork, he'd left at the end of his ninety-day probation period by mutual agreement. Not much grounds for discontent there. Then again, as Liz was always reminding people, anything we wrote, including e-mails, could be subpoenaed by someone suing Mutant Wizards. Perhaps Personnel felt it safer not to go into too much detail about why we hadn't wanted to keep Mason on.

I hadn't learned anything more that afternoon — not that I didn't try to interrogate anyone unlucky enough to pass through the waiting room. By five o'clock, when I finally locked the doors and put the switchboard on night mode, I suspected most of the staff members were sneaking out the back door to avoid me.

I decided that I'd gone as far as I could with what little information I had to go on. I was going to come back tonight and snoop around.

Before I left, I strolled through the office. Either the afternoon's build had gone far better than usual, or the programmers had decided to run the evening build on Luis's spare server over at the Pines. At any rate, the Mutant Wizards staff was clearing out. Not entirely, though, and a few of the therapists had evening office hours and would be seeing patients as late as eight or nine o'clock.

Under the circumstances, I thought, pausing in a corridor, it didn't make sense to come back before eleven, at the earliest. Perhaps even midnight. Or —

"Can I help you?"

I glanced up and realized I was standing outside the door of one of the therapists' offices. The short, mousy, bespectacled man who was Dr. Lorelei's partner. He was hunched over his keyboard, and his hands covered the monitor, as if to protect it, even though it was facing away from me.

Get a life, I wanted to say. Even if I could see, from here, what you're typing, why would I want to? I doubt anyone wants to pry into your poor patients' secrets. At any rate, I don't.

"Sorry," I said. "Trying to remember where I left something."

He didn't speak, and continued to clutch his monitor.

"Good night," I said, and walked away.

When I was a few feet away, I heard the rattle of the keyboard start up again.

"Weird," I muttered. And then pushed him out of my mind. I had more important things to worry about.

Like seeing what I could find in Ted's house.

I looked up the address on the map before I set out. Not that I really needed to; I had a pretty good idea where it was. After so many months of house-hunting in Caerphilly, I could probably have walked blindfolded through any of the promising neighborhoods — promising, these days, began with any house that actually had indoor plumbing, and stopped only a little short of houses large enough to have their own zip codes.

Ted had lived in the country, about a twenty-minute drive south of town, an area I didn't know as well because it was almost entirely farmland. As I drove, I brooded on the injustice of the fact that the beastly Ted had actually managed to snag a house in the country, while all Michael and I had found was the Cave.

At least he'd said it was a house. Maybe it would turn out to be someone's old toolshed or a converted tobacco barn.

I finally came to a mailbox with the name CORRIGAN scrawled in black Magic Marker over another, faded name beginning with an *S*. I craned my neck to see the house, but the driveway was lined with boxwoods, ten feet tall and so overgrown they nearly met in the middle. I backed up, but the hedge continued across the front of the yard until it met the woods on either side.

"Here goes," I muttered, and pointed my car down the driveway — whose condition suggested that the owners had given up maintaining it about the same time they'd abandoned the poor boxwoods. The driveway seemed longer because I had to drive three miles an hour, but still — this was a large lot. And when I emerged from the boxwood tunnel in front of the house, I was so startled that I almost ran into a crumbling sundial.

If Alfred Hitchcock hadn't modeled the house in Psycho on this place, then surely Edward Gorey had found inspiration here. It was a three-story gray Victorian, complete with a widow's walk on the top, and sporting several dozen odd turrets, gables, bay windows, balconies, and other architectural flourishes. I spotted one tall, stately window that wasn't marred with either cracked glass or boarded-over panes, but if there was a square foot of unpeeled paint or undamaged gingerbread, it had to be on the back of the house. A lugubrious weeping willow appeared to be dying of some wasting disease in the front yard. I followed a trampled path through the foot-high weeds to the porch.

"A real fixer-upper," I said, craning my neck to see if the shingles had finished falling into the yard or if there were still a few lurking up there, waiting to land on unwary visitors.

Someone had nailed unpainted boards in place of the missing porch steps, and the porch floor seemed sound enough to hold me. Fighting the tendency to look over my shoulder — not to mention the superstitious expectation that if I did, I'd see a tall, cadaverous figure with a black cape and very pointed teeth — I managed to unlock the door.

And almost turned and ran. Not that the inside was scarier than the outside. Quite the contrary. Although equally neglected-looking, the interior was so unrelentingly cozy that I had a moment of panic, thinking that I must have come to the wrong house and was about to be arrested for trespassing.

"Don't be daft," I told myself. "It's the right address, and the key fits."

I closed the door behind me — yes, it creaked — and began slowly and carefully making my way through the house. Slowly and carefully, because nearly every square foot of floor was covered with furniture or small, fussy throw rugs, and nearly every square inch of horizontal table or shelf space with objects, most of them small and breakable.

Three sets of wind chimes and a bumper crop of cobwebs dangled from the crystal chandelier in the foyer. Three drab coats, a tangled mass of canes, and several dozen battered black umbrellas occupied the huge Victorian coat stand to my left, while to my right, a hall table displayed a heterogeneous collection of marble obelisks, painted china eggs, miniature foo dog statues, seashells, mineral specimens, and brass bells. I made the mistake of trying to draw aside the velvet curtain that partly filled the archway from the foyer to the living room, and the resulting dust cloud sent me into a fit of coughing so violent that all the tiny spiders I'd dislodged had managed to hide themselves by the time I recovered.

The living room held four mismatched

velvet couches, their colors softened by time except where someone had recently moved one of the lace doilies or antimacassars, and so covered with needlepoint pillows that I doubt a small child could have found room to sit on them.

The massive velvet curtains might be wonderful insulation in the winter, but I longed to jerk them aside and fling open a few windows. The temperature outside had finally begun to drop, but inside it was near one hundred degrees. But touching the curtains would disturb months — maybe years — of accumulated dust. I didn't want to leave that much evidence of my visit.

So I blotted the sweat from my face with the hem of my shirt and tiptoed past glass-fronted bookcases bulging with faded, dusty books and odd bric-a-brac. A collection of elegant glass paperweights shared space with several dozen souvenir models of buildings and landmarks from around the world. I particularly liked the way the plaster Statue of Liberty seemed to be conversing with the miniature of *The Thinker*, and how the Eiffel Tower seemed to be in the backyard of the White House.

"Okay, Ted," I said aloud as I dodged a giant dead fern perched on a tiny fretted

Victorian plant stand and narrowly missed overturning a whatnot filled with tiny china cats and shepherdesses. "I can think of three explanations for this. One — you were going to give up programming for an exciting new career selling antiques, collectibles, and kitsch. Especially kitsch."

On the whole, I thought that explanation unlikely. Wouldn't a dealer have better taste? I paused for a moment, distracted, to inspect a small curio cabinet that seemed to be entirely filled with the kind of little ceramic birds and frogs florists use to decorate inexpensive potted plants.

"Two — you're a medium and you've been channeling one of the legendary packrats of history."

I reached the doorway to the kitchen and looked around. The calendar beside the phone was still turned to April, with its overly cute picture of a quartet of fuzzy yellow kittens spilling out of an Easter basket. On the windowsills, the earthly remains of dozens of houseplants rustled gently in the faint draft created by my arrival. And on the counter, among the trivets, trinkets, and tea cozies, I found a nest of pill bottles, all in the name of a Mrs. Edwina Sprocket. Who had apparently suffered from an impressive variety of ailments, including heart problems, high blood pressure, osteoporosis, indigestion, and constipation. The most recent refill dated from the end of March.

"Three — you convinced the landlord, or the heirs, to let you move in before they held the estate sale."

The more I looked around, the likelier that explanation seemed. The kitchen cabinets held dusty canned goods. Mostly cream soups and other bland prepared foods. The refrigerator contents were definitely Ted — several six-packs of Coors, leftover pepperoni pizza, kung pao chicken trimmed with feathery gray mold, and frozen enchiladas. The only kitchen items that seemed recently used were a few utilitarian pans, utensils, and plastic dishes — stored in the dish drainer, probably because it would have taken a magician to fit another saucer into Mrs. Sprocket's tightly packed kitchen cabinets.

Other than the kitchen, the other rooms on the ground floor seemed undisturbed for weeks, except where someone — probably the Caerphilly police — had recently walked through, as I was now doing, leaving a trail through the dust. Most of the bedrooms on the second and third floor appeared to have been shut up for years. I sneezed a lot.

I had poked head and shoulders through the trapdoor to the attic and was peering around, trying to decide if it was worth searching, when the doorbell rang. I started, hitting my head on a low beam. And then I went downstairs to investigate.

The doorbell rang again as I tiptoed through the living room to peek out the lace curtains covering the glass panes in the door.

It was Frankie, looking as eager as ever, though minus the phony police uniform. But still, what was Frankie doing here?

I opened the door to find out.

"Oh, Meg — hi," he said, looking rather surprised to see me.

"Hi, Frankie," I said. "What can I do for you?"

"Um . . . I saw your car," he said, teetering a little as he nervously wound one leg farther than usual around the other. "So I thought I'd see if I could help you out."

I looked pointedly from my car to the giant hedges surrounding the driveway. Unless Frankie had X-ray vision, there was no way he could have seen my car from the road.

He squirmed. "So have you found any of

Ted's files? We could really use some of his files."

"The police took all his computer equipment," I said. "I'm just locking up."

Maybe that was a sneaky thing to say — implying, as it did, that I was here as part of the police search.

"Oh, okay," he said. "Well . . . I'll be going now."

I watched him drive away and waited until I was sure he was gone. Ted's files were urgent — but were they urgent enough to bring Frankie this far out of town? After work?

Strange.

I went back to explore the one part of the house I hadn't yet seen — the basement.

Chapter 12

Of course, I thought, if this were one of those women-in-jeopardy movies, the basement would be where the escaped lunatic was hiding, or where the secret treasure was buried, and the soundtrack would swell with ominous music when I reached for the door handle.

And, I confess, I did start when I looked down the steps and saw a figure in the gloom. Santa Claus, to be precise. He was propped up in the corner where the stairs made a ninety-degree turn, his head slumped on his chest and his hat askew. I deduced from the improbable way his left leg was twisted that he was a life-size Christmas decoration, but I still checked him for a pulse before turning my back on him. The moth-eaten, life-size reindeer — irritatingly, only seven of them — were hanging by their antlers from hooks in the ceiling beams.

I noticed, with a sigh of relief, that the basement seemed ten degrees cooler than the rest of the house. And there I found more proof of Ted's brief occupation. A space at the foot of the stairs had been cleared of clutter, and here Ted had set up housekeeping. A futon. A makeshift desk, still bearing the outline, in dust, of a CPU.

The clothes Ted hadn't hung from the overhead beams were jumbled into a copier-paper box. In fact, the copier-paper box seemed to be the cornerstone of his decorating and storage scheme. Beside his futon, one box served as a bedside table, holding a digital alarm clock and half a dozen empty Coors cans. His desk was a board held up at each end by a stack of three boxes. The desk boxes contained computer manuals or small pieces of electronic equipment. A stack of about two dozen boxes formed a low wall between his niche and the rest of the basement — they contained a vast collection of science-fiction and mystery paperbacks and a small collection of relatively unkinky girlie magazines. In the tiny basement bathroom, Ted's towels, ragged and brightly colored, had been thrown unfolded into a copier-paper box, since the linen closet was overflowing with Mrs. Sprocket's vintage toiletries and faded, lace-trimmed towels.

I wasn't seeing much paper, anywhere. Which was unusual. No matter how much so-called computer visionaries touted the paperless future, in my experience, heavy computer users tended to have more paper around, rather than less. And I found no disks, Zip drives, tapes, or CD-ROMs. Unheard of. One thing I'd noticed about my coworkers at Mutant Wizards — they adored their hardware and software with a passion I couldn't even begin to understand, much less share. But at the same time, they trusted their cybernetic idols even less than I would have. I'd seen only one programmer whose work space wasn't littered with printouts and backups, and I'd heard Frankie and Jack arguing about whether the best metaphor for that guy was "bungee jumping without a cord" or "playing Russian roulette with an Uzi."

And it hadn't been Ted. His cube at work had been as bad a rat's nest of paper and disks as anyone's, until the police hit it. Evidently the police had stripped his home office, too, and the only things I'd find were objects the police had left behind — probably for good reason.

I stood, looking around, and feeling

sorry for myself gave way to feeling sorry for Ted. I wondered if he'd actually rented the house, or if he'd only worked out some kind of deal to live in the basement as caretaker until it was sold. No matter how tight housing was, I wasn't sure I'd want to live here, surrounded by the warren of metal shelves Mrs. Sprocket had used to store such treasures as her back issues of the *Saturday Evening Post*, her empty mason jars, and several dozen rusty metal cemetery flower baskets.

I was working on a good case of melancholia when the doorbell rang again. As I was racing up the stairs to answer it, I tripped over something and fell sprawling on the landing where the L-shaped stairs turned, halfway up. I didn't stop to see what had tripped me — I wanted to take care of the new visitor first.

This time it was Rico. A dressed-up Rico; he'd thrown a plaid sport coat over his design school T-shirt. He was leaning casually against one of the porch pillars. I was tempted to tell him that he didn't have the height to pull off a really classy lean, but I settled for some more practical advice.

"I wouldn't put any weight on that if I were you," I said. "One good push could bring the whole porch roof down."

"Oh, hi, Meg," he said. "What are you doing here?"

"Locking up, at the moment," I said. "The police have taken all of Ted's computer stuff, so it's no good looking here for the missing Lawyers files."

"I figured as much," he said.

"Then why are you here?"

"To tell you the truth, I was hoping to run into Ted's landlord. He hasn't returned my calls."

"And why are you looking for Ted's former landlord?"

"Same reason you are, I guess," Rico said. "Sooner or later he'll want to rent the place out again. I was hoping to be first in line."

"The landlord's not here," I said. "I guess you'll have to keep trying. See you, Rico."

"Okay. Any chance you could let me in to — ?"

"Good-bye, Rico."

I stood, pondering for a moment. Ratty as Ted's living quarters were, he had a place to live. And I couldn't remember anyone describing his basement den — all I'd heard were envious comments on how lucky he was to have actually snagged a place outside town. I suspected he'd never had anyone over. And Frankie and Rico both lived back at the Whispering Pines Cabins, four or more to a room. Could Caerphilly's tight housing market actually be a motive for murder? It had certainly caused not a few heated discussions between Michael and me during our yearlong search for living space. And we were sane, rational human beings, for the most part. My coworkers at Mutant Wizards? Yeah, maybe one of them would kill for a place to live. I'd keep it in mind.

Meanwhile, I headed back for the basement stair landing. I hadn't stopped long enough to see what had tripped me, but what I'd seen out of the corner of my eye intrigued me.

"Talk about literally stumbling over evidence," I said as I stared down at my discovery.

It was a trapdoor. It had fallen back in place, but fit so tightly that it hadn't quite closed, and I was able to pry it open with a kitchen knife.

"Eureka!" I exclaimed as the trapdoor popped open to reveal a space about two feet square and filled to the brim with stuff.

I sat down beside the trapdoor and began removing the top items from Ted's secret stash.

On the top were a trio of romance novels, which surprised me a lot more than Ted's small collection of mildly dirty magazines. I'd never have pegged Ted for a romance reader.

But someone had read these books. They were not only heavily thumbed, but marked throughout with a yellow highlighter, as well. All three were by the same author — someone named Anna Floyd who, according to her author biography, lived in the country with her adoring husband and her three darling cats. Two were set in the present day and one in Regency England. I flipped through one of the modern ones and read highlighted quotes. Enlightenment was not forthcoming. If there was a clue here, I'd probably have to read the damned books to figure it out. Later. Much later. Maybe never, if I could first figure out who really killed Ted.

Next was a blue file folder with THE HACKER scribbled on the tab. In it, I found printouts from the *Boston Globe* Web site — articles about the "Robin Hood Hacker" case, which I vaguely remembered hearing about a year ago. I browsed a couple of the articles, but they didn't say anything I didn't remember reading before. Young programmer caught hacking into the system of a major New York bank and erasing about five thousand dollars in charges from his girlfriend's account. Major embarrassment for the bank when it turned out that the girlfriend had been trying to dispute the charges for two years — they'd come from Panama, a country she could prove she'd never visited — and she had finally attempted suicide, due to stress resulting from her ruined credit history and the bank's repeated collection calls.

"Maybe I should sic the assertiveness therapist on her," I muttered. And hacking the bank was the best Robin Hood could come up with to solve Maid Marian's problem? Didn't these people know why God invented lawyers?

Never mind. All's well that ends well. Robin Hood got off with a warning, and the girlfriend got her good credit rating restored.

So what was so interesting about the case that Ted created a file about it and had to hide the file in his secret compartment?

Maybe Ted *was* the Robin Hood Hacker? No, the photo of the police escorting the hacker out of his apartment building was pretty blurred, but it couldn't possibly be

Ted, who was taller than I and had blondish hair. The hacker had dark hair, and the arresting officers towered over him. Perhaps Ted kept it as a reminder to himself to keep to the straight and narrow? Or was it part of the research for a scheme to hack some other bank? I'd have to work on that.

And I was equally puzzled by the next object — a set of rules from Lawyers from Hell. Not the computer version, but the original role-playing game. I couldn't figure out why Ted would need to hide that. But it looked like an actual original — I could see some annotations in Rob's handwriting. Which meant the thing might have considerable value if Ted planned to sell it on the black market to rabid fans. So maybe he was hiding it because it was valuable. And he didn't trust banks. Or maybe he'd swiped it from someone.

Under the rules, I found a three-year-old copy of *PC Gaming* magazine. Surprise, surprise. He had a few more of them scattered around the basement, and we had dozens down at the office. What was so special about this copy that he had to hide it? I spotted a paper clip marking a page and turned to that article. Representatives from half a dozen gaming companies talked about the future of the industry. I chuckled. Since Rob was still inventing the paper version of Lawyers from Hell three years ago, anything they'd said about the future was probably a little off base by now.

Ted's secret stash wasn't turning out to be as exciting as I expected, I thought, suppressing a yawn.

Next I found a sheet of paper containing a number of strings of numbers with dots in the middle. A month ago, I'd have been puzzled; now, thanks to my time at Mutant Wizards, I knew that a Web site address, like www.mutantwizards.com was the pretty name humans used, while our computers looked for long strings of numbers. When I got back to the Cave, I could log on to the Internet and type in the numbers to see where they led. Not that I expected one of them to turn out to be www.whokilledtedandwhy.com or anything really useful like that.

Beneath the IP addresses, I found several long, abstruse legal documents. I got through a few paragraphs before deciding I'd better keep them for bedtime reading.

And at the bottom of the compartment, I found what looked like a small flashlight.

I checked it out — aha! It was actually a small portable black light. Which did solve my problem of how to get my hands on one so I could check the mail cart path. But I couldn't think of any good reason for Ted to have hidden it here. Everyone knew he was fascinated with the mail cart and had been fooling around with changing its path. Why bother to hide the evidence of his pranks?

"For this, you need a secret compartment?" I said aloud. Then again, maybe he hadn't built the secret compartment; maybe he'd found it and decided to use it. But even I could have found a better collection of things to hide in a secret compartment. "Jeez, Ted. Is that the best you could do? Is that it?"

I peered down into the compartment. Yes, that was it. Well, almost it. I saw a small, triangular white shape — the corner of a piece of paper that was trying to disappear through the crack between the side of the compartment and the bottom.

I grabbed the kitchen knife I'd used to open the trapdoor, and carefully teased the rest of the paper out, before it could disappear into whatever spider-infested crawl space was behind the stairs.

It appeared to be a printout of a computer spreadsheet, like the ones I used to calculate my budget. Down the left half of the paper was a series of words or phrases, like "the Voyeur," "the Ninja," "Mata Hari," and "the Iron Maiden." Eleven entries in all, and beside each one were a dozen columns of notes in tiny, barely readable type. Some of the words I could decipher — things like "struck out" or "no dice." But most of it . . .

"I need more time and better light to deal with this," I muttered. Although I figured it would be worth dealing with. From the date on the upper right-hand corner, it had been printed on Saturday — only two days before the murder. And one of the labels on the left was THE HACKER. So maybe the printout would help me figure out the meaning of the strange collection of objects I'd found beneath the trapdoor.

I found an empty grocery bag in Mrs. Sprocket's pantry — actually, I found several hundred, but I needed only one — loaded the contents of the secret compartment into it, and stashed it in my trunk.

But after I locked the house back up, I decided to explore the yard a little. The driveway continued behind the house, although I deduced from the three- and four-foot dogwood seedlings in the middle of it that no one had driven that way for several years. I followed the driveway and discovered an enormous weathered barn.

My cell phone rang. Michael.

"So what are you up to?" he asked.

"I'm not sure," I said. "Do you have to be breaking into someone's actual house for it to be burgling? Or would someone's barn count, too?"

"I know I'm going to regret this, but whose barn are you burgling?"

"Ted's. Or his landlord's."

I wedged the phone between shoulder and ear and explained, briefly, what I'd been doing, while rummaging through my purse for something that would serve as a makeshift screwdriver. The door was secured with a relatively new padlock, but since the screws holding the hasp onto the door were already half-loose, it took only a few minutes to remove the hasp entirely.

"There, I've got it," I reported to Michael. "And I bet the police didn't search in here. They couldn't have, unless there's another way in — the padlock was swathed in spiderwebs."

"You don't think maybe the spiderwebs are a sign that there's nothing worth finding in the barn?"

"Not necessarily," I said. "I mean obviously there's no evidence of the murder in here, given the spiderwebs; but there could be something that gives me a clue to why he was killed."

"Meg, be careful," Michael said.

"I will," I said. "Stand by, and I'll give you a blow-by-blow description of what I see."

I began pulling open the barn door. I was wondering if I should fetch the flashlight I kept in my car, when something struck me on the head and I lost consciousness.

Chapter 13

I awoke to find myself gazing into the glassy eyes of a moth-eaten taxidermied moose.

"Meg! Answer me!" it pleaded in a small, hollow voice.

"Yes?" I said.

Apparently the moose didn't hear me.

"I'll keep her on the line," it said, in the same oddly distant voice. "See if you can get a number for the Caerphilly police department. . . . What? . . . C-A-E-R—"

The police department? There was something about the police department that I ought to remember. If my head would stop hurting, I might remember.

I glanced around and saw my cell phone lying in the grass beside the moose's cheek.

"Michael," I said, grabbing the cell phone. "I'm fine. Don't call the police. Chief Burke would be really angry."

"Meg! Are you all right? What happened?"

"I'm fine. It was only a moose."

A brief pause.

"Keep trying to get the Caerphilly police," Michael said. Apparently to someone else. "I think she's going to need an ambulance."

"Michael, I told you, I'm fine," I said. "It was only a stuffed moose head."

"Only a stuffed moose head?" he repeated. And then, to whoever else was on the other end. "Get the number but don't call yet. Meg," he said, more loudly. "Are you sure you're okay?"

Was I okay? What if our deranged killer was following some kind of punning weapons motif, I wondered, as I patted the top of my skull. First strangling Ted with a mouse cord, and now assaulting me with a stuffed moose? I winced — by probing my scalp, I had confirmed that, yes, I had a remarkably large lump on the top of my head, and while it didn't appear to be bleeding, touching it made my headache temporarily worse.

I looked around and realized that the killer probably wasn't responsible for my predicament. I was lying at the edge of a small delta of objects that had erupted out of the barn when I opened the door. In addition to the moose, I spotted a crab pot, a rope hammock, several bicycle tires, a bad-minton net, a headless garden gnome, half a dozen flowerpots, several croquet mallets, a broken toilet, a large wasp's nest — fortunately, unoccupied — and several dozen other less recognizable bits of junk.

"I'm fine," I said. "I was opening the door to the barn, remember? A stuffed moose head fell out and beaned me. I have a lump on my head, but I'm fine."

"Don't go in the barn," Michael said. "It could be dangerous to go into the barn."

"I'm sure it would be dangerous, and I'm not going in there," I said. "I'd need a forklift to clear a path before I could even think of going in there. I'll be lucky if I can put back everything that fell out when I opened the door."

"That's good," Michael said. "Don't try to put things back, just get out of there; obviously it's not safe."

"Okay, okay," I said.

"And get your father to look at your head."

"Okay, I will," I said.

I was lying, of course. I stayed long enough to put back the stuff that had fallen out of the barn, which with only one and a half working hands seemed to take forever. But did Michael really expect me to leave it all spread across the lawn, advertising my snooping in case anyone like Chief Burke came back? I was tempted to just stow it all in the basement, on the theory that the police would be so overwhelmed by the magnitude of Mrs. Sprocket's clutter that they'd overlook the fact that some of it was sneaking around when their backs were turned, but decided it was a bad idea. They might have taken photos.

When I got back to the Cave, I tried to settle down and study Ted's collection of artifacts, but then I just put them aside in favor of half an hour with an ice pack and some aspirin.

I did put the portable black light in my purse. Depending on what time the pizza fest broke up, I might come back here afterward, or I might want to go straight from Luigi's to the office. I changed into jeans and a T-shirt that was presentable enough to wear to the restaurant, yet old enough that I wouldn't mind dirtying it up if my snooping led me into something messy, like the Dumpster.

When my head started feeling better, I realized I still had a little time to kill — I didn't want to be the first one there. On a whim, I turned on my laptop and logged on to the Internet. I searched for information on Anna Floyd, the romance writer, but apart from learning, on Amazon.com, that she had written two more books besides the ones I'd found in Ted's house, I couldn't find anything about her. One of Anna's book covers featured a handsome one-eyed pirate holding the buxom, swooning blond heroine. The pirate looked a little like Michael, I thought with a sigh. I fingered the cell phone. Should I call Michael? Change my mind about a virtual date? No, I checked my watch — he would probably still be filming, so I decided not to interrupt him. Besides, I was definitely going to go to Luigi's to interrogate the guys, and I wasn't sure how he'd feel about a virtual office party.

So I put the cell phone away. But I still had time before leaving for Luigi's, so I decided to do something useful. I grabbed the paper I'd found in Ted's cache, the one with the numbers I suspected were IP addresses, and carefully typed one of them into the address line of my browser.

My screen went black. Had my battery suddenly given out? No, it was the Web site's background. Suddenly, the words, HOT! HORNY! XXXXXXXX!!! began flashing in red on my screen, accompanied by several grainy pictures of women doing things better left undescribed.

"Ick," I said, and hit the back button to escape.

Instead of taking me back to Amazon, and Anna Floyd's overripe but fully clothed heroine, hitting the back button brought me to another black page pocked with pornographic images and leering red captions. I hit the home button and sighed with relief, thinking I'd escaped — but within seconds, small windows began popping up all over my screen, like toadstools after a rain, showing suggestive corners of pictures or offering badly spelled links to a bewildering variety of perversions.

I finally had to turn the laptop off to end the barrage, and sat there looking at it, fighting an irrational urge to spray the keys of my laptop with disinfectant before I touched them again. And feeling a familiar anger — the same anger I'd felt when, as a teenager, I'd felt a tap on my shoulder in a movie theater and turned to find a man exposing himself. At least with the flasher I could lash out, breaking his nose with a backhanded punch before dumping a thirty-two-ounce Coke in his lap. What could I do to the distant, anonymous creator of a sleazy Web site?

"Cute, Ted. That was a nasty little piece of work," I said aloud. "But what does it mean?"

There were half a dozen more IP addresses on the slip of paper. I shook my head as if to clear it. I'd have to check them out, of course; just because one of them was a porn site didn't mean they all were. But I had a feeling they would be, and I wasn't in the mood to face any more of them now.

I checked my voice mail. A message from Michael, reminding me to have my Dad check my head and promising to call me tomorrow if he didn't hear from me tonight. A message from Dad, reporting that he was having dinner with the ME and would fill me in tomorrow if he learned anything new. A message from Rob, reporting that he was still on the lam and would see me tomorrow, from which I deduced that he was still out of jail and enjoying his status as prime suspect.

Excellent. No one expected to hear from me till tomorrow. I washed my face and hands and grabbed my purse. Time to head over to Luigi's.

Even on a Tuesday night, Luigi's was hopping. I didn't see any of the Mutant Wizard crowd, so I loitered by the front counter till I could flag down one of the waitresses.

"I'm looking for the Mutant Wizards group," I said.

"The what?" the waitress asked.

Apparently there were still a few people in Caerphilly who hadn't heard about us. Possibly a good thing, under the circumstances.

"It's an office get-together," I said. "A bunch of people — probably guys, mostly, I really don't know how many."

"We got a couple groups," she said. "You want to walk through the dining rooms, see if you spot them?"

Just then Roger strolled up.

"Roger, hi. Do you know where the — ?"

"Two," Roger said to the waitress.

"Two?" I echoed.

"Two," the waitress said. "Right this way."

"Hang on," I said to the waitress. "Two?" I repeated, turning to Roger. "I thought you said there was going to be a group having pizza here tonight."

"No, I asked you to have pizza," he said. "Two," he added, to the waitress.

She looked back at me.

"Two, my sainted grandmother," I said. "You did not say 'Would you like to have a pizza with me.' You said, and I quote, 'We're having pizza tonight. Luigi's, seven-thirty.' That is how you tell someone she's welcome to join a group who already have plans. That is not how you ask someone out on a date."

"You tell him, hon," the waitress said, leaning against the counter and putting her hands on her hips.

"Well, you're here now," Roger said. "Why don't we just have some pizza and — ?"

"The hell we will!" I said.

"Is there a problem here?" said a man. The manager, presumably.

"No," Roger said.

"Yes," I said.

"The jerk lured her here on false pretenses," the waitress said.

"Do you need help, miss?" the manager asked me.

"No, I'm fine," I said. "He's the one who needs help — like some training in basic social skills. In the first place, Roger, that is not how you ask someone out, and in the second place, I'm already seeing someone and not interested in going out with anyone, and in the third place, if I were interested in going out with someone, you would be only slightly above Ted on my list of prospects and well below George, and in the fourth place — in the fourth place —"

Oops — tactical mistake. I hadn't thought of a fourth place.

"In the fourth place —," I repeated, hoping for inspiration.

"Here we are!" exclaimed a voice from behind me. "Are we on time?"

Jack. With Luis trailing in his wake.

"What are you doing here?" Roger said, frowning.

"Meg told me about the pizza party," Jack said. "Good thing Luis and I came, huh, or you'd have had a pretty boring time. Guess everyone else was busy. We'll have fun anyway, though, won't we? Four, please," he said to the waitress.

The waitress looked at me. So did the manager.

"Four," I said.

"Table for four," the waitress said. "You got it, hon."

"But —," Roger began.

"So," Jack said, flinging his arm around Roger's shoulders and herding him along after the waitress. "How's it going, Rog?"

Luis put his hand over his mouth to hide a snicker, and he and I fell in behind Jack and Roger.

"Glad you guys showed up," I told Luis.

"Roger's such a jerk," Luis said.

"No kidding. So since there wasn't really a pizza party, how did you two happen to show up?"

"Something you said to Jack clued him in," Luis said. "After all, he's seen the jerk pull stuff like this before."

Was it reassuring that I wasn't the sole object of Roger's awkward attentions, or should I be embarrassed I hadn't figured him out earlier? I decided not to worry about it.

As we sat down — with Luis and Jack flanking me — the waitress plunked a wax-encrusted Chianti bottle onto the table and used an orange Bic to light the candle stuck in its mouth. As she did, I happened to be glancing at Luis's face and realized something.

Luis was the Hacker. The Robin Hood Hacker. No wonder the blurred black-and-white newspaper photo from Ted's secret cache looked so familiar; the lighter flame was enough like the glare of the reporters' flashbulbs to let me recognize his face.

But Luis wasn't the name in the article — in the caption under his picture, the first name had been Michael or Mike — a name that tends to stick in my mind. So either Luis had been using a false name when he was the Robin Hood Hacker, or he was using one now. Suspicious, in either case.

When I got home, I was definitely going to have to spend some time with the printout I'd found in Ted's cache. Maybe the chief wasn't so far off after all. The note he'd found in Rob's in-basket had made him suspect that blackmail could have been the motive.

Maybe Rob wasn't the only one who got a blackmail note. Maybe he was just the only one stupid enough — or innocent enough — to leave it lying around where the police could find it. I definitely needed to study the printout some more.

I would also definitely have to make a copy of the printout and get the original to the police. Preferably without telling them how I found it. Maybe if I turned in his keys, told them how I'd picked them up after one of his trips through the reception room, and then claimed the paper had been with them. Yeah, that would probably work. And confront Luis to find out what was really going on. Sometime when we didn't have onlookers, though — particularly not Jack, who seemed to be Luis's mentor. And then —

"Meg?"

"Sorry," I said. "My mind was wandering."

"You like vegetables, right?" Jack said. "We can get a vegetarian pizza if you prefer."

Roger and Luis looked glum.

"No, I like meat," I said. "I'm through trying to reform everyone's diet. From now on, you can keel over from scurvy for all I care."

That shut down conversation. Until the beer arrived — their beer and my red wine, actually.

"So what's the latest from Rob?" Jack asked.

"Out on bail," I said.

"What have they got on Rob, anyway?" he asked.

"They seem to think the murderer had to be a martial arts expert," I said.

"And they arrested Rob?" Luis exclaimed.

I nodded. Roger snorted with laughter, spraying most of a mouthful of beer on the table, and Luis and Jack both looked as if they were trying hard not to explode.

"Oh, go ahead and laugh, all of you," I said, tossing a wad of napkins over at Roger.

"Martial arts expert," Roger said, using

the napkins to wipe his T-shirt. "That's such a crock."

"Don't worry," Jack said, appropriating some of the napkins and using them to clean the table. "Rob will be fine as soon as they realize . . . um . . ."

"That he can't fight his way out of the proverbial paper bag?" I suggested. "What's to keep them from deciding by that time that the killer was a martial arts beginner with dreams of glory."

"Unless there really is some good reason for them to think it was a martial arts expert," Luis said. "In which case they might pick on Jack."

"I wondered if you did martial arts," I said. "What kind?"

"A little karate, a little jujitsu," he said.

"A little!" Luis exclaimed. "He's a black belt in both. An expert!"

"Advanced enough to know what I don't know," Jack said. Which was more convincing evidence of his skill than anything Luis could say — most of the really outstanding martial artists I'd ever met came across more mild-mannered than your typical ninety-eight-pound weakling.

We kicked the days' events around over a sausage-and-mushroom pizza. I tried to get them talking about Ted's character, with limited success. Apparently people were past the initial shock and excitement of Ted's death and had reached the stage where survivors want to feel sentimental about their fallen comrade and tell stories of his virtues and accomplishments and the good times they'd had together. Since Ted didn't appear to have any virtues and accomplishments, or at least none of which present company were aware, this pretty much limited them to practical jokes Ted had played that were at least remotely funny and didn't involve bodily functions best left unmentioned while eating pizza.

Not the most scintillating dinnertime conversation I'd ever heard. And I was mildly distracted throughout dinner, trying to figure out how I was going to make my exit unaccompanied by the persistent Roger. As the pizza slices disappeared and the conversation slowed, I found him watching me with the single-minded focus of a cat outside a mousehole. Not that I was worried about my safety — even if Jack and Luis hadn't been there, I had no doubt of my ability to fend him off. I just wasn't in the mood for a scene.

But fate smiled on me. Even Roger's libido couldn't prevent several mugs of beer from having their usual effect.

"Don't eat the last piece," Roger said as he got up.

Now this was a lucky break, I thought as I saw him head for the rest rooms. I dug in my purse and fished out some bills.

"Here," I said handing them to Jack. "Just in case Roger doesn't know how to take drop dead for an answer, I think I'll take off now."

"And here I was going to offer to escort you home if Roger proved persistent," Jack said. The tone was joking, but I had a feeling he was serious.

"I'd feel better if you just stayed here to baby-sit Casanova," I said. "If I head out now, I can catch Michael before he goes out to dinner."

"Curses, foiled again," Jack said, pocketing the cash with a smile. "I'll give you your change tomorrow at the office."

I made it to the door before Roger returned, and thus escaped without having to do anything reprehensible.

I did tell one small lie. I wasn't heading home to call Michael. I was taking Ted's portable black light over to the office to check the mail cart path.

I felt bad, in a way, about Jack. Not that I had given him any encouragement. But he was a nice guy — hell, he was attractive.

223

If I didn't have Michael, I could see myself accepting some of the lunch and dinner invitations he'd made. In a heartbeat.

An attractive, gainfully employed bachelor — if my mother and my aunts were around, they'd already be trying to set him up with someone.

Not that I shared my family's addiction to matchmaking . . . but the thought did hit me: What if I arranged to have lunch with him and Liz? I wouldn't do any of the sort of obvious things Mother and the aunts would try, like arranging to meet them both somewhere and then forgetting to show up. But if I could get them together outside the office, when Jack wasn't running as fast as he could to keep the release on time and Liz didn't feel she had to be Ms. Corporate Attorney.

Then again, if Rob really was getting interested in Liz . . .

Snap out of it, I told myself. They're all grown-ups; they can run their own lives.

I arrived at the Mutant Wizards office to find the parking lot nearly empty. The only vehicle there was Frankie's fifteen-year-old van, which would probably sit there until he'd saved enough for a new transmission. Of course, Caerphilly was small enough that a lot of people walked to work, but the empty lot was a good sign. As were the darkened office windows.

I let myself into the building and climbed the stairs to the second floor, where the Mutant Wizards offices were. I stuck my key in the suite door lock, but before I could turn it, the door slipped open.

Damn, I thought. Probably the therapists again. They were used to leaving the front door unlocked so they wouldn't have to interrupt a session with one patient to buzz in another. I'd been trying to explain to them that they couldn't keep doing this — not considering Mutant Wizards' extensive investment in hardware, to say nothing of the possibility of corporate espionage. I would read them the riot act tomorrow. Point out that their actions could have enabled the murderer to enter the building, or reenter to destroy evidence.

I was fuming and already beginning to compose my stern lecture as I stepped into the office and groped to the left of the door for the light switch.

"Lorelei!" someone whispered.

As I turned, startled, toward the sound, two hands gripped my shoulders and a mouth closed over mine.

Chapter 14

At least the mouth tried to close over mine. One of the things martial arts is supposed to do, if you're paying attention, is train your reflexes, so you react quickly and effectively when you think someone's attacking you. As Michael found out rather painfully one day when he decided to drive up and surprise me upon my return from a craft show. Unfortunately, he decided to surprise me by sneaking up behind me and grabbing me.

"I won't ever do that again," he'd said, nursing his bruises.

"Don't," I'd replied. "Because if you do it again, I'll react the same way. If someone grabs me, I can't stop to worry about whether it might be someone I know."

It was nice to see my reflexes were still okay. In fact, better than okay, I thought as I flipped on the light switch and looked down at my would-be assailant. Or, perhaps, would-be admirer. I made a mental note to call my karate instructor and thank him. Then again, maybe not; he was sure to want a blow-by-blow description, and I was already having a hard time remembering exactly which technique I'd used to shake off the clutching arms, and exactly how I'd knocked the attacker to the floor. I could report that the side kick to the groin worked splendidly, though. The intruder had curled into a fetal position, his face almost touching his knees, and he was making faint whimpering noises. I didn't recognize him immediately, but then, what little I could see of his face was starting to bruise. And, wonder of wonders, I didn't seem to have reinjured my left hand in the fray.

George, awakened by the light, blinked sleepily at the sight of me.

"Okay," I said to the groveling intruder. "Who the hell are you, and what do you mean by attacking me like that?"

I had to repeat myself several times before he stopped whimpering and looked up.

"Why did you do that?" he asked.

"You attacked me in the dark," I said. "I defended myself."

"I thought you were someone else," he said, heaving himself up on his knees.

"I figured out that much. Don't get up just yet," I said, turning my body slightly so I was ready to deliver another good, solid kick.

George added to the effect by choosing that moment to shriek rather loudly. I knew he had just recognized me and assumed, in his single-minded way, that I had arrived to feed him, but it must have sounded rather ominous to the intruder. He dropped back to the floor and curled up again, watching me warily.

I recognized him now — a therapy patient. One of Dr. Lorelei's flock, a small, plump, graying man who could have been any age between thirty and fifty. This was the first time I'd seen him unaccompanied by his wife, also small, plump, graying, and of indeterminate age.

"You thought I was Dr. Lorelei?" I asked.

He reduced his chances of getting kicked again by blushing.

"So you were coming to see Dr. Lorelei."

He nodded.

"Why?"

"I'm a patient of hers," he said.

"Her office hours were over a long time ago," I said.

"This was urgent," he said.

"Men usually seem to think so, yes."

"I needed to talk to her. Urgently. She agreed to meet me here."

"Right," I said.

He could see I didn't believe him — he didn't look as if he expected me to. But at least he stopped babbling inanities.

"Show me some ID," I said.

He reached into his pocket, pulled out his wallet, and handed over a driver's license. The picture matched his face, or would when the swelling went down, and the name sounded vaguely familiar — about the way it would from seeing it on the visitor's list a couple of times. I pulled out my notebook-that-tells-me-when-to-breathe and wrote down his name and address; my handwriting was somewhat more ragged than usual because I was still keeping one eye on him.

"I think you should leave now," I said as I flipped the driver's license onto the floor beside him. "If you still need Dr. Lorelei, why don't you meet her in the College Diner? It's open twenty-four hours, and they didn't have a murder on the premises yesterday, so the waitresses are probably a little less apt to kick first and ask questions later. I can send the doctor over when she shows up."

"No, no. I'm feeling much better," he said. "Just apologize to her for dragging her out so late, okay?"

Somehow he didn't look better. He looked a little traumatized. I'd probably set his therapy back years. I'd feel sorry if it wasn't clear that the little swine was cheating on his wife.

He looked relieved. Perhaps he was expecting me to call the police. Which I still could, later, if I decided it was a good idea. Like if I checked the visitor's logs and found out he was at the office Monday.

I stood at a safe distance as he hauled himself to his feet and staggered out of the suite. I kept my eye on him for the whole five minutes it took for the elevator to lurch up to our floor and drag its doors open so he could limp inside.

If he really was expecting Dr. Lorelei, it might be interesting to catch her off guard when she arrived. Which might be very soon, if he had mistaken me for her. I turned out the overhead lights and my flashlight, and was about to hide behind the partition that separated the reception area from the rest of the office when it occurred to me that Dr. Lorelei might already be inside her office. But no, surely if she'd heard the commotion in the reception area, she'd have appeared already.

While I was debating where to hide, I heard a noise out in the hall. I pulled open the coat closet door, only to find the space in which I was planning to hide filled with a giant cardboard box. Dammit, nothing was supposed to be in the coat closet but visitor's coats and the fire extinguisher. I made a mental note to figure out tomorrow who had junked it up. Meanwhile, I ducked under the reception desk, barely making it out of sight before the door opened.

I heard cautious footsteps.

"Randall?" a voice called. "Are you here?"

I stood up, turning on my flashlight as I did, and aiming it toward the voice. Dr. Lorelei stood, blinking, in my beam. She was wearing a slinky black dress and four-inch heels — which made her about six feet four inches.

"Fancy meeting you here," I said, putting one hand on my hip while keeping her pinned with the beam.

She looked uncomfortable but didn't say anything. Was she too surprised to talk, or was she trying to figure out what to say? Or perhaps just trying to wait me out. Two could play at that game.

But long before the pressure of my withering glance had a chance to demoralize Dr. Lorelei to the point that she would confess her rendezvous — heck, if she wanted to confess to Ted's murder while she was at it, I wouldn't complain — the office door popped open behind her, and I saw the pasty face of the rabid fan who had been trying to sneak into the offices all week.

"Aarrgghh!" I yelled, and flapped my arms, much the way I'd do to chase squirrels off Dad's bird feeder. The fan reacted much as the squirrels did: after a moment of frozen shock, she turned and ran.

And like the squirrels, she would probably lurk just out of sight, waiting for a chance to come back and steal something. I turned angrily to Dr. Lorelei.

"You see!" I said. "That's why we can't have people leaving the doors unlocked all the time. I don't know whether it was you or one of the other therapists who told my brother that playing Lawyers from Hell was a silly, useless way for grown people to spend their time — well, fine, no one's forcing you to play it. But you have to realize that there are people who take it very, very seriously, and will stop at nothing to get some kind of inside information about the new release, and if you persist in leaving the doors unlocked, it's going to cause problems. For all we know, these crazy fans could have had something to do with the murder!"

Dr. Lorelei didn't say anything, but I saw her eyes dart sideways a couple of times to glance at the door. Did she think I was so unbalanced that she'd need to make a run for it?

Then I realized she might be thinking what had just occurred to me: if a crazy fan really did have something to do with the murder — and while I admit that having the police suspect my brother made me biased, I still thought the fans were logical suspects — then maybe the police should check them out. Only I'd just chased the craziest of them all away, instead of trying to sic the police on her.

Oh, well. Odds were she'd be back tomorrow. In fact, if she didn't show up again fairly soon, that would be even more suspicious.

Dr. Lorelei finally found her voice. "I didn't leave the door open," she said. "I was just as surprised and shocked as you were to find it open."

"Really," I said.

"I came down to meet a patient who's having a crisis," she said, glancing again at the door. "I need to let him in when he arrives."

"If you mean Randall, he managed to find his own way in, and he seems to be over his crisis, so I sent him home."

She opened and closed her mouth a few times, as if not sure what to say. "I don't know what you're thinking," she began.

Actually, from the look on her face, she'd probably already figured out what I was thinking. I'd have to ask one of my therapist relatives to be sure, but I had a pretty good idea that having an affair with a patient would be a first-class violation of Dr. Lorelei's professional ethics. Not to mention a violation of ordinary human morality — Randall was married, and so was Dr. Lorelei, unless the ring she wore on her left hand was some kind of camouflage to deflect the romantic fantasies of her patients.

But I wasn't mean enough to say all that. Okay, maybe I was mean enough, but something more interesting occurred to me instead, and I decided to take a wild chance.

"Is that what Ted was blackmailing you about?" I asked. "Your affair with Randall?"

Bull's-eye. Even with just the flashlight

beam for light, I could see her flinch.

"He wasn't blackmailing me," she said. "I mean, he tried, but I told him off. I never paid anything. Why should I — ? I'm not having an affair. I'm having a small problem with a patient who has become obsessed with me, true, but I'm working that out."

"And meeting him here at one a.m. was part of working it out?" I asked, checking my watch.

"I should have known you'd assume the worst," she said, drawing herself up and turning on her heel.

"Doesn't much matter what I assume," I said, to her departing back. "Be interesting to hear what Chief Burke makes of it."

Maybe it was my imagination, but I think her shoulders fell a little as I said that.

I watched as she crossed the lobby and disappeared down the stairway.

I'd guessed correctly — Ted had tried to blackmail her. Wasn't there an entry for The Valkyrie on his list of targets? That would fit Dr. Lorelei perfectly. But did this have anything to do with his murder?

Perhaps not, if her reason for showing up here was as innocent as she would like me to think. Then again, maybe even the appearance of an ethics violation would damage her career — especially her brand-new national radio show. And if she really was having an affair — ?

Whether or not she was having an affair wasn't important, though I admit I was curious. What mattered was whether or not she'd kill to protect her professional reputation and her growing fame as the star of *Lorelei Listens*. And for my money, yes, she was ambitious enough. Not to mention the fact that, given her size and strength, she could probably have strangled Ted even without stunning him first.

Maybe I should be glad she left quietly.

Maybe I should have stayed in hiding instead of confronting her. And speaking of hiding — I checked the box in the coat closet and found it full of pink Affirmation Bears. So Dr. Brown would receive tomorrow's complaint about people usurping shared space for personal use. Or maybe I should focus on the safety angle — if a fire broke out and I reached into the closet, I wanted to put my hands on the extinguisher, not a fuzzy pink cheering section.

Should I wrestle the box into her office now? No. For now, I was going to make myself a copy of Ted's blackmail list, so no one would see me doing it in the morning, and leave it at the reception desk, with the keys. And then crawl around with the black light, studying the mail cart track. The bears could hibernate where they were until morning, when Dr. Brown was available to move them herself.

I strolled through the opening and turned right, rounding a corner and walking down the north hall, which led, eventually, to the copier room.

And then I saw something down the hall and ducked into a nearby cube.

Chapter 15

I peered carefully out of the cube. I'd seen someone in the computer lab. During the daytime there were always people in the lab, of course; even at midnight, which it very nearly was, seeing someone working late would not be odd — but this someone was sitting in the dark.

I'd never found out why, unlike the rest of the office, the computer lab had floor-to-ceiling glass walls. I didn't find the view of a large room full of hardware that aesthetically pleasing, but maybe I wasn't the intended audience. Maybe to the technically oriented, it was a symphony in plastic, metal, and silicon, a tone poem in black, white, gray, and beige.

Or maybe it was a security measure, so no one could easily get up to any kind of sabotage. Anyone who walked down the north corridor could see everything that was happening in the lab.

And anyone in the lab could see anyone who walked down the corridor.

I peered carefully out of the cube where I was hiding. My eyes were more adjusted to the dark now, and the flicker from several monitors gave enough light for me to recognize the occupant of the lab.

It was Roger.

He was making CD-ROMs. "Burning" them, as the guys said. Mutant Wizards had several CD burners in the lab, so the programmers could make a small quantity of CDs when they wanted to get people to test new versions of the game. As I watched, Roger punched a button on one of the CD burners. The drawer slid open. He removed the CD inside and put it on top of the inch-high stack of CDs beside the burner. Then he took a fresh CD from a stack to his left, placed it in the holder and pushed the drawer back in. His fingers flew over the keys for a few minutes, and then he sat back, clasped his arms behind his head, and went back to watching the various monitors and CD burners.

Of course, it was always possible that he had some legitimate reason for being there. Doing some urgent task related to the new release. And that he hated the fluorescent lights and preferred to sit in a room lit only by the glow of the monitors. And found it more convenient to sneak in the back door, rather than through the front door, where I'd have seen him. But still . . .

I ducked back into a cube and looked around. Luis's cube, I noticed. I rifled the papers by his phone and, as I'd hoped, found a copy of the emergency contact list. Roger was on it, and, more important, his work, home, and cell phones were listed.

I called his cell phone. After a couple of rings, he answered. "Yeah?

"Roger!" I exclaimed. "Thank God someone's got his phone on; I've been ringing people for fifteen minutes. Listen, you live pretty near the office, right?"

"Right," he said.

"Is there any chance you could do me a big favor and drop by the office really quickly?"

"Why?" he asked. Not mentioning, of course, that he was already at the office, which anyone who was here for any honest reason would have said right away.

"I left Spike in his cage in the downstairs hall," I improvised. "Rob was supposed to pick him up, but I can't reach Rob — I'm beginning to worry that the police have taken him in again, and I don't want to abandon Spike there all night if Rob didn't have a chance to pick him up. Could you go over there and take a quick look?"

"Yeah, I guess so," he said. "Hang on."

I heard some tapping noises through the phone, and then a door opening and closing as he left the computer lab. I waited until I heard the same noise again, this time from the reception area, and then I ran back to the computer lab, carefully opened the door, and tiptoed over to where I could see his monitor.

"Okay," I muttered. "I see why you're slinking around in the middle of the night."

From the looks of it, Roger was being a very bad boy. One monitor showed a pornographic Web site. Not, as far as I could tell, a very good one. But perhaps the visitors didn't much care about the bad lighting and composition of the photos, or the fact that the women in them weren't particularly beautiful or enthusiastic about what they were doing. And I was sure no one else cared that the text — what there was of it — was poorly spelled and hideously ungrammatical. I was probably the only person who'd ever tried to read the text, aside from its author.

And, turning to a second monitor, I was pretty sure I knew who that author was.

The screen was covered with unintelligible code. But if I glanced back and forth between the two monitors, I could see some of the text from the porn site on the second screen, interspersed with lines and lines of unintelligible gibberish pocked with brackets.

Apparently I'd interrupted Roger in the middle of updating his site. The cursor blinked right after the phrase "completely nekkid and reelly . . ." — I restrained my impulse to correct his spelling, and I didn't particularly want to know what adjective he'd been about to type.

Was this how he normally spent his evenings? I wondered. Or just the evenings when his inept attempts at connecting with real live women fizzled?

I turned back to the first monitor. Something about the site looked familiar. I grabbed the mouse and scrolled up to the top of the page. Red and yellow words flashed at me, just as they had done on the site I'd seen at home — the site whose address I'd found in Ted's cache. Different words, but same style — which means, unless all porn sites had the same graphic look, it was probably the same site.

I glanced at a third monitor, which seemed to be tracking the progress of

Roger's CD creation. He was copying vast quantities of files onto the CD. File titles flashed briefly across the screen as they were copied, and from the titles, I deduced that he was copying porn files. Backing up his site, perhaps? Adding new material to it?

I didn't know enough to tell, and didn't really care. Whatever he was doing, it shouldn't be happening on Mutant Wizards property, with Mutant Wizards hardware. Tomorrow, I'd look for someone who could figure out what was happening. I grabbed a slip of paper and wrote down the address of the porn site, in case whoever I enlisted needed that to track it down.

"Meg?"

I jumped, and then realized that Roger's voice was coming from my cell phone.

"I'm in the lobby. The dog's not here. Anything else?"

"No," I said. "Thanks a million, Roger. Sorry to drag you over there at this time of night."

If I were Roger, I'd at least have pretended to allow enough time to walk over to the office, I thought, with irritation. Was he too stupid to think of that, or did he think I was? Either way, I needed to leave, now. But I wanted some evidence. I slipped a CD from the middle of Roger's completed stack. And then, in case he was keeping count, I tiptoed across the lab, grabbed a blank CD from the box where they were stored, and slipped it back at approximately the same place.

The lab itself seemed relatively soundproof — perhaps that explained why Roger had not emerged to check on any of the earlier events of the evening. But as I opened the door to the corridor, I heard the front door open and close. Clutching the contraband CD with my left fingertips, I eased the lab door slowly closed and slipped back down the hall and into a nearby cube.

Just in time. I saw Roger's shadowy figure pass by, and then I heard the computer lab door open and close.

I peeked out and peeked through the glass walls again. Roger was settled back in his chair, hands clasped behind his head, staring impassively at his monitors.

Time for me to disappear.

I tucked the CD into my purse and sneaked the long way back to the reception area. Even though I didn't think Roger could hear it, I made sure to open and close the office door as quietly as possible.

And I knew better than to wait for the geriatric elevator; I tiptoed down the stairs and eased the door closed. And breathed a sigh of relief. Unless Roger left the windowless computer lab, I'd be undetected. I was safe.

Or maybe not, I realized as I turned and stepped out into the parking lot. Which was still almost empty. Aside from Frankie's van, my blue Toyota was the only car in the parking lot. And apart from me, the only person in sight was the huge biker who'd been lurking in our parking lot. At the moment, he was lurking beside my Toyota.

As I watched, he leaned down and peered under the car.

His back was to me, so I decided to sneak a little closer to see what he was up to.

He was at least six feet six inches tall, and remarkably broad. Aside from a slight potbelly, he seemed mostly muscle. He wore enormous canvas boots, greasy jeans, a T-shirt with the sleeves ripped out, and a denim vest with a florid painting of a winged ferret on the back. Chains jingled merrily from various parts of his outfit, and his arms sported a remarkable collection of tattoos, though his thick body hair made it hard to appreciate any of their details. Except for one: on a thinly forested patch of bulging bicep, I could decipher the words BORN TO LOSE. The effect was somewhat spoiled by the skull inserted between the *o* and the *s* of "lose." Although a miniature work of art in its own right — one eye-hole sported a rose, and the other a writhing worm — the skull was so nearly identical in size and shape to the o that it was clear that the tattoo artist hadn't been the world's best speller, and had originally inscribed "Born to Loose." You had to give the arm's owner points, I decided. He was at least literate enough to consider fixing the typo worth additional pain and possibly more money.

But literate or not, he wasn't the sort of person one wants to find hovering over one's car in a deserted parking lot at — good grief! — 1:05 a.m. Perhaps if it had been earlier, I would have gone back inside to wait him out or call the police. But I was tired, cranky, and, I suppose, a little reckless.

Assailants aren't looking for opponents, I said to myself, recalling the words my karate instructor had always used. They're looking for victims. Don't look like a victim.

I slid my purse down to where I could use it for a purse fu block if needed, made sure my weight was balanced evenly, took a deep breath, stood up as straight as I could, and prepared to project fierceness and self-confidence as I strode forward.

Chapter 16

Apparently I wasn't projecting anything with sufficient force for the biker to notice. I stopped a few feet short of the car and wondered what to do next. My supposed assailant was still peering under the car. What could he possibly be doing? Was there some kind of nefarious sabotage he could do to the undercarriage of my car? And he was holding a ratty old towel on one hand — soaked in ether, perhaps, the better to subdue his unwary victims? Or did thugs use some more modern anesthetic these days? And how long was I supposed to stand around waiting for him to notice my fierce, alert, threatening presence, anyway? Should I clear my throat or something to get his attention?

"Hey!" I shouted. "What do you think you're doing? Get away from my car!"

He stood up, bumping his head on the door handle on the way. "Shh!" he said, putting his finger to his lips and whispering. "You'll scare her."

Fingers massaging where he'd hit his head, he bent down again and looked back under the car, leaving me standing there, purse in hand, feeling ridiculous.

"Here, kitty-kitty-kitty!" he called in a falsetto.

"You're looking for a cat?" I asked.

"A pregnant cat," he said.

"Ah," I said. "I was wondering where she went."

"She's under your car," he said, standing up and puffing a little, as if prolonged bending over tired him. "She won't come out."

Sensible cat.

"Perhaps the noise is scaring her," I said.

"Noise?" he repeated.

"You know — the chains and stuff," I said, gesturing to his outfit. "All that jingling."

"I should have realized!" he exclaimed, and began divesting himself of chains. "The poor little pussycat! I never realized how terrified she must be."

He'd shed the bracelet chains and belt chains, and was just discovering that he'd have to shed his jacket and jeans to rid himself of the ones permanently attached to them. I was about to protest — although I was mildly curious to see if his striptease act would reveal any other amusing tattoos — when the cat, evidently alarmed by the noise of his chains hitting the asphalt, made a break for freedom. Luckily she was so focused on the biker that she failed to notice my arrival. I dropped my purse and managed to snag her, though she was struggling so hard I wasn't sure I could hold her.

"Here, let me take her," the biker said. With a few deft moves, he swaddled the cat in the towel so that only her head showed. She mewed faintly in protest, then gave up and closed her eyes.

I sucked a few of the worst scratches on my right hand and was grateful, for almost the first time in two weeks, for the bandage that had shielded my left hand.

"Poor widdle thing," the biker cooed, scratching the cat behind the ear. "I've got a box all ready for you."

"A box?" For a moment I visualized a perfect feline-size coffin, topped with a wreath of catnip; then I told myself to stop being so morbid.

"It's behind the car," he said. "Would you mind getting it?"

He'd have had to drop the cat to attack

me, and I was beginning to get the feeling he was harmless. Either the cat felt the same way or she had given up all hope. While I didn't think she was enjoying having her head scratched, she'd stopped fighting.

I found the box and set it on the hood of my car. It was a copier-paper box with a six-inch-square hole cut in the lid and covered with a piece of old window screen.

I managed to get the top off, and the biker put the cat inside. He deftly unwrapped the towel with one hand and then set the top in place before the cat realized she could move again.

"Poor kitty," he cooed, peering down through the screen. "You had me worried."

"Oh, is she your cat?" I asked. "We thought she was a stray and took her in."

"That was nice," he said. "No, I think she's a feral cat."

He looked up at me.

"Which means she's essentially a wild animal, you know, and it's no good trying to domesticate her."

"Nobody was —," I began.

"Just like that buzzard you people are keeping," he went on. "That's a very bad practice. Wild birds were not meant to be house pets."

"Tell me about it," I said. "I'm the one who gets to clean up after him."

"I haven't been able to find out for sure yet," he said. "But there very well may be a Virginia law against keeping buzzards captive."

I was getting a little tired of lectures.

"Listen, I appreciate your dedication to wildlife and all that, but who the hell are you, and what business is it of yours if we're keeping a whole bevy of buzzards in our office?"

"I'm —," he began, sticking out his hand.

"Rrrowrrr!" the cat wailed, an eerie noise that sent a chill up my spine.

"Oh, I think it's time," he said. "It's a good thing we caught her when we did. I'll take care of her now. Yes, you're a very brave cat, aren't you?"

The last comment was to the cat, of course, who continued to howl disconcertingly as he walked slowly away with her, his nose glued to the square of screen, telling her every second what a good, brave cat she was. He reached the corner, made a left, and continued walking.

I suppose it would have been nice to offer him a ride, but however relieved I was to find my supposed mugger was actually a feline midwife, I was still shaken. I retrieved my purse, got into my car, and drove off in the other direction.

I didn't really worry about leaving the cat in his hands. Clearly, whoever he was, he was a softie for animals.

But if he knew about George, he had obviously been inside the Mutant Wizards office at some time. Not necessarily since we'd moved to our new quarters since I didn't remember seeing him. But then again, I hadn't been there every moment. What if he had thought Ted was responsible for keeping George in captivity? Or had suspected Ted of some other unkindness to animals?

Which didn't seem that implausible to me. The office dog pack pretty much roamed at will during the day, in and out of all the cubes and offices, begging food and other attention from almost everyone. Except, perhaps Ted. Even genial Katy had always ignored Ted, and I didn't remember ever seeing her or any of the other dogs padding into or out of his cube. I'd never seen him mistreat them — I'd have had his head if I'd seen anything of the sort. But I had seen him teasing them, with perhaps the faintest suggestion of cruelty — enough to make me keep an eye on him.

What if our animal-loving biker had actually seen Ted mistreating a dog or cat? And had been angry enough to take revenge?

It sounded a little far-fetched, even to me. The chief would probably laugh at the idea that Ted might have been killed for cruelty to animals. Unless he saw the biker crooning over the pregnant cat, maybe. Then again, if the guy were a little over-enthusiastic on the subject of animal welfare, odds were he'd have already butted heads with the police sooner or later.

"I'll worry about it tomorrow," I muttered as I stumbled down the stairs to the Cave and unlocked the door. "It's way too late for any of this."

It was 1:30 a.m. I had to be at work at 8:30 tomorrow — correction, today. I ought to go to bed, get as much sleep as I could, so I would be alert and rested for the busy day that awaited me. Sleeping was the only logical, sensible thing to do.

I called Michael.

"You're up late," he said. "Insomnia?"

"Investigating," I said, and I poured out everything that had happened since we'd last talked. Dr. Lorelei's love tryst, my discovery of Luis's notorious past, the midnight visit from the obsessed fan, Roger's porn site, and my encounter with the biker in the parking lot.

Well, not everything that had happened. I decided he didn't need to know about Roger's failed attempt to enlist me into his social life.

"You need to do something about the porn site right away," Michael said. "And if you ask me, this Roger creep is the most likely suspect for the murder, too."

"He's up there, yes. Ted could have been blackmailing him about using Mutant Wizards servers for his porn operation."

"You don't know that for sure. What if he was only using the CD burners?"

I thought back. He could be right. I didn't actually know for sure that his pornography was stored on Mutant Wizards hardware. I'd only assumed it.

"Good point," I said. "It's going to take someone a lot more tech-savvy than I am to figure that out."

"And even if he is using the Mutant Wizards servers," Michael went on, "you want to make sure he's not doing it legitimately before you cause a stink."

"Michael, Mutant Wizards is not in the pornography business," I protested.

"Not exactly, but how do you know what business deals Rob and the rest of them might have made to keep the company afloat during the first few months?"

That floored me.

"You think they might be running a porn site to make money?" I demanded.

"No, but what if they sublet part of their hardware, or even just space in the computer lab, to someone who is running a porn site? It's not actually illegal, you know — and I hear it's highly profitable."

I considered this. Mutant Wizards had gone through a few lean months in the early days. That was one reason I had become a major stockholder — I'd come up with the money to get Rob through one cash flow crisis. What if he'd had another financial pinch and didn't want to hit up the family again? What if he'd made a deal with the devil, so to speak?

"It might be legal, but it isn't respectable," I said. "And it would be a major PR disaster if it were true and the press found it out."

"Exactly."

"Thanks," I said. "I hadn't thought of that possibility. I'll have to get a little more information before I decide what to do about Roger."

"Any idea how you're going to get the information?"

"I have a couple of possibilities," I said.

"Luis, for example. He's got the skills, and now that I know his secret, I can probably motivate him to use them."

"Of course, there is the fact that he's a suspect," Michael pointed out.

"Everyone I know who could possibly figure this out is a suspect," I said. "I'll ask someone else to look into the same thing, and compare what they come up with."

"Who?"

"I don't know; I'll have to think about it when I'm more awake. Maybe I can figure out someone else that I have a hold over, like Luis. Or someone Ted hasn't yet tried to blackmail."

Or maybe Jack, who would probably do it just because I was the one asking. Not that I was going to mention that to Michael.

"I need to spend more time with the printout first," I said. "If you ask me, it all comes down to the printout. It adds up — the blackmail note to Rob, the file on Luis, his having the address of Roger's site. He was trying to blackmail everyone on the list. So the murderer is almost certainly someone on this list."

"Yes, but since no one on the list is identified by his or her real name, I'm not sure that gets you anywhere," Michael said.

"Yes, but I've already identified a couple

of them. Luis as the Hacker, for example."

"You're really sure about that?" Michael asked.

"Let me get the file and look at the photo," I said, shuffling through the papers scattered across the sofa. "Yes, it's Luis — and my God, I should have noticed this before! The Robin Hood Hacker's name is Mike Crews — that's *C-R-E-W-S*."

"So?"

"Luis's last name is Cruz — *C-R-U-Z*. Different spelling, but pronounced about the same."

"I get it."

"And I bet Dr. Lorelei is the Valkyrie. She's perfect for it."

"Of course, that only leaves — what? — nine more names on the list?"

"Spoilsport," I said.

"Sorry," he said. "Listen, read the list, from the top; let's see if any of the other code names suggest anything."

"Okay. The Emperor. The Space Cadet."

"A lot of people call Rob a space cadet," Michael suggested.

"Yes, but he's not the only candidate at Mutant Wizards. Maybe not even the most logical."

"Sad, but true."

"And the way everyone at Mutant Wizards feels about Rob, they're just as apt to call him the Emperor."

"Yes, but would Ted call him that?" Michael asked.

"Good point. Anyway. The Hacker — are we agreed that he's Luis?"

"Right," Michael said.

"The Voyeur — that's Roger, because of the porn sites."

"Hey, remember the blackmail note the police found in Rob's office?" Michael asked. "Maybe that wasn't intended for Rob at all."

"You mean, maybe the reference to naked pictures was about Roger's porn site?" I exclaimed. "I like it!"

"Any chance Roger might also be the one who programmed Nude Lawyers from Hell?"

"Roger?" I echoed. "No way."

"Why not?"

Good question. I'd answered off the top of my head, and I had to think about why not.

"It's too nice," I said, finally. "There's something about it that's . . . I don't know . . . witty. Charming. A certain sly intelligence. And if Roger has an ounce of wit, charm, or intelligence, I'll eat one of his CDs."

"Makes sense," he said. "So go on with the list."

"The Ninja," I continued. "Mata Hari. The Bodice Ripper. That's Anna Lloyd, whoever she is. She may not even be at Mutant Wizards."

"Or Anna Lloyd could be a pseudonym for someone you know. Maybe your friend Liz has a secret second life as a romance writer?"

"Doesn't seem likely to me. Getting back to the list: the Valkyrie."

"Perfect for Dr. Lorelei, as you guessed," Michael said.

"And what if the blackmail note wasn't to Rob or Roger, but to her," I suggested. "What if Ted found some compromising pictures of her and her boyfriend?"

"Or took them, if they're getting up to things at the office."

"Exactly," I said. "I like that idea a lot. Anyway, getting back to the list. The Luddite. Professor Higgins. And last but not least, the Iron Maiden. If you ask me, that's more likely to be Liz."

Michael laughed. "You said it, not me."

"I like her, but she grates on a lot of people. I'm sure she did on Ted, for example. And the note beside the Iron Maiden says, 'Still no angle.' I remember someone saying, the last day or so, how miffed Ted was that he couldn't get anywhere with Liz. What if what they thought was his trying to ask her out was his trying to blackmail her?"

"It's possible," Michael said. "Or maybe the payment he wanted wasn't in cash."

"That's true," I said.

"Here's another interesting one," I said. "Beside the Ninja it says 'xxx pix.' Do you suppose that means the Ninja has something to do with Roger's porn scheme?"

"Seems possible," Michael said. "Is there anyone who seems particularly friendly with Roger?"

I pondered for quite a few expensive long-distance moments.

"Not really," I said at last. "I think of him as just hanging at the edge of a group, not exactly ignored, but tolerated, just barely. When I was a kid, we had an old dog who smelled so bad no one really wanted to have him around, but it wasn't really his fault, so you couldn't exactly chase him off. You just put up with him and hoped he'd go away eventually. That's how everyone treats Roger."

"So if you notice someone who puts up with him more than most, maybe that's the Ninja."

"Good point," I said. "I'll keep my eyes open."

Wrong thing to say, I thought, glancing at the clock, and then trying instantly to forget what I saw.

Chapter 17

I yawned, reached to cover my mouth, and then changed my mind and covered the mouthpiece of the phone. I didn't want Michael ordering me off to bed before we finished talking.

"Three fairly definites and two possibles," he was saying. "And didn't you say the list had some entries that seemed to indicate they weren't caving in?"

"Yes," I said, rubbing my eyes and scanning the list. "The entry on the Bodice Ripper says, 'Not ready to tackle yet.' And beside the Emperor it says, 'No response.' And Professor Higgins apparently said 'Go to hell.' I'd say he hadn't hit everyone yet, and also had struck out a few times. It'll take time to figure out what some of the abbreviations mean, but only about half of them were actually paying blackmail, I think."

"So if they're not paying blackmail,

maybe once we know who they are we can strike them off the suspect list."

"No," I said. "Once we know who they are, I think we need to pay particular attention to the ones who wouldn't pay."

"Why, if they didn't care enough about whatever secret he'd uncovered to pay blackmail?"

"Maybe someone cared too much, and didn't trust Ted to keep quiet, even with the blackmail. Maybe someone didn't pay because he planned to kill Ted. We need to worry about that, too."

"I *am* worried about it," Michael said. "What's with this 'we' stuff, anyway? I'm in California, and can't exactly be much help, and you shouldn't be doing this anyway."

"I'm crushed. I thought you shared Dad's admiration for my amateur sleuthing skills."

"I do. I think you've uncovered some important evidence here," he said. "But if you're right, and Ted was killed because he was blackmailing someone, what makes you think that same person will react calmly if you unmask him as the killer? Or her. Don't take any chances. You need to turn that printout over to the police."

"I will, of course," I said. "Tomorrow morning."

"Good."

"After I've made a copy of it."

"Oh, good grief."

I sighed. It was too late, and I was too tired for yet another argument over my taking too many chances.

"Michael, don't worry so much," I said. "I'm not going to confront someone and accuse them. I'll let the police do that. But I'm certainly in a better position than they are to try to figure out the real names of the people on the list. I'm there at Mutant Wizards all day."

"What if some of the people on the list aren't at Mutant Wizards?" he countered. "Ted did have a life outside the office, right?"

"Not in the last six months he didn't," I said. "And anyway, even if all the suspects aren't from Mutant Wizards, we know the killer was there Monday. I know who was there Monday, and I have a lot better chance of catching them off guard than the police."

"Just don't take any foolish chances," he said. "Sneaking around the office in the middle of the night is not a smart thing to do."

"Don't worry — I'm not feeling suicidal," I said. "I'm not going to do anything but try to identify the rest of the people on the printout."

"Yeah, right."

He didn't sound as if he believed me.

"And find out who Ted's landlord is, of course," I said. "If he rented the place, I'm more than half-convinced he was supposed to be some kind of caretaker until they could settle the estate and sell it."

"You know, that's not a bad idea," Michael said. "You should definitely concentrate on the landlord angle. See if the place is for rent or sale."

"Michael, were you paying attention when I described that house?"

"I gather it was a little run-down, but what's wrong with a place that needs a little fixing up?"

"A little run-down? It's a wreck!"

"So it'll need a lot of fixing up," he said. "We can handle it."

"It's *Invasion of the Body Snatchers*, and you must be the pod Michael," I said. "It can't possibly be the real Michael, Mr. 'Neither one of us has time to bother with all that,' who refused to even consider that nice but run-down farmhouse last summer. The farmhouse was in mint condition compared to this place."

"That was last summer," Michael said.

"And you've grown more reasonable?"

"More desperate," he said. "Just check it out, will you?"

I closed my eyes. The place was way too big, and probably way too expensive, and I couldn't even imagine what it would look like without Edwina Sprocket's possessions crowding every inch of it. But something about Michael's voice told me it wasn't the right time to bring up any of that.

"Don't get your hopes up. Everyone in town knows the place is vacant, you know."

"Just check it out, okay?"

"Okay."

When would I have time? I wondered. Maybe I could get Dad to do it.

After saying good night to Michael, I got ready for bed. I fussed with the ancient window air conditioner until it deigned to produce the occasional puff of cold air. And then I crawled into bed, but for a little while, I lay there, staring at the printout some more, looking, in vain, for more inspiration.

"Tomorrow," I said, and turned out the light.

But tired as I was, sleep seemed to retreat the second I put my head on the pillow. After tossing and turning for a few minutes, I decided that if I was going to have insomnia, I might as well get something done. I turned on the bedside light and looked around.

I picked up *Living Graciously in a Single Room* and began flipping through it. Like most of the decorating books Mother had given me in the last few months, it was long on pretty and short on practical. But still, I liked decorating books. I could easily have lost myself in all the eye candy if the pictures hadn't kept reminding me of Ted's murder.

Looking at one strikingly minimalist room, I found myself murmuring, as usual, "Nice — but where on Earth do they put their stuff?" And then found myself mentally back in the midst of Mrs. Sprocket's stuff. Had I searched her house thoroughly enough? I assumed Mrs. Sprocket had no connection with the murder — but what if she did? Another death within a few months of Ted's — was there anything suspicious about it? Was anything suspicious happening around Mutant Wizards in March or April, when Mrs. Sprocket died? Apart from the first appearance of Nude Lawyers from Hell, nothing that I knew of. I scribbled an item on my to-do list to ask

Rob when he first began to feel something was wrong around the company. And another to ask Dad to check out Mrs. Sprocket's death. It wouldn't be hard for him, by now he and the local medical examiner were probably playing poker together.

The book contained one section all about creative space dividers. Mother had bookmarked that section, so my first reaction was that we needed to bring her up to see the Cave; apparently nothing else would convince her that we were not in need of creative ways to divide space. We just needed more space. Not to mention the fact that to judge by the examples in the book, its author considered space dividers creative only if they were made of strange and expensive objects that included lots of sharp points and dust-catching crannies. I wondered what the author would think about Ted's copier-box dividers. Probably too practical to rank as creative. And Ted's basement lair certainly didn't qualify as gracious one-room living. And exactly how had Ted snagged his living quarters? Was he really renting them, or just acting as caretaker for Mrs. Sprocket's heirs? Was there some way I could find out? And —

I tossed *Living Graciously in a Single Room* aside. Obviously it wasn't going to keep my mind off anything. Instead, I picked up the romance books I'd brought back from Ted's secret stash. I began browsing through them, half reading, half skimming.

They weren't deathless prose, but they weren't badly written, either. And while Anna Floyd, whoever she was, had definitely found a single plot and was busy running it into the ground, I did find her plot a little more to my taste than the ones in the romances some of my aunts devoured.

All the heroines were tall, assertive blond women. Not conventionally beautiful or in the first flush of youth, but still compellingly attractive, to judge by the number of gorgeous men chasing them. But — and this was the part that interested me — in all three books, the actual heroes were not the gorgeous guys. They were shy, mild-mannered, bespectacled, studious chaps, oddly appealing despite their outward goofiness or scruffiness.

Not that the silly heroines noticed this right off the bat; they would dismiss the heroes as uninteresting wimps and spend most of the book drooling over the most buff, square-jawed, perfectly groomed and dressed stud in sight. Who invariably turned out to be a villain, of course, once the heroine made the mistake of boarding his luxurious private yacht, flying to Vegas on his personal Learjet or, in the case of the historical novel, showing up for what was supposed to be a respectable house party attended by a trio of widowed aunts as chaperons, only to find herself trapped in a remote Scottish castle with the local chapter of the Hellfire Club.

Enter the heroes, who, when it came to a pinch and the women they'd been adoring from afar were in danger, would cast off their spectacles to reveal flashing if myopic eyes and shed their mousy garb to reveal lean, muscular bodies that enabled them to rescue the heroines from the clutches of the rogues — now revealed as having the courage of marshmallows.

I liked the fact that the heroines invariably played an active role in their rescue, fighting side by side with the heroes against whatever sinister crowd of minions the villain could muster for the grand finale — piratical deck hands, seedy security guards, or loutish thanes. Although the fighting wasn't particularly well described — what little detail she gave was somewhat inaccurate, at least when it came to swordplay and martial arts, about which I knew enough to be picky. But of course, her focus wasn't on the fighting — in the heat of battle, her heroines would find time to notice the heroes' firm, cleft chins and high cheekbones. During the final clinches each buxom blonde would already be planning to refurbish her rescuer with a better wardrobe and contacts — or, in the case of the historical romance, more flattering spectacles.

Fascinating, I thought, as I put the third one down. But why in the world did Ted feel he had to hide them in his secret compartment?

Presumably, Anna Floyd was the Bodice Ripper. That much was easy. But what was her connection with Mutant Wizards?

I'd worry about that later. Right now, I really needed to get some sleep. Was it dawn yet? I glanced over at the Cave's single, tiny window. Either it was still dark outside, or Michael's landlord had dumped another wheelbarrow load of mulch into the window well, obscuring what little light was not already obscured by the nearly useless air conditioner. I turned out the light and this time fell asleep almost instantly.

Chapter 18

As soon as I woke up, I realized that between dodging people and slinking about the office, I hadn't gotten a chance to use the black light. Which was one of the main reasons I bothered to go over in the middle of the night — so I could wield Ted's black light unobserved. I'd have to go back tonight.

I also realized that I was already late for work and destined to be even later by the time I arrived, even if I omitted all my usual little personal grooming rituals — like running through the shower, combing my hair, and throwing on some clothes.

Since I was late anyway, I stopped by the hardware store on the way in to get Ted's key copied, in case I wanted to snoop in his house again.

I arrived to find Dad seated at the switchboard, looking befuddled, while nine or ten lines were flashing.

"There you are!" he said. "I seem to have lost the knack of this."

"I was expecting a temp to show up to take care of the switchboard," I said as I scrambled to take his place.

"One did show up," he said. "But she left."

"Left?" I said. "What do you mean, she left?"

But Dad had escaped. Ah, well. I decided it was academic exactly which staff member had scared away today's temp.

When I'd cleared out the stacked-up calls and put in a complaint to the temp agency, I slipped away long enough to make a copy of the paper I'd found in Ted's cache. Then I called the police station to report finding it and his keys, and sat down to await the chief's arrival.

"Great," I muttered as I leaned back in my chair. "The police are trying to railroad Rob, and here I am, stuck at the switchboard again."

Of course, getting stuck at the switchboard would have been a lot worse if I had any idea what I ought to be doing to clear Rob. But my brain was a blank. So I answered calls and pondered.

And, just to feel I was doing something useful, I took out one of the romance books I'd found in Ted's cache, stuck an emery board in it as a bookmark, and left it lying on the reception desk, so I could watch people's reactions to it.

"Doesn't look like your kind of thing," Liz noted.

"Found it," I said, waving at the chairs across the room, as if to imply I'd found it there. "Thought I'd put it where the owner could claim it."

Jack had much the same reaction, and Luis pretended to ignore it. Everyone else who passed by felt obliged to comment on it. Three of them made fun of the male cover model's physical development and questioned his masculinity. Three insisted on reading passages aloud, and two asked me if I would read to them. Five pretended to think I was reading the book for educational purposes, and four of those offered to help me with my homework.

Rico, the graphic artist, was doing the reading aloud routine when Chief Burke strolled in.

" 'You're mine!' he exclaimed, as his cruel hand savagely ripped the silken fabric of her blouse. He ravished her with his eyes —"

"Am I interrupting something?" the chief asked.

"Yes, thank God," I said. "Go emote someplace else, Rico; I need to talk to the chief."

"You're no fun," Rico complained, tossing the book back on the desk.

"None at all," I agreed. "Go spread the word."

"So what's this thing you think you've found?" the chief asked.

"Here," I said. "I found Ted's keys — he dropped them when he was riding through the reception area Monday, and I picked them up, but with everything else that was happening, I forgot about them till today, when I opened the drawer they were in. And this was with them."

The chief took the printout and held it at various distances from his eyes, tilting his head up and down, left and right, then up and down again, with an occasional irritated glance in my direction. Was it my fault that the print was so small? He finally gave up, tucked his chin on his chest, pulled his glasses down so he could see over them more easily, and studied the paper.

"And you think this thing is connected with the murder?" he said finally.

"Of course," I said. "Don't you see what it is?"

He lifted his eyes from the paper and looked over his glasses at me.

"It's his list of people he was black-mailing!" I exclaimed.

"What makes you think that?"

"Look at the notations in the far right column," I said. "Stuff like 'coughed up' and 'caved' and 'won't pay' — doesn't that sound like blackmail to you?"

"Maybe," the chief said, studying the paper again.

"For heaven's sake, you're the one who's so excited about the blackmail note you found in Rob's office," I said. "If the guy would try to blackmail one person, why not several? And here's his whole list of victims."

"It doesn't have names," the chief pointed out.

"Of course not," I said. "I expect even Ted knew better than to leave evidence of his crime lying around for anyone to find. But I bet if you figure out who these names match, you'll be a lot closer to convicting the killer."

I'd said convicting rather than catching because I suspected the chief thought that by arresting Rob he'd already caught his man. He stared at the list a little longer and then reinforced my suspicion.

"You realize your brother's probably on this list," he said.

"He may be," I said. "And ten other people, too."

"Maybe he's the Ninja," the chief mused.

"In his wildest dreams, maybe," I said. "More like the Space Cadet."

"One of these columns looks like dates," he said. "You have any theory on that?"

"No," I said, trying to peer over his shoulder to see the column in question.

"We'll look into this, then," he said, curling the paper so I couldn't see the contents.

Of course, I had to wait until after he left to pull out my own copy of the paper. Dates? What did he mean, dates?

"Oh, by the way —"

The chief. Standing right in front of the reception desk — I'd been so absorbed in scanning the printout that I hadn't heard him come back in. I nearly fell out of my chair, and if I were the chief, I'd have been highly suspicious of the way I was acting, and would have demanded1 to see the paper I was so quick to hide with such a guilty look. Fortunately the chief's mind wasn't on the case. He was holding an Affirmation Bear.

"Damned thing turned up down at the station," he said, slapping it down in the desk.

"I gladly accept new challenges and new situations," the bear chirped.

The chief scowled and walked out again.

"What's that?" I looked up to see Frankie standing near the entrance.

"Here," I said, tossing him the bear. "Whack it in the belly."

"I am not afraid to show my feelings," the bear announced when Frankie whacked him.

"Cool — I've got to show this to Rico."

"Be my guest," I said to his departing back. I turned back to the spreadsheet.

Damn, the chief was right. There was a column that probably contained dates. I hadn't realized it because I usually separate the month, year, and day with slashes or hyphens, rather than periods, but once he suggested the idea of dates, I realized that's what they had to be. And they were all this year — within the last three months, in fact.

Of course, I wasn't sure what good this new insight did, since I still had no idea what he was tracking — the first time he approached his victims? The last time the victims had paid? Their most recent turn

279

to bring doughnuts for staff meeting? No way of telling.

Let's tackle something else, I thought. Ted's house, for example. I made a few phone calls to the Caerphilly Courthouse and found out where I could go to find out who owned the house.

"Meg?"

I looked up to see Frankie.

"Okay if we keep this for now?" he asked, brandishing the bear.

"As long as you like," I said. "It belongs to Dr. Brown, but I don't think she'd mind. There's a whole box of them in the closet."

"Really?" Frankie said. "What are they doing there?"

"Getting in my way," I said. "Why don't you stash them someplace else until Dr. Brown needs them?"

Frankie left, dragging the giant box of bears.

For the next hour or so, I heard a great deal of squeaking from the rest of the office. Squeaking and laughter. Then Cubeville grew suspiciously silent.

I thought of going back to see what was going on, but I was lying in wait for Luis. I didn't see him until lunchtime. He nodded as he passed through the reception area, but I was stuck on a call until after he'd disappeared.

Damn. I mentally cursed the temp agency. Then with a sudden inspiration, I punched in the code that would let me change the answering message and recorded a new version — instead of "Our offices are closed now" it said "Our switchboard is closed now" and reminded people that they could reach whoever they were calling if they knew their party's extension. Then I put the phone in night mode, grabbed my purse, and raced for the stairs.

Luis was strolling at the languid pace most people adopted if they had to go out in the near hundred-degree heat. By walking briskly, I caught up with him when he was only half a block away.

"Fetching lunch?" I asked.

"Want something?"

"I'll stroll along with you, if you don't mind," I said.

Luis nodded, and I fell into step beside him. I'd been planning to bring up the subject of the Robin Hood Hacker in casual conversation, but I was having a hard time figuring out how to start a conversation that I could drag in the right direction. And Luis wasn't one for casual conversation, anyway. We had already ambled on half a block, and I got the feeling he was perfectly capable of walking all the way to whatever carryout he planned to visit and then back again without saying another word.

Forget subtlety, I told myself. "Luis," I said. "I know what Ted was up to."

Luis frowned and glanced at me, but said nothing.

"What he was trying to do to you, I mean," I added.

"I don't think he deliberately mangled the code so I'd have to clean it up, if that's what you mean."

For Luis, that was a long speech.

"Dammit, Luis. I know you were the Robin Hood Hacker," I said.

Luis seemed to shrink a bit, and he hunched his shoulders as if expecting a blow.

"And Ted knew," I continued. "And he was trying to blackmail you with it. I don't know why — all the charges were dropped and almost everyone thinks you were a hero. I mean that's where the Robin Hood nickname came from, right? But I knew you were paying him blackmail, and I want to know why."

"I don't want to lose my job," he said.

"No reason why you should," I said. "I

282

mean, it's not as if you were convicted of a crime."

"Yeah, but the bank — the one I hacked? They'll never let it go."

"What could they possibly do to hurt you?"

"They've gotten me fired from two jobs already."

"Rob wouldn't fire you for that."

"He might not want to, but what if the bank figures out a way to put pressure on him? What if suddenly his line of credit gets canceled? Or one of our competitors' systems gets hacked and word leaks out that I work here. Stuff like that happened, my last two jobs."

"So that's why you changed your name?"

"Yeah," he said. "Changed it back, actually. That's the funny part. Mike Crews was me trying to be somebody I wasn't, when I went away to college. Luis is my middle name. Miguel Luis Cruz."

"Does anyone else know?"

"Jack," Luis said. "He hired me for my first job when I got out of college. One of the two I lost. He was the one who recommended me to Rob. And suggested going back to my real name."

"What did he say about Ted trying to blackmail you?"

"I didn't tell him about that," Luis said. "I was afraid of what would happen."

"Afraid of something like what did happen?"

"No," Luis said. "If you mean you think Jack killed Ted, no, that's not what happened. I just figured he'd come down hard on Ted, and Ted would find some way to get even."

"Like what? What could he possibly do to get even with Jack?"

"I don't know," Luis said. "If there was anything you wanted to hide, Ted would find out about it. He had this thing about knowing everything, all the dirt, even if he didn't do anything with it."

"And you think Jack has something to hide?"

"Everyone has something to hide," Luis said with a shrug.

We walked along for a little while in silence. On the one hand, I was feeling a little triumphant. My suspicions had been correct — Ted was blackmailing people. One person, anyway, and it stood to reason that if it worked on one person, he'd try it again. I was making progress in unraveling the secrets behind Ted's strange little cache.

But I wasn't altogether sure I liked what

I'd found. I couldn't imagine quiet, self-effacing Luis as a murderer, but I had a hard time imagining him as a daring hacker, either, and he certainly had been that. And he had a motive for the murder. For that matter, I couldn't see calm, sardonic Jack as a murderer, but he had motive, too. He was Luis's friend and mentor — if someone threatened Luis, I could see Jack intervening.

"What are you going to do?" Luis asked.

"I don't know yet," I said. "Depends on what else I find out."

He nodded. I thought some more and decided, what the hell. I needed someone computer savvy to help me. Why not Luis? Now that I knew his secret, I had some influence over him.

"You could help," I said.

"How?"

I dug into my bag, pulled out my notebook-that-tells-me-when-to-breathe, and ripped out a sheet of paper. I flipped through it until I found the URL of the porn site I'd seen Roger tending and wrote that down on the sheet. Then I flipped through some more until I found where I'd stuck the sheet of paper with the IP addresses I'd found in Ted's basement, and copied those down, as well.

"Here," I said. "Check these out."

"What are they?" he asked.

"Porn sites," I said.

He looked up, surprised.

"At least two of them are," I said. "I have a feeling maybe they all are. I want to know for sure, and I don't want to look at them if I can help it. And I want to know everything you can find out about them."

"Like what?" Luis asked, puzzled.

"Who owns them," I said. "Where they're located. And most important, whether anyone at Mutant Wizards has any connection to them."

"Okay," he said.

"And don't tell anybody," I said. "Not Rob, or Jack, or anyone else at Mutant Wizards, or even your own mother."

"Right," he said. "This has something to do with the murder?"

"Maybe," I said. "Or maybe I'm just on a crusade to stamp out pornography."

"You going to stamp out Nude Lawyers from Hell while you're at it?" he asked with a rare, fleeting smile.

"Maybe," I said. "Do you know who programmed it?"

He didn't say anything for a moment, and it suddenly hit me that I might have solved another of the small mysteries that plagued Mutant Wizards.

"If I knew, it probably wouldn't be smart to tell you," he said finally. "Look, on this porn thing — how far do you want me to go?"

I was opening my mouth to say, "As far as you need to go to get answers, for heaven's sake," but something stopped me.

"I'm not sure I understand what you mean," I said instead.

"Do you just want me to get what I can from legitimate sources?" he asked. "What we could turn over to the police without getting in trouble? Or do you want me to go all the way? As far as it takes?"

"See what you can get legitimately first," I said. "If that's not enough — well, we'll worry about that later."

"Right," he said. He looked relieved.

I wondered if he'd have agreed if I'd said, "As far as it takes." Did he now have qualms of conscience about illegal hacking, or was he just running scared?

And what should I do if he couldn't find out everything I needed from legitimate sources? I confess, I didn't feel too guilty about using any means necessary to stop Roger's porn operation, which if not illegal was certainly distasteful and potentially risky for Mutant Wizards. But could I live with myself if I got poor Luis into trouble? Was encouraging a supposedly reformed hacker to relapse as morally suspect as, for example, serving bourbon balls to an alcoholic aunt?

And, of course, what if Luis was in cahoots with Roger?

"By the way," I asked. "What exactly does Roger do, anyway?"

"He's the sys admin," Luis said.

"And that is — ?"

Luis blinked as if it had never occurred to him that someone might not know what a sys admin was.

"That stands for systems administrator," he said. He was talking in the same overly loud, slow way tourists talk when they can't quite believe that the hapless foreigners around them don't understand English. "He's in charge of all the hardware and software that runs the network."

"Oh, is that why he's always sitting around in the computer lab?" I said.

"Yeah, that's more or less his job," Luis said. "Not that it really should take as much time as it seems to take him. He even had Ted helping him with some of the stuff lately, and it still seemed to take him forever to do anything."

"Are you suggesting that perhaps Rob

needs to hire a more competent sys admin?" I asked.

"Don't quote me on that," Luis said. "But yeah. Roger's pretty lame, not to mention a head case. As you found out last night."

Interesting. Maybe Ted had been the one in cahoots with Roger.

I was still pondering this when we arrived at Luis's destination. Good thing I'd finished interrogating him. He was heading for the College Diner, a Caerphilly institution most people outgrew by their senior years, except for the occasional trip down nostalgia road. Or the occasional case of munchies at 3 a.m., since the diner was the town's only twenty-four-hour restaurant.

"Catch you later," I said. I continued on to a small deli that made an edible ham-and-swiss sandwich.

Then I headed over to the courthouse to joust with bureaucracy.

Chapter 19

In the office of the Recorder of Deeds I learned that the house where Ted had lived — if you can call his basement lair "living" — was still listed as belonging to Mrs. Edwina Sprocket.

"How often are these records updated?" I asked the clerk.

"They're updated as soon as we get the information."

"This property is listed as belonging to someone who died a couple of months ago," I said. "At least I think she died."

"Then it probably still belongs to her estate," the clerk suggested.

"How can I find out for sure if she's dead," I asked.

"Environmental Health Office," he said. "Room 414."

"Why the Environmental Health Office?" I asked. "As far as I know, she died of old age, not pollution."

"That's the name of the office that keeps all the death certificates," the clerk said with a shrug.

For eight dollars, the ominously named Environmental Health Office gave me a copy of Mrs. Sprocket's death certificate. Cause of death was heart failure, which wasn't particularly helpful, but at least I had the attending physician's name and could sic Dad on him if it seemed useful.

And then, down in the Circuit Court office, I managed to find out the name of the attorney who was handling her will.

It all took an hour and a half, which seemed maddeningly long to me, even though I had the feeling it would have taken twice as long if Caerphilly were a larger, busier county. Of course, a larger, busier county might have bothered to air-condition its offices. I felt I'd done a whole day's work and had an overlong stay in the sauna by the time I headed back to the office to eat my wilting sandwich.

The world hadn't come to an end while I was away from my post, so I decided I'd repeat the experience later in the day. As soon as I figured out something useful I could do with my time away from the switchboard. And I could check out what kind of construction was going on; I'd heard hammering from someplace in the back when I walked in.

But for now, I cleared out the accumulated messages and started on my sandwich. I'd picked up a copy of the *Caerphilly Clarion* while I was out and I opened it to — well, not my favorite section, but the section with which I'd grown most familiar: the real estate section.

Slim pickings as usual.

"Damn, and here I was going to see if I could whisk you away to the steak house for lunch."

I looked up to see Jack in the doorway.

"Thanks," I said. "But I'm trying to stick pretty close to the office except for really important things. Like going to visit any houses for sale or rent."

"I'm house-hunting myself," he said.

"Isn't everyone?"

"Everyone at the Pines, anyway," he said with a shudder. "Anything interesting?"

"Nothing Michael and I didn't already see this weekend," I said, handing him the paper.

"You didn't like the 'luxurious lakeside retreat'?"

"You mean the million-dollar starter castle on the handkerchief lot?" I said. "A little steep for our budget."

"Especially since they're asking two million for it," Jack agreed. "The 'dynamite fixer-upper' was a holdover from last week, too. What's wrong with it?"

"They had a serious house fire," I said.

"Needs a whole lot of fixing up?"

"Needs bulldozing, if you ask me," I said. "It's a charred shell — no way you could ever make it habitable. You'd need to bulldoze the ruins, haul away the rubble, and build a new house."

"You're not interested in building?"

"Maybe, if we could find a reasonable lot," I said. "We're not interested in paying the cost of a house for a lot that would still need thousands of dollars of demolition work before we could even begin building."

"Check," he said. "Hey, this one's new — 'unique rambler in woodland setting' — sounds promising."

"Yeah, belongs to a friend of Michael's," I said with a sigh. "We got a chance to see it before it went on the market. Could have made an offer if we wanted to. Beautiful lot. Beautiful house. Just one problem."

"Price too big?"

"House too small."

"I don't care how small it is, it has to be bigger than the motel room I'm sharing. See — three bedrooms."

"Trust me, it's too small. The owner's only three and a half feet tall. He had it built to scale. Five-and-a-half-foot ceilings."

"You're kidding, right?"

I shook my head.

"So why's he selling?"

"He got married. His wife's almost my height; she's tired of crouching."

"Now I know you're kidding," he said. "Trying to keep everyone else from jumping on the place, right?"

"Go see for yourself."

"I will. Mind if I borrow this to make a copy?"

"Keep it. Nothing I can use," I said. "Listen, what do you know about Ted's house?"

"I know he found someplace to rent outside town," Jack said.

"You never saw it?"

"No — have you?"

"Yes," I said. "I went over to see if I could find any work papers or files that the police hadn't taken."

"Was it a dive?" he asked. "I figure, as quickly as he found it, it must have been a real dive."

"Not really," I said. "Was there any talk

about his finding a place to live? Resentment, jealousy?"

"Not that I remember," he said. "Of course, I bet a lot of people probably thought what I did — that there must be something really wrong with it if he found it so quickly. He was only at the Pines maybe a month. Even when he was there, he didn't really socialize much with the rest of us, so it's not as if he invited people over for a housewarming party or anything. I don't think most people even knew where he'd moved."

"A couple of people did," I said. "A couple of staffers showed up there while I was doing my search. I think they wanted to see if they could snag the place before someone else did."

"You're not really thinking that one of them killed Ted so they could get his house, are you?"

"Why not?" I asked. "I know at least three quarters of our staff are still living at the Pines or bunking with friends or maybe driving an hour or more to get to work. And here Ted snags a place in the country after a few weeks?

"I still think it's going a little far, killing someone over a house."

"Oh, and there are acceptable reasons

for killing someone?"

"You know what I mean," he said with a laugh. "It seems a little weak for a motive."

"Wait till you've been doing that a few more months," I said, pointing my thumb at the real estate section.

"Maybe you have a point," he said as his eyes scanned the same sparse pickings I'd already rejected. "What's wrong?" he said, glancing up to find me frowning as I looked at him.

"Nothing," I said. "Or rather . . . could you do something for me?"

"Just name it," he said. He folded the paper, shoved it under his arm, and leaned over the reception desk.

I fished out my notebook again and gave him the same information I'd given Luis, with the same instructions — including, of course, orders not to tell anyone, even Luis.

"What's this all about, anyway?" he asked. "Where did you get these addresses?"

"Tell me what you can find out first," I said. "Then I'll tell you the whole story."

He looked at me for a moment, then nodded and left.

Back to the house hunt. I looked up the telephone number of the lawyer who was handling Mrs. Sprocket's estate. I got the man on the line before I realized I hadn't figured out what to say, and something about the lawyer's precise yet oratorical tones made me suspect he'd enjoy playing cat and mouse with me before refusing to give me any useful information.

"I'm calling . . . I assume you've heard about Ted Corrigan's death?"

"Yes, and I'm afraid we will not be looking to engage another caretaker for the house," the lawyer said. Sounding rather bored, as if he bothered to talk to me only for the fun of practicing his elocution.

"Caretaker?"

"Isn't that why you called?" the lawyer said. "To apply for the caretaker's job?"

"Actually, no," I said. "But you've already answered the question I was going to ask."

"And what, pray tell, was your question?" he asked. Oh, dear. Now he sounded suspicious.

"I'm with Mutant Wizards, the firm he worked for," I said, improvising. "We were going to see if there was something we could do — to help out the family, you know. Make a month's rent or mortgage payment, if we could find out where to send it."

"Not needed," the lawyer said. "But you could help me out. Do you have any information on his next of kin? I need to know where to send his final paycheck. Not that the miserable beggar really earned it, that I can see, but still, one doesn't like to speak ill of the dead, does one?"

"I can have our Personnel department call you with that information," I said. "If we don't have it, I assume we'll find a way to get it ourselves, for much the same reason."

"I'd appreciate it," he said, sounding genuinely grateful, so I decided to push my luck.

"Just out of curiosity," I said. "Why aren't you hiring a new caretaker? The house could certainly use it. Is someone moving in?"

"No, but it's going on the market," he said. "The Realtor will be getting it ready to show and handling maintenance till it's sold."

"Big job," I said. "Getting it ready, that is; in this market, the maintenance probably won't be needed for long."

"It could be needed indefinitely if the heirs don't scale down their expectations," he said.

"Why, what are they asking?"

My jaw dropped when he named the price. I think I gasped.

"Breathtaking, isn't it," he said. "Totally unrealistic, even in this market."

"Is it on a large piece of land?" I asked.

"Not enough for that price," he said. "Couple of acres."

"With a working diamond mine in the backyard, perhaps?"

He chuckled.

So much for buying the house, as I'd tell Michael the next time we talked. I thanked the lawyer for his time, signed off, and then called to ask Darlene in Personnel to send him the information he needed. Offhand, I couldn't think of anything else I might need from him, but you never knew; so it seemed useful to keep on his good side.

So few people passed through the reception area for the next hour that I began to wonder if they'd all fled down the fire escape. I finally grew so curious that I put the switchboard in night mode and went back to see what was going on.

I'd hoped to find them all busily doing evil things to the Affirmation Bears. I was disappointed. Yes, nearly every cube sported a bear, one or two of them partially disassembled. But most of the staff were in the computer lab, apparently receiving a pep talk from Jack.

I found out what Dad had been up to all morning when I walked into the lunchroom.

Chapter 20

As I stepped over the threshold, I felt something catch at my ankle. I was glancing down to see what it was when I saw something falling from the ceiling onto my head. I threw my good hand up to protect my face and intercepted a flying mouse cord.

"Damn," I heard someone say. "That almost worked."

I glanced over and saw Dad and Rico crouched behind one of the tables.

"Not really," Dad said.

"If she hadn't put her hand up, it would have worked."

"What are you two trying to do?" I asked.

"Testing a theory of mine," Dad said.

I glanced around. The tables and the floor around the doorway were littered with nails, hammers, screwdrivers, bolts, and assorted bits of string, not to mention a dozen or so mouse cords. Only one or two had intact mice still attached.

"Let me rig it up again," Rico said, grabbing another mouse from the clutter

He dragged a chair over to the doorway and began attaching the mouse to a complicated device made of levers, pulleys, and rubber bands, which dangled over the doorway from a set of hooks and eyes. When he'd finished attaching the mouse, he ran a string down the wall and then across the doorway.

"There," he said. "Meg, could you go out and walk in again? And this time, don't try to protect yourself; just walk in and —"

"Nothing doing," I said. "I'm not sure how you think you can launch that thing with enough force to strangle someone, but just in case this is not as stupid as it seems, I'm not going to play guinea pig. Why don't you walk in yourself?"

"But I know how it works and —"

"Damn!"

The chief financial officer had walked in. Apparently he'd been walking faster than I had — when he hit the trip wire, instead of the mouse cord, the whole contraption came down and tangled itself around his head.

"I think we'd have noticed if someone had rigged a booby trap like that anywhere on the premises," I said as I helped them disentangle their captive.

"I thought if we could figure out how to propel the mouse cord with the right trajectory and sufficient force to strangle someone, then we'd worry about reproducing the effect with less hardware," Dad said. "But so far, we haven't achieved anywhere near enough momentum or accuracy. I'm beginning to think maybe this is a dead end."

"Why complicate things?" I said. "I know it would be more fun if someone had built an elaborate machine to kill Ted by remote control, but I really don't think whoever did this went to that much trouble. I think they just got mad and strangled him on the spot."

"It's just that it's hard to imagine anyone having the nerve to do that, here in such a crowded office," Dad said.

"Someone did," I said. "And they probably knew the office well enough to know just when and where it was uncrowded. Like maybe during a meeting; look how empty the place is now, with everyone in the computer lab."

"Hmmm," Dad said, but I could see he wasn't convinced. He and Rico began rigging up their mouse-cord launcher again.

"If you wait a few minutes, we can try to trap you again," he said.

"Maybe later," I said, strolling out.

The meeting in the computer lab was still going on, and most of the rest of the staff were there.

The few exceptions were all clustered around Frankie's monitor, reading something.

"What's up?" I said.

"Hi, Meg," Frankie said. "You know anything about this?"

The others stepped aside so I could get close enough to read the monitor. I could see that they'd been reading a Web site that published gossip about the computer gaming industry. I followed Frankie's pointing finger.

The latest inside scoop from Mutant Wizards is that the much-awaited new release will be a companion game, Veterinarians from Hell.

Oh, dear, I thought.

"Vets from Hell," Frankie said. "Must be a new idea Rob's been working on. Man, what an incredible brain that guy has! One idea after another!"

I was a little startled at this picture of

Rob as a gaming mastermind. To me, Rob seemed to have only one idea, on which he was determined to ring in as many variations as possible. Lawyers from Hell, Doctors from Hell, Cops from Hell, and now, if public reaction to the rumor I'd inadvertently started was favorable, Vets from Hell.

"Hey, we could use Doc as a consultant," Frankie said.

Doc? Did they mean Dad? Considering that all of Mother's farmer cousins habitually asked him for free medical advice for their livestock, I supposed he could contribute usefully to Vets from Hell.

"Just think of it!" one of the developers suggested. "We don't just have cats and dogs . . . We have anacondas, Vietnamese potbellied pigs, zebras. . . . It's a teaching tool."

"Unicorns, wyverns, manticores," suggested another.

"Mutant Vets from Hell!" they shrieked in chorus.

"Mutant" was a code word; it meant they were about to stray even further than usual from reality. In about five minutes, they'd be arguing over how to implement a coherent system of magic. I'd heard this all before. Maybe it was time to nip this particular brainstorming session in the bud.

"Actually, I think I was the one to blame for that article," I said. "It wasn't something Rob was planning at all."

They stared at me.

"Wow, I bet it's, like, genetic," one of them murmured in awestruck tones.

"So have you got a development team yet?" another asked.

"I'll get back to you," I said, and left, hastily. I knew Rob was already giving serious thought to Mutant Lawyers from Hell, in which the competing lawyers could win trials not only with evidence and witnesses, but also by casting spells to confuse the jury and turning the opposing lawyers into swine. With my luck, Rob would actually like the Mutant Vets idea.

I was relieved to get back to the switchboard. At least I was until I heard the door open and looked up to see the biker entering. Okay, he made me a little less nervous than he did before I saw him with the cat, but that didn't mean I wanted him clinking into the Mutant Wizards reception room. And what was he carrying in the battered black leather satchel? Not to mention the crumpled brown paper bag?

"I've come to see Cathleen Ni Houlihan," he said.

"I'm afraid we don't have anyone working here by that name," I said while shifting so I could more easily reach the panic button.

"Nonsense, she doesn't work here," he said. "She — Katy!"

Katy, the Irish wolfhound, bounded into the room and launched herself at the biker, ending up licking his face with her front feet on his shoulders, while he said unintelligible things to her. Unintelligible because they were, apparently, in Gaelic. I didn't speak Gaelic, but I remembered what it sounded like from the summer Dad was preparing for a trip to Ireland.

Rhode Island Rico trailed in after her and shook the biker's hand, looking smaller than usual beside him. And beside Katy — why would someone ever want to own a dog that clearly outweighed him? Then again Keisha, who barely topped five feet, owned both of the Saint Bernards.

"Thanks for coming over, Doc," he said.

Doc?

The biker reached into the brown paper bag and pulled out an object. I recognized the logo on the bag now — it was from Caerphilly's most militant vegetarian restaurant, which meant that the light brown patties he was feeding to Katy had to be some kind of soy-based hamburger substitute.

"What happened?" Doc asked — I supposed I ought to begin thinking of him as Doc.

"Another dog bit her ear," Rico explained. "I was worried that it might get infected."

"Did you catch the other dog?"

Rico looked nervously at me. I looked down at the crate beneath my desk.

"I suspect he's here," I said with a sigh. "How did he get out, anyway?"

"Rob had him in his office," Rico said. "We thought he'd calmed down. He was behaving like a lamb until Katy came in."

"Never trust Spike when he's behaving himself," I advised. "He does it only to lull you into a false sense of complacency."

"I'm sorry," the biker said. "I don't think we've actually been introduced. Clarence Rutledge. I've just moved to Caerphilly to set up my veterinary practice."

He extending one large, colorfully tattooed hand to me. I tried not to stare at the cartoon ferrets frolicking around his wrist. The other hand was still occupied with Katy — or Cathleen Ni Houlihan. Apparently she and I had never been introduced, either.

"If you don't already have a vet for your dog —," he continued.

"He's not mine," I said. "I'm just taking care of him for a few weeks while his owner decides if she's allergic to him."

"If he needs some medical care while he's with you, then," he said.

Business must be slow, I thought.

"I emphasize wellness and natural remedies. Of course," he added, glancing down at Spike, "what I really plan to specialize in is behavior therapy."

"Wonderful," I said.

"Often, aggressive behavior in canines is a result of underlying psychological problems."

"If you're suggesting that you could cure Spike of biting people, it's been tried," I said. "Frequently. His owner has probably spent more money on his education than my parents spent on mine."

"Really?" Doc said, looking even more interested. "I'm getting together a study to try some new approaches on dogs that have proved resistant to previous attempts at aggression reduction. I don't suppose you'd be interested in enrolling Spike? . . ."

"Maybe," I said. "Especially if it requires a period of residence at wherever you're conducting your study."

I took Doc's card, which proclaimed that he provided "holistic care for your animal companion." He and Rico strolled off to repair the damage Spike had done to Katy's ear.

So he wasn't a thug. Did that make him more or less likely to have killed Ted?

If Doc were in the habit of making house calls on his patients, it was all the more likely that he'd known Ted. And witnessed any instances of cruelty to animals Ted might have committed. And also all the more likely that Ted had tried to blackmail him. When I'd thought him merely a biker, I hadn't considered Doc a very likely blackmail target — unless, I suppose, Ted could prove that he'd never done anything wild or wicked, which could probably ruin someone's reputation as a hellion. But Doc, the reformed biker turned vegetarian holistic animal doctor? If I were an aspiring young blackmailer looking to expand my clientele, Doc would be exactly the sort of person I'd want to meet. I bet at some time in his unenlightened past Doc had worn leather boots instead of canvas ones. And probably kicked a dog or two with them.

Yes, I should look into Doc, I thought. When he came out, I'd reopen the subject of aggression reduction for Spike.

Meanwhile, to kill time, I picked up Anna Floyd's romance book and began absently skimming through it again. I confess, my mind was more on Ted's fate than the perilous plight of the statuesque blond heroine.

A finger planted itself on the page I was theoretically trying to read. I looked up to see Dr. Lorelei.

"I strongly advise against reading that," she said, frowning. "It can be very dangerous."

Chapter 21

Dangerous?

I glanced up. No, she wasn't joking — I wasn't sure she knew how. And if she was trying to make some kind of veiled threat, it was too well veiled for me to understand it.

Silly I might agree with — and I couldn't help feeling a little embarrassed, sitting there holding the thing, when I'd been so intent on establishing my reputation as a tough-minded, no-nonsense kind of person. But dangerous?

"Dangerous? What, do they have subliminal messages or something?" I asked.

"Life, and particularly relationships, are not always the way they're portrayed in those books."

"I think that's the point," I said. "If I wanted realistic stuff about life, I'd go read Tolstoy or something. I mean, I don't really believe in dwarves and hobbits, but that doesn't stop me from reading fantasy. And in real life, murders often go un-solved — does that mean it's dangerous to read mysteries that wrap everything up neatly on the next to last page?"

"One has to be careful of seeing the world through the lens of popular fiction," Dr. Lorelei intoned. "Books like that create unreasonable expectations in their readers."

"It's not creating unreasonably expecta-tions in me," I said with a shrug. "I don't believe the stuff; I just read it to kill time when I'm stuck in line someplace. Or when I'm here at the desk."

Dr. Lorelei sniffed.

"I don't really buy into the heaving this and throbbing that, and midnight assigna-tions in deserted places," I went on, fixing her with a stare.

She turned pale and left, rather hur-riedly.

"You've upset her."

I looked up to see the mousy, bespecta-cled face of Lorelei's partner.

"Sorry," I said. "But she didn't have to give me a hard time just because I picked up something to read that isn't on the list of the world's hundred greatest works of literature."

"She's very fierce about what she believes," he said with a smile. "I think that's what I've always loved about her."

I made a noncommittal noise. Loved about her? This was interesting.

"I think it took two years of discussions before she finally agreed that it would not compromise her principles for us to get married," he said.

"You're her husband?" I asked, astounded.

"We prefer the term 'life partners,'" he said. "Not only is that a gender-neutral term, but it carries much less negative psychological baggage, particularly for the female in the partnership."

To me, life partners sounded more like a title at a law firm, but to each his own.

"So my taste in reading offended her feminist principles," I said. "Someone should have warned me."

"I'm sorry," he said, patting my hand. "Sometimes Lorelei forgets that other people aren't as evolved as she is in these matters. She's very impatient with all the trappings of romance — she feels society uses them to indoctrinate women into the conventional roles that a paternalistic society attempts to impose upon them."

Was it just my imagination, or did his

words sound a little flat, as if he'd used them far too often. And did he look a little wistful? And what, pray tell, did he think of the outfit Dr. Lorelei had worn last night? Didn't last night's four-inch heels and slinky black dress count as "trappings of romance"? Not that she'd have waltzed out of the house wearing them, of course — even the most oblivious of husbands wouldn't have overlooked that. Obviously she'd have put on her usual sensible business attire to make the "Sorry, dear — I have a patient who's having a crisis" announcement. But if he didn't even know her slinky outfit existed, that was a really bad sign, wasn't it?

While I was pondering, Dr. Lorelei's life partner sighed, checked his watch, and padded back toward his office. I flipped through Anna Floyd's book again. Tall blond heroines . . . mousy, bespectacled heroes.

What if either Dr. Lorelei or what's-his-name, her life partner, was secretly writing under the pseudonym of Anna Floyd?

I waited until Luis passed through again.

"Luis," I said.

"I'm working on it."

"I have another job for you."

"What now?" he said, rolling his eyes.

"Do the therapists have a network, or just their personal PCs?"

He frowned. "They have a network," he said. "Separate from ours, but Roger administers it, too."

"Great," I said. "Can you search our network and theirs for any occurrences of this name?"

I wrote "Anna Floyd" on a piece of paper and handed it to him.

"Who's she?" he asked.

I held up the book. He wrinkled his nose.

"This is connected with the murder?"

"Who knows?" I said. "Just find out if anyone here has ever mentioned the name Anna Floyd in any of their documents."

He stuffed the slip of paper into his pocket and headed toward his cube.

I had barely found my place in the book again when Doc returned, doing his Saint Francis act with the office dog pack trailing in his wake — eight of them today. Apart from Katy the wolfhound, I spotted a collie, a German shepherd, a Norwegian elkhound, a keeshond, and Keisha's two Saint Bernards. All friendly, easygoing creatures, individually, but when you put them all together, quite a lot of dog. More than the office needed, if you ask me; then again, I considered one Saint Bernard about half again as much dog as any reasonable person could ever need.

As usual, Spike went crazy when the pack loped in, which gave me the opening I needed to tackle Doc.

"Could you send them out?" I called out over Spike's hysterical barking and the good-natured barks and yaps of the others. Doc complied, gently shooing out the other dogs.

"About this aggression reduction thing," I said when the reception room was quiet again, except for Spike's occasional triumphant bark at having caused his foes to flee.

"He isn't going to learn to interact peacefully with the other dogs as long as he's locked up like that," Doc said.

"If business is slow, I'd be happy to let him out," I said. "On one condition, though: you have to give the dog owners on staff a group discount on patching up any damage he inflicts."

Doc chuckled as if he thought I were kidding. "Let me talk to him," he said, reaching into his pocket and pulling out a small chunk of soy burger. He squatted down in front of Spike's cage and held it out in his right hand. "There's a good boy," he cooed.

Spike cowered in the back of his cage as if terrified by the sudden appearance of food-bearing fingers at the door of his prison. Doc waggled the soy burger enticingly until Spike condescended to creep forward far enough to sniff at the food. I noticed he wasn't in any hurry to gobble it up.

"You see," Doc said, looking up at me. "He's really a very — arrrrrrr!"

As soon as he realized Doc wasn't watching him, Spike lunged forward to snap, not at the food, but at Doc's left hand — he'd carelessly curled his fingers through the wire mesh to balance himself.

"Sorry about that," I said, opening the drawer where we kept one of the office first aid kits.

"He needs . . . a great deal of work," Doc said, holding out his hand so blood wouldn't drip on his clothes. Of course, this meant he was dripping on the carpet.

"Maybe you could hold it over the newspapers?" I suggested.

"Blood can be washed out very easily," Doc said, frowning. "I'm sure whoever cleans your offices knows how."

"Yes, but it would almost be easier to do it myself than to get them to do it," I said, offering him the Band-Aid selection. "Not to mention the fact that you're bleeding along the mail cart's path."

"Given all that, maybe this isn't the best place to keep a dog with an aggression problem," he said. I noticed he wasn't calling Spike a poor little thing anymore.

"Speaking of aggression reduction," I said. "Your program sounds like a good idea to me, but I'm not the one who has to make the decision. Do you have any information I can send to his owner? A brochure, maybe some credentials?"

He opened his black bag and began pulling out papers, including a framed copy of his veterinary school diploma. Fifteen minutes and a trip to the copy room later, I had all the information I wanted about Doc's aggression-reduction program, and, more important, about Doc himself. Although he was either older than me or much more weathered, he'd graduated from veterinary school only two years ago. Definitely a midlife career change — and he was cagey about what he'd done before going to veterinary school.

"I'll get back to you after I check with Mrs. Waterston," I said as Doc hoisted his black bag.

"Wonderful," Doc said. "I'm sure the aggression-reduction therapy will be just the thing."

With that, he exited.

"Aggression-reduction therapy? Who's that?"

I looked up to see one of the therapists looming over my desk: the assertiveness guru who was always feuding with Dr. Brown. Though perhaps they weren't feuding any longer; he was holding a pink Affirmation Bear in one large hamlike hand.

"Dr. Clarence Rutledge," I said. "He does aggression-reduction therapy for —"

"Nonsense!" the therapist snapped. "I know everyone in the field, and I've never heard of him. What kind of credentials does he have?"

I handed over my photocopy of Doc's diploma.

"This man's not a psychotherapist!" he shouted, ripping the diploma in quarters and throwing the pieces in my face. "He's a bloody horse doctor! He has no business tinkering with the human mind!"

"He's not," I said. "He's —"

"I'm going to report this! If he thinks he can —"

"Quiet!" I shouted.

He stopped in mid-tirade.

"He's not tinkering with the human mind. He's going to tinker with him," I said, hoisting Spike's crate up and plunking it on the desk.

The therapist blinked, and Spike lifted one side of his lip and growled.

"Aggression-reduction therapy?" the therapist said. "I'll show you aggression-reduction therapy!"

He mashed his face against the wire front of Spike's crate and growled. Or maybe "roared" would be a better word; it sounded more like something you'd expect to hear when a lion was chasing you through the jungle than anything I'd heard come from even the largest of canine throats. And while both Spike and I were still startled into immobility, he opened the door latch, threw the Affirmation Bear inside the crate, slammed the door shut, and stormed out of the room.

"I take responsibility for my own destiny," the bear proclaimed, as Spike pounced.

The bear continued to squeak affirmations at intervals after Spike dragged him to the back of the crate and began dismembering him, the optimistic chirp contrasting strangely with Spike's savage snarls. I knew from seeing disassembled bears on various programmers' desks that apart from the small sound box that played the affirmations, the bear contained nothing but cotton batting, so I wasn't too worried that Spike would hurt himself. Destroying the bear kept Spike quiet and occupied for most of the afternoon, and all I had to do was open the crate door occasionally to brush out the accumulated shreds of plush and cotton.

Meanwhile, I pondered the question of how to investigate Doc. I could ask Luis to do it, of course, but when I'd asked him to snoop around for traces of Anna Floyd, Luis had sounded a little testy. I didn't want to push him too far. Not to mention the fact that Luis hadn't yet brought me the lowdown on Roger's porn operation, either. Not surprising, since Luis was working a more-than-full-time job, but still — I'm used to more speed and enthusiasm when I send someone off to snoop for me.

So, since investigating Doc's background wouldn't necessarily require the same kind of computer expertise needed to uncover Roger's porn operation and Anna Floyd's files, I decided to return to my tried and true method of snooping. I called Mother.

"Hello, dear," Mother said when she recognized my voice. "Did you get the book I sent you?"

"Book?" I repeated, drawing a momentary blank.

"*Living Graciously in a Single Room*," she prompted. "I mailed it last week; it should have arrived by now."

"Oh, yes," I said. "It came Monday. But I haven't had time to read it yet."

"You don't actually need to read it," she said. "Just look at the pages I bookmarked and let me know which idea you like. I can come up Friday to take measurements."

"Measurements?"

"The seamstresses can't very well start making the curtains and slipcovers without measurements."

"What curtains and slipcovers?"

"If you'd read the book I sent . . . ," Mother said, her tone dripping disapproval.

"Mother, I've been a little busy," I said. "Didn't Dad tell you about the murder?"

"Well, yes," she said. "But it sounded as if he had that well in hand."

"It's been keeping him busy, all right," I said. "Speaking of that, there's something we thought you could help with."

It took a few tries to get her off the subject of chintz and chair rails, but once she understood that what I wanted — what we wanted (I let her assume Dad was also interested) — she took down all the information I had on Doc. If the veterinarian cousin didn't come through, odds were she could get what we needed from an aunt who raised show Pomeranians.

Of course, to get her to cooperate, I'd had to promise to consider letting her decorate the Cave with something called toile de Jouy. I had no idea what toile de Jouy looked like, but the name alone alarmed me. The Cave was, technically, Michael's, going by the name on the lease, or Michael's and mine, if you considered who was usually in residence. And if you could pin him down to an opinion on a subject as esoteric as upholstery fabrics, Michael, like many guys, would vote for something simple and unfussy. In my experience, simple, unfussy fabrics tended to have simple, unfussy names. Tweed. Plaid. Wool. Stuff like that. Toile de Jouy did not sound like the sort of fabric on which one could safely eat pizza, drink champagne, or do any of the other fascinating but untidy things one can do on a sofa.

I was starting to get a little worried about Mother's decorating obsession. Over the last several months, she had been talking more and more seriously about opening a decorating business. Should I encourage her? I wondered. I couldn't help savoring the idea of Mother bullying un-suspecting strangers into buying the kind of expensive, over-the-top rugs, furniture, and household objects she adored and ac-tually getting them to pay her for the privi-lege. But I had the sneaking feeling if she ever did start her business, she'd expect me and my sister to let her redecorate once or twice a year and then keep everything ab-solutely spotless so she could drag poten-tial clients through our homes with little or no notice. Not to mention the suspicion that if Mother went into decorating, she'd inflict things on us that would make toile de Jouy seem down-to-earth and homey.

I brooded about the prospect until closing time, and then went back to the Cave.

I scanned Ted's blackmail list. So far, I'd still identified only three of the targets — Roger, Luis, and Dr. Lorelei as the Voyeur, the Hacker, and the Valkyrie. I racked my brains over the others for a while, and then gave up to take a much-needed nap before stealing back to the office for the evening's snooping.

Chapter 22

When midnight rolled around, I walked back to the office, enjoying the cooler night air. One of the Cave's few virtues was its central location, only a few minutes' walk from the campus, the Mutant Wizards office, Luigi's, or any other important location in Caerphilly. And while some people had begun to complain about safety — imagine they actually had to lock their doors these days — the crime rate here was so minuscule compared with the Washington, D.C., area that I rarely hesitated to walk by myself.

Especially at times like this, when I wanted to be unobtrusive. I would never have expected to find anyone else around the office after hours — at least, not after midnight. But after running into such a crowd last night, I decided maybe I'd rather not have my car sitting quite so visibly in the parking lot.

The lot was empty when I arrived. Of

course. It had been last night, too. Apparently, last night I had been the only surreptitious visitor to Mutant Wizards without the sense to conceal her mode of transportation.

And by the time I arrived at the parking lot, I was rather hoping I'd see a car. Serves me right for being careless about safety, I told myself as I entered the lot, already fishing in my purse for the office key. About halfway through my walk, I'd begun to get that creepy feeling that someone was watching me. If I stopped suddenly, the echo of my footsteps stopped just a little too late. Was that my shadow on that building — or the shadow of someone else, slinking along behind me.

If this were one of those teen horror flicks, I told myself as I approached the front door, we would now have reached the part where the character on screen makes the mistake of thinking that she's safe just because her destination is within reach. And she'd let down her guard, and bingo! Casualty number one.

So I pretended to have trouble finding my keys, while concealing them in my hand, and had a good look around the parking lot while pretending to rummage through the purse. No one.

Then, to put my pursuer off guard, I put my hands on my hips, said "Damn," and took a step or two away from the door, as if I were leaving.

When I thought whoever had been following me would surely have retreated to avoid being seen, I whirled, ran back to the door, keys at the ready, unlocked it, and ran inside.

I'd also seen plenty of horror movies where the heroine assumed she was safe just because she was inside a building. No such mistake for me. I pulled out my flashlight and made sure there was no one in the downstairs entrance. Or in the stairwell. While I was checking the stairwell, I heard a faint noise. Someone trying the knob of the outside door.

I clicked the beam off and hid in the stairwell, just beside the door. If anyone came into the stairwell, I could jump him. And of course, if whoever was following me came in and took the elevator, I'd have plenty of time to call the police before it arrived at the second floor.

Nothing, for thirty seconds. Then I heard another faint noise. The rattle of a key in the lock. Aha! So whoever had been following me had a key to the building. That narrowed my possible pursuers down to maybe a hundred people. Unless, of course, I'd caught the eye of a mugger who traveled with a collection of skeleton keys. But my money was on someone who worked in the building.

My eyes were adjusted to the dark now, not that it was completely dark — a streetlight outside lit the hall faintly, and some of the light reached the wall opposite the door into the stairwell. A trapezoid of shadow appeared on the wall as a faint squeak told me the door was opening. Then the door closed and I could see the shadow of a man on the wall. I tensed. The shadow grew, and then he stepped through the doorway into the stairwell.

"Aaiiee!" With a bloodcurdling yell, I sprang toward the intruder, giving him a glancing blow to the shoulder with the flashlight and then knocking his feet out from under him with a swift kick. He fell with a thud and a yelp, and I was about to stomp on his knee and crush it when I realized there was something familiar about that yelp.

I turned on the flashlight instead, and saw that I had felled Rob.

"Hi, Meg," he said, and rubbed the back of his head, where I'd hit him.

"Rob, what are you doing here?"

"I was following you," he said, feeling his ribs. "I saw you walking this way, and I thought I'd see what you were up to."

"It never occurred to you to just walk up and say, 'Hi, Meg. What are you up to?' "

"I thought it would be more fun to surprise you," he said, rubbing his knee. "Gee, I blew it didn't I? I should have done the Crash of the Eagle when you attacked me. Or maybe Striking Mace."

"If you say so."

"Could we take that over again?" he asked. "I'll go out in the hall and come back in again and —"

"Rob?"

"Yes?"

"Go home," I said.

He stood up, tested his knee, winced, and nodded. "Okay," he said.

I watched as he limped slowly off. I hoped he was exaggerating the limp. I felt bad about hurting my own brother, but not too bad. If he was going to slink around stalking people, he'd have to learn to take care of himself.

I climbed the stairs. Quietly, though I figured anyone who had anything to hide probably heard the commotion Rob and I had made and fled long ago. I unlocked the office door and then drew back into the shadows and waited until I was sure anyone lurking inside would have gotten impatient and peeked out. And then I waited another five minutes, because I knew perfectly well patience wasn't my long suit.

I flung the door open suddenly and flipped the light switch, figuring that the sudden illumination would temporarily blind anyone lurking inside. Of course, it wouldn't help my vision, but I figured I'd have an edge if I was expecting it.

No armed thugs or nimble ninjas lurked inside the door. I could see George, stirring slightly, but I turned the light off before he woke up completely. Apart from him, the reception area was unoccupied.

So was the rest of the office. I could probably have figured that out in five minutes if I'd just walked around yelling "Hey, anyone here?" Or better yet, "Pizza's here!" It took me four times that long, listening outside doors and then leaping through, doing my best imitation of what the cops do in TV shows. It occurred to me, halfway through, that this tactic probably worked better for cops with firearms than for someone armed only with a large flashlight. And that if anyone was recording my antics with a hidden camera,

I'd never live it down.

But by the time I'd finished creeping and leaping my way through the floor, I was reasonably sure no one was there. Yippee. Time to begin the real business of the evening.

I balanced the black light on my bandaged left hand, wiped my embarrassingly sweaty right palm, took a better grip on it, and fumbled for the on switch. The light was about the size of a flashlight — in fact, it did have a small flashlight built into one end. But running all along the length of it was a glass cylinder, rather like a very short fluorescent lightbulb. I'd tested it, at home, of course — at least as far as I could test it without anything ultraviolet to detect. I'd put in fresh batteries and switched it on to admire the weird purple glow. I was ready to stalk the mail cart.

But using the black light to do so proved harder than I'd thought. I'd imagined the mail cart's path would look rather like the markings on an asphalt highway, a wide, solid line, several inches wide. Or perhaps more like the baselines on a ball field. I dredged up a childhood memory of seeing someone mark the baselines with a little cart that rolled along the infield, depositing a thick trail of white powder behind it. I presumed the mail cart company used something like that, only with powder that was colorless in daylight. And when I flicked on the black light, the trail would suddenly appear, glowing luminously. And all I'd have to do to find some key evidence was follow the trail, like Dorothy skipping down the yellow brick road.

I flicked on the black light and saw . . . nothing. Nothing out of the ordinary, anyway.

I waved the light around.

Still nothing.

It wasn't as if I had expected to find that the killer had left secret clues in ultraviolet ink or anything, but there had to be something, or the mail carts couldn't run.

I went back into the reception area where, thanks to my several days as substitute switchboard operator, I had a very good idea where to look for the mail cart path. I got down on my hands and knees and held the black light within a few inches of the carpet.

I saw something all right, but it was hardly the broad, unmistakable path I'd imagined. More like a faint spackling of yellow dots. After I'd studied them, I began to see something like a pattern.

I also saw green flecks, but they seemed

too small and random to have anything to do with the mail cart, especially since they appeared in some areas of the floor where the mail cart couldn't possibly go. Like under the reception desk. And faint pink spots that appeared in a regular pattern, like a grid, all over the room. I finally concluded that the pink spots were actually one of the fibers in the carpet.

I studied the floor of the reception room until I thought I understood the mail cart markings, and then crawled along the trail, out the opening into the main part of the office, checking my theories. Yes, that pattern of dots signaled that the cart was supposed to turn. This other pattern, which I'd first seen beside the reception desk, cued the cart to stop at a desk and beep for a human to take his or her bundle of mail.

Here and there I found larger, fainter spots, ranging from silver dollar size to dinner plate size, though less regular. They seemed to cluster. Puzzled, I studied them until I finally remembered Dad talking over dinner one evening about how forensic technicians used black lights to detect bodily fluids. Deducing that the larger spots might have resulted from the Bring Your Dog to Work program, I went to the kitchen, washed my hands, and resolved to give the larger spots a wide berth for the rest of my investigation.

I'd hunted out a blank floor plan of the office — left over from the Space Race, as I called the premove turfing over who got to sit where — and marked the cart's path on that. I started from the reception area, went down the hall past the computer lab — which was dark and Rogerless tonight, to my relief — and then through the cube-filled main space, ending up back in the reception area. It took two hours, but I felt a moment of satisfaction when I sat down on one of the guest sofas and looked down on my floor plan — now clearly marked with the mail cart's entire route.

Somewhere along that path, Ted was killed.

I studied the floor plan, noting the places where the mail cart was out in the open — unlikely spots for anyone to strangle Ted — and the places where a sufficiently daring murderer might possibly risk an attack.

Frankly, there was no place I'd have risked an attack. Perhaps I wasn't cut out to be a daring murderer. Or perhaps I was missing some critical clue, some plausible theory.

Perhaps they'd all joined forces to off

Ted; the programmers on one end of the mouse cord and the graphic artists on the other, like some lethal game of tug-of-war.

I decided to inspect a couple of the most promising sites again. I picked up the floor plan and headed down the hall toward the lunchroom.

The no-longer-darkened lunchroom. Someone was in there again.

As I crept down the hall toward the room, I heard a familiar rattling sound. The sound of dice shaken in a plastic cup, followed by the slightly different rattle of half a dozen dice landing on a hard surface.

The sound, combined with the late hour, took me back in time. To when Rob was still perfecting Lawyers from Hell, which also happened to be just after Michael and I started dating. I was staying with my parents until I could evict the sculptor who'd sublet my apartment. Michael would come down for weekends, and we'd play Lawyers from Hell with Rob and the rest of the family for hours. Not that we were that interested in the game, but with no place we could really be alone together . . .

I shook my head to bring myself back to the present and peered into the room. Frankie, Keisha, and several others from the staff were sitting around a table. The familiar paraphernalia of role-playing games lay scattered across the table. A box full of dice in all sizes and colors. Not just the standard six-sided dice, but also eight-sided, ten-sided, twenty-sided, and my favorites, the four-sided dice, which looked like three-dimensional triangles or tiny three-sided pyramids. All the players had pencils and sheets of paper, and they were all staring intently at Frankie. Apparently Frankie was acting as game master, the referee who runs the session. He was frowning over a rule book, evidently trying to make a decision based on the dice roll he'd just thrown.

The faces were different, but the scene was the same, and I felt oddly transported back to those earlier evenings, with their odd mix of excitement and frustrated sexual tension. What am I doing here instead of in California with Michael? I wondered. I could —

Something jarred me out of that fantasy. The scene before me was a little too much the same as those early days of Lawyers from Hell. Frankie was sitting behind a game master's screen, a piece of cardboard folded into three parts so it would stand upright and keep the players from seeing all the notes and statistic sheets he was using to run the game.

In the original live role-playing version of Lawyers from Hell, Rob had always used a special game master's screen — we'd called it the judge's bench. Our niece who went to art school had painted it. Around the bottom was a frieze with caricatures of several dozen family members who'd helped play-test the game, all depicted wearing prison stripes and leg irons as part of a chain gang.

I recognized the screen in front of Frankie as that original Lawyers from Hell judge's bench. A little battered, but unmistakable. I recognized the trio of rule books at Frankie's elbow, too. Pre-trial, jury selection, and trial phases — Rob's original final version, run off on his inkjet printer and stapled in purple paper covers, the same copies we'd given to the graphic designer cousin to typeset. No doubt with Rob's handwritten notes in the margins. At least two out of the three volumes were the originals. The third was a printed copy, and I was willing to bet the missing volume was the one I'd found in Ted's cache. Not that the printed copy wasn't rare enough, given the short period of time Rob had tried to sell the paper-based game before moving to the computer version. But not nearly so rare as the original.

"What's going on here?" I asked.

The half-dozen players all started and whirled to see what was up; then their faces all took on a sheepish, guilty look.

"We're playing Lawyers from Hell," Keisha said.

"Don't tell Rob," Frankie begged.

"That you're playing his game?"

"That we're playing the unautomated version," Keisha said.

"With Rob's paraphernalia," I added.

They all looked guilty. I folded my arms and looked stern. It's what I always did when I wanted to make Rob confess something. I'd learned my first day at Mutant Wizards that it seemed to have the same effect on the whole staff.

"It's okay," Frankie said. "I mean, we all love the computer version. It's wonderful!"

The others nodded and murmured agreement.

"But if you first got into gaming playing role-playing games — face-to-face ones — it's . . . well, it's kind of . . ."

"It's not as much fun," Keisha said bluntly.

"I keep telling them they should let the users hear the dice rolls," one player put in. "We could generate the sound of rattling dice."

"I thought one of the advantages of the computer version was that you didn't have to spend so much time rolling dice and calculating things," I said.

"Yeah," Frankie said. "But you lose something, too. That adrenaline surge you get when the Judge rolls the dice and you know something's about to happen."

"And the human interaction," Keisha added. "One of the weaknesses of the computer game is that it's at most a two-player game — you don't have all the fun of a group of people playing all the different witnesses and stuff. I know the online version is supposed to fix that, but it's still not like sitting in a room with people and playing. There's no ambience."

I looked around the room. On the face of it, the lunchroom was pretty short on ambience. Deltas of paper spread across the floor, interspersed with pencils, stray dice, and bags of snack food. Half a dozen pizza boxes were scattered over the counters. Beer and soda cans, solo or in clumps, festooned the entire room.

But on another level . . .

"So sometimes we borrow Rob's stuff and play a game, the old-fashioned way,"

Frankie said. "Just . . . because."

"Yeah, I know what you mean," I said. "We had a lot of fun, playing the game, back when Rob was still polishing it."

"You were a beta tester?" Keisha exclaimed. "Cool!"

"Do you still play?" Frankie asked.

"I haven't for months," I said. I'd almost said years; it felt like that long. "It got to be pretty time consuming, especially after Rob decided that he needed someone else to judge so he could concentrate on experiencing the game as a player, and I got drafted. Being judge is a whole lot more work."

"You've played the judge?" Frankie asked.

"Oh, my God," Keisha exclaimed. "Do you realize who she is?"

The others looked at her, puzzled. For that matter, so did I.

"She's Judge Hammer!" Keisha said.

The others looked at me openmouthed.

"You were, weren't you?" Keisha demanded.

"Yeah," I said. "Rob was already Judge Langslow, so I picked hammer. For my blacksmithing."

"Wow," Frankie said.

They were still looking at me, with the

sort of awestruck expressions they usually wore when listening to Rob's pronouncements. As if I were some kind of heroic figure out of legend.

Which to them, I suppose I was. Although he had little or nothing intelligible to say about topics such as game mechanics, marketing techniques, or the future of the electronic entertainment industry, Rob kept getting invited to speak at conferences. And to many people's astonishment, he'd become a highly entertaining speaker. He confined himself largely to telling anecdotes about things that had happened during the development of Lawyers from Hell. Lightweight stuff, but Rob managed to make the development of the game seem like a scientific quest at least as important as the Alamo Project. Occasionally, someone who heard one of his tales would find it a powerful metaphor for some business truth, and if they told Rob about their insights, he was always happy to add them to his repertoire. And otherwise sane people, after hearing his nostalgia-laden tales of playing the early version of the game, seemed to regard those late nights in my parents' family room with the same kind of envy other generations would feel for people who'd actually experienced Paris in the twenties or Haight Ashbury during the Summer of Love.

"Would you consider judging a game for us?" Frankie asked, and several others began clamoring, as well.

None of us ought to be here at all, I thought, on a work night; I should confiscate Rob's paraphernalia and send them home, so I could get on with studying the floor tiles.

"Just a short game," I said.

Chapter 23

In my fit of nostalgia about the good old days of playing the original Lawyers from Hell, I'd forgotten a few small details. Like how absolutely horrible you feel the next day if you're trying to survive on two and a half hours of sleep.

At least I'd identified another of Ted's blackmail targets. Frankie, ringleader of last night's gaming party, was almost surely the Luddite.

I was too exhausted to protest when I discovered that the box of Affirmation Bears had reappeared in the closet. From time to time, Dr. Brown would trudge through the reception room and deposit several disheveled bears in the box. In between her trips, various staff would sidle into the room to abscond with an armful of bears. I couldn't focus well enough to keep count, but I got the feeling she was losing ground steadily.

The effort of punching the buttons to answer phone calls was almost more than I could manage, and I cringed when one call turned out to be Mother.

"I've got exactly what you need, dear," she said.

Please don't let this be about faux finishes, I thought.

"That veterinarian of yours has quite an interesting history," she went on.

"Just how interesting?" I said, uttering a silent prayer of thanks for gossip, the only thing on Earth that could distract Mother from interior decorating.

"He used to belong to one of those militant animal-rights organizations," Mother said. "Remember how Aunt Cecily told us about the protests they kept having at dog shows a few years ago?"

"Only vaguely," I said. As a child, I'd found Aunt Cecily fascinating, because she was the only grown-up who got away with talking about sex — not to mention using the word "bitch" — at my grandmother's dinner table. But like most of my cousins, I learned to tune Aunt Cecily out once I'd reached the age where hearing about Pomeranians mating became boring instead of titillating.

"They would register dogs for a show —

genuine dogs — but then they'd show up with some of their human members in cages, wearing collars, and try to take them into the ring. And then there were the anti-hunting protests, when the members dressed up like deer and went running through the woods."

"I remember that," I said, recalling a newspaper shot of the earnest protestors, wearing synthetic fur ponchos and head-gear topped with giant papier-maché antlers.

"Apparently your veterinarian friend left the group after a hunting protest that ended in a very unfortunate shooting incident."

"Really," I said. I could feel adrenaline starting to wake me up. "Do you think it could be another murder?"

"No one was killed, dear," Mother said. "But your friend was shot . . . in the derriere. And instead of taking him to the hospital right away, the other protestors tied him to the hood of their Volvo and drove around town honking for several hours. He was quite put out, and they had a parting of the ways. I gather he's become much less radical — shortly after that he joined the ASPCA and applied to veterinary school."

Mother grilled me for details of what Doc was doing now, and then signed off, presumably to relay his current whereabouts to Aunt Cecily. I made a note to share her information with the chief, next time I saw him. Would his history as a radical animal-rights activist make Doc more plausible as a murder suspect? Probably — after all, Ted had only two legs.

After that flurry of excitement, my energy level dropped again. I actually dozed off at the switchboard at some point in the morning and woke up to find Luis shaking my shoulder.

"Are you all right?" he asked.

"I'm fine," I said, although I noticed that I didn't sound fine; I sounded cranky. Realizing that only made me feel more cranky.

"Here," Luis said, handing me a diskette.

"What's this?" I asked.

"The collected works of Anna Floyd," he said, glancing around to make sure no one was there.

"So I was right," I said. "It is a pseudonym for someone at the office."

"Bet you can't guess who," he said with a Cheshire Cat smile.

"What's-his-name," I said. "One of the

347

therapists, the mousy little guy. Dr. Lorelei's husband."

"You knew all along," he said.

"I suspected, but I didn't know," I said.

He shook his head.

"How's the other research project going?" I asked.

"More slowly," he said. "I assume you'd rather not tip off whoever runs the porn sites that someone's checking them out."

"You assume right," I said. "Just let me know when you have something.

He nodded and left.

So now I knew who the Bodice Ripper was, I thought as I stuck the diskette into the computer and began checking the files Luis had copied.

I found copies of letters to and from publishers — fairly big publishers, I presumed, since I'd heard of them. Complete drafts of two of the books I'd seen in print. And a file that was clearly the first half of another novel.

I couldn't think of anything else I could do while stuck on the switchboard, so I began to read the unfinished book.

Which turned out to be rather interesting. You found out in the first chapter that the heroine, a typical blond, statuesque Anna Floyd kind of gal, was already married to a mousy, bespectacled man who greatly resembled Anna's usual heroes. But the wife was bored with him — she was contemplating having an affair with a sexy neighbor who'd been flirting with her. A sexy neighbor who, the reader quickly deduces, might well be the local Jack the Ripper or Hannibal Lecter. Was the heroine so mesmerized by Sexy Neighbor's pecs and cleft chin that she couldn't see fava beans and a nice Chianti in her future? Or had I heard so many analyses of real and literary serial killers from Dad that I suspected the worst from Sexy Neighbor long before most people would?

Eventually, even the heroine began to have a few nagging doubts about Sexy Neighbor — though of course she paid no attention to her intuition, probably because doing so would bring the book to a screeching halt about one hundred pages short of the minimum required length. Still, having read three of Anna's books, I figured I didn't have to worry about the heroine. Sure, she'd let Sexy Neighbor lure her to his den of iniquity, but Mousy Husband would turn up just in time. He would burst on the scene, eyes flashing, and save her from certain death, or a fate worse than death, whichever Sexy Neighbor intended to come first.

Imagine my surprise when Sexy Neighbor turned up dead. And Mousy Husband began acting . . . well, highly suspicious. Was this just a ploy to keep the two lovers apart for a few more chapters? Or would Mousy Husband turn out to be the real serial killer, thereby allowing the heroine to find happiness with the mousy, bespectacled but perhaps secretly heroic homicide detective who had just turned up to investigate the neighbor's death?

The husband and the homicide detective were in the middle of a duel of waspish wit and mousy spectacle polishing when the manuscript broke off in midchapter.

"Aarrgghh!!" I exclaimed. I wasn't sure which was more provoking: not knowing how the story ended, or realizing that I'd actually gotten caught up in Anna Floyd's hokey plot.

Although perhaps my interest was less related to the plot than to the question of what, if anything, it had to do with Ted's murder? Was this rather dark and brooding story really the product of the same mind that had produced the other three mildly amusing if somewhat predictable works I'd previously read? Was there any significance to the fact that Anna Floyd was writing about murder instead of the usual abduction and seduction themes?

Most interesting of all — since all Anna Floyd's statuesque blond heroines and mousy heroes clearly resembled Dr. Lorelei and her husband, was this plot inspired by something in real life? If Lorelei was having an affair with a patient, she'd probably done a certain amount of sneaking around. And if Ted had been blackmailing her, an observant eye — say, a jealous husband — could have detected a certain emotional tension between them. What if the husband had put the evidence together and come to the erroneous conclusion that Dr. Lorelei had been having an affair with Ted? Was the book some kind of wish fulfillment? Or, better yet, a game plan? In the book, Sexy Neighbor had been bludgeoned, not strangled, of course, so the book wasn't a finished game plan. But what if the blow to Ted's throat was a bludgeoning attempt that had failed, forcing the killer to fall back on the mouse cord to finish his victim off?

I'd have to consider the husband a suspect. And decided that if he was a suspect, I should make a better effort to remember his name. I looked him up on the phone list. Dr. Glass. I'd work on remembering that. Dr. Glass whose motive, if he turned out to be the killer, would be transparent.

I was rereading passages of the manuscript, trying to figure out if the mousy homicide detective resembled anyone else around the office or if he was another version of Dr. Glass. And also looking for clues that the deceased Sexy Neighbor was intended to represent Ted. He wasn't my idea of a dreamboat, but maybe he looked that way to Dr. Glass. He was taller and younger, anyway. And perhaps his breezy attempts at charm had gone over better with Dr. Glass than they had with me.

I still had my nose buried in the book when the door opened. I glanced up to see a cleaning cart rattle into the reception area. I focused back on the screen, and then realized that there was something odd about the figure pushing the cart. I looked up at her. Her shoulders sagged in typical tired fashion beneath the usual faded blue smock the building cleaning service staff wore. A few wisps of gray hair escaped from her bandanna.

Odd that she would be here so early, I thought. Usually the cleaners didn't show up till after five. Probably someone had called for a special cleanup of some kind, I deduced, and was about to turn my attention back to my computer screen.

The cleaner stopped for a moment before pushing her cart through the opening into the rest of the office, and sighed heavily as she eased her obviously aching back. As she did, her bandanna slipped up a little, revealing an earlobe pocked with odd, assorted earrings.

The rabid fan.

"You again!" I shouted, furious that the intruder had very nearly gotten past me in her cleaning lady disguise. I vaulted over the reception desk to catch her. She turned and tried to ram me with the cleaning cart, but I had more momentum. I batted the cart aside, shoved the bandanna-clad figure to the floor, and sat on her.

Four of the office dogs thought this was enormous fun, and danced around us barking. Jack and Frankie, who had been talking in the hallway, ran over and waded through the dogs to help.

"Hold on to her," I said. "And turn her over."

"Her again," Frankie said.

"This time we arrest her for trespassing, I hope," Jack said.

"Definitely," I said. "And just maybe a little more than trespassing."

I went back to my desk, rummaged in

my carryall, and pulled out the computer gaming magazine I'd found in Ted's cache. I opened it to the article he'd marked and studied the pictures briefly.

"Take a look," I said, holding out the magazine to Jack. "That's her in the middle picture. Read the caption."

"What's up?" Frankie asked.

"She's not a fan," Jack said, looking up from the magazine. "She's a spy."

"Let me see that," Frankie said, reaching for the magazine.

"She works for The Four Gamers of the Apocalypse," I said.

"Those sleazy copycats," Frankie growled, which was mild compared to what some of the programmers said about Mutant Wizards' biggest and most hated competitor.

"Hang on to her while I call the police," I said.

"I'll leave quietly," she said.

"No, you'll stay here till the police arrive," I said, from the switchboard, where I was dialing. "I think they'll want to hear why the vice president of one of Mutant Wizards' major business rivals has been hanging around here in disguise for several weeks. And I bet they'll be fascinated when they hear that the first person to see through her disguise turned up dead shortly afterward."

"I had nothing to do with that," she said quickly.

"Yeah, right," I said. I was mentally congratulating myself. I'd identified another of the code names on Ted's blackmail list. Our rabid fan turned corporate spy had to be Mata Hari.

As I expected, the police were very interested to hear about a case of trespassing on the scene of the murder. The chief, they promised, would be right over. I hung up feeling quite cheerful. Surely Mata Hari would draw some of the heat away from Rob.

"What's the problem?" We looked up to see Liz standing a few feet away, looking anxious.

"It's that fan again," Frankie said.

"She was attempting to enter the building, disguised as a cleaning woman," I said. "Do you think we can charge her with trespassing?"

"We can't possibly charge all the persistent fans with trespassing," Liz said.

"I don't see why not, but never mind," I said. "This one's more than a fan."

I handed Liz exhibit A in the case against Mata Hari. She studied the photo and our captive.

"I'm not a prosecutor, but I suggest we call the police and see what they can do," she said finally.

"I already did," I said.

"Wait a minute," the intruder protested. "You don't understand. I was just —"

"And someone be sure to jot down anything she says," Liz added. "Some of it may prove useful in court."

The intruder stopped protesting.

"By the way," Liz said, motioning for me to follow her out into the hall. "While the chief is here, do you think you could find out if he's learned anything about our other unwanted visitor?"

"Other unwanted visitor?" I said, drawing a blank. "Oh, you mean Eugene, the disgruntled employee."

"Eugene Mason," she said, glancing over to make sure the door was closed. "Yes."

"I meant to ask — what's he so disgruntled about, anyway?"

"It's completely ridiculous," Liz said. "He signed a noncompete agreement when he came on board. Standard practice; all the staff do. And part of the exit interview is that he's supposed to initial the agreement to confirm that he understands the terms and will abide by them. And he won't."

"Why not?"

"He claims that the agreement is too onerous, and the copy we have on file isn't what he signed."

"I don't get it," I said. "He's phoning in threats and lurking around just because we asked him to initial something he doesn't want to initial?"

"He doesn't get his final paycheck until he initials the form," Liz said.

"Okay, now I get it," I said, frowning. "Isn't that a little harsh?"

"Not really," she said. "He knows a great deal about the software architecture, not to mention our plans for future releases. We need to make absolutely sure he isn't going to peddle what he knows to one of our competitors — or if he does, that we've got the documentation we need to sue them. Or defend ourselves if he tries to sue us."

"Is that likely?" I asked.

She shrugged. "Depends," she said.

"Depends on what?"

"On whether he finds an attorney stupid enough to take his case," she said. "It'll never hold up in court — he can't even find his own copy of the noncompete agreement, which is probably why he's so off base about what it says. Of course, he claims someone stole it, for heaven's sake. At any rate, it's not very likely he'll get someone to take it on contingency, and so far he hasn't convinced anyone he's got the wherewithal to pay."

"I almost think you enjoy these legal battles."

"Of course not," she said, frowning. "I'd rather prevent them. But I do feel a certain satisfaction when I know I've done whatever needs to be done to take care of a problem. Which reminds me — according to your father, you're close to solving the murder."

"I wish," I said. "Dad's an optimist. I'm a realist. I'm just trying to keep the chief from railroading Rob."

"Wouldn't solving the case be the best way of doing that?"

"Naturally," I said, fighting back a yawn. "But that's easier said than done. I'm just trying to dig up enough dirt on enough people to convince the chief that Rob isn't the only one with a motive for killing Ted. As soon as I've accomplished that, I'll give up sleuthing so I can catch up on my sleep."

She studied my face for a moment, then nodded. "Makes sense," she said. "I should get back to work."

I followed her back into the reception area.

"Make sure the police know about as many of the trespassing incidents as possible," she said, and headed back to the library.

"Tough lady," Frankie said.

Why did I have a feeling he'd have said something shorter and less complimentary if I hadn't been there. Jack's face didn't give away anything; he just nodded and headed back to his desk, leaving Frankie to guard our captive.

So she was tough — did they really want one of their former coworkers to steal everything they'd been working on so hard and hand it to the competition? They were all so excited about their stock options — didn't they understand that the stock options weren't worth beans unless Mutant Wizards continued to prosper?

Light suddenly dawned. I'd be willing to bet that Liz was the Iron Maiden on Ted's list. And what had Ted said about the Iron Maiden? I went back to my desk and fished in my drawer for the blackmail printout.

"No dice," read the notation beside the Iron Maiden. "Can't even get time of day."

Made sense.

And what about Eugene Mason's claims that someone had stolen his copy of the agreement? What if someone had? What if Ted had stolen it, and Mason had found out, and Ted's murder was the result?

Next time Liz spotted Mason lurking outside, I'd have to go out and interrogate him, I decided. And I should study his personnel file, to see if perhaps he seemed to match any of the names on Ted's blackmail list.

The front door opened and the chief walked in, accompanied by several uniformed officers.

"That was fast," I said.

"We were already on our way over," the chief said.

I wasn't sure I liked the sound of that.

Chapter 24

"Anything we can do for you?" I said.

"You've done a great deal for us already, thank you," the chief said.

I frowned and looked more closely at him. Usually when people said something like that to me, they were being sarcastic. The chief seemed serious.

"How?" I asked.

"That computer printout you gave us," the chief said. "That proved to be very useful. So what seems to be the trouble here?"

"We caught her trying to break in," I said, indicating the intruder.

I could tell Frankie really wanted to hang around, but now that I didn't need him for guard duty, I didn't think Jack would appreciate my keeping him from work, so I shooed him off. The chief took a short statement from me and then dispatched two of the uniformed officers to take her down to the station.

"Anything else we can do for you?" the chief asked.

"That's about it," I said.

"Then we'd like to go back and talk to one of your staff, if you don't mind."

"Of course not," I said.

Actually I minded plenty, but asking my permission was obviously only a formality. The chief nodded pleasantly and went through the opening to the main part of the office, followed by a very young officer in a uniform that looked brand new.

What the devil, I thought, and flipped the phone to night mode so I could see what they were up to. The chief didn't look as if he wanted my company, but he didn't actually order me away, so I followed them into the main part of the office.

And all the way to the back corner, to Jack's cube.

"John Ransom," the chief said.

Jack looked up, saw the chief, and frowned. Then he saw me and removed the glasses he only wore when staring at a monitor.

"What can I do for you?" he said.

"You're under arrest for the murder of Theodore Corrigan," the chief said. "Read him his rights, Sammy."

362

"Yes, sir," the young officer said, reaching into his pocket.

"You've got to be kidding," I said. "What makes you think Jack is the killer?"

"Like I said, that computer printout you brought us," the chief said. "We figured out from the date column that the day before his murder, Mr. Corrigan made an approach to his most recent potential blackmailing target — code named the Ninja."

"And you think Jack's the Ninja?" I said. I looked at Jack, who shrugged, leaned back in his chair, and lifted one eyebrow as he watched the young officer. Perhaps Sammy had never arrested anyone before — at least not for murder. He was still nervously patting and fumbling with his uniform pockets, apparently searching for his Miranda cue card.

"It all added up, once we determined he was the only really accomplished martial artist among our suspects," the chief said.

"Apart from me," I said. "Are you really discounting me as a suspect purely on the strength of a few broken bones?"

"You don't have the same kind of motivation Mr. Ransom has," the chief said.

"And what motivation is that?" I asked.

The chief smiled. "Let me use your computer for a minute," he said to Jack.

Jack hesitated.

"Okay if I save what I'm doing first?" he asked.

The chief nodded magnanimously, and Jack's fingers rattled the keyboard rapidly for a few seconds.

"Be my guest," Jack said, standing up and taking a seat on the countertop at the back of the cube.

The chief sat down and hitched his chair up to the computer. He bobbed his head up and down several times, looking like one of those toy dogs with the nodding heads, until he found an angle that let him see the screen, and then he picked up the mouse and began laboriously moving it around the screen. We all leaned over to see what he was doing, except for Sammy, who was removing stray bits of paper from his wallet and staring at them, apparently hoping that one of them would turn out to be his Miranda card.

"I could probably do that faster if you tell me what you want done," Jack suggested as the chief continued pecking keys and peering at the monitor. Faster, and no doubt with less danger to Jack's computer, I thought.

"No, our computer guy showed me how

to do this," the chief said. "Aha! That's got it!"

A familiar, colorful graphic appeared on the screen: a cartoon gavel smashing down on a surface.

"You've started Lawyers from Hell," I said.

"No," the chief said. "I've started Nude Lawyers from Hell."

"I stand corrected," I said, watching as tiny naked cartoon figures began marching across the screen. "What does either of them have to do with Ted's murder?"

"Watch this," the chief said.

He peered at the keyboard and pressed several keys.

The picture on screen changed. Strings sprouted from the wrists and ankles of the cartoon figures, as if they were puppets. The scene shifted, the way it does in a movie when the camera pulls back for a long shot. Now we could see the wooden frames from which the puppet strings hung, and a pair of hands moving the frames.

"What is this?" I asked. I thought I'd seen every possible sequence in the game, more times than I wanted to imagine — but I'd never seen this.

"It's an Easter egg," Jack said.

"What's that?"

"That's what they call it when one of these programmer fellows sticks in a little something extra that isn't supposed to be there," the chief said. "You can see it only if you know what keys to press."

He was preening himself as if he'd figured it out himself. "Now watch this," he said, pointing back at the screen.

Jack sighed.

The view widened again. I could see the rail on which the puppeteer was leaning, stacked with little discarded garments — tiny cartoon suit jackets and trousers, crumpled doll-size judges' robes and minuscule loud ties. Then the face of the puppeteer came into view.

Jack.

It was a cartoon version of his face, but larger and more detailed and realistic than the Lawyers from Hell characters, and instantly recognizable. He winked at us, and a curtain began closing over the picture. In a few seconds the game reappeared.

"You programmed Nude Lawyers from Hell?" I said, looking up at the real Jack.

He shrugged sheepishly. "I just wanted to see if I could," he said. "And I thought it would make a nice April Fools' gag."

"See," the chief said. "He admits it."

"Some gag, sending it out all over the world," I said.

"I didn't do that," he protested. "I just put it on a couple of machines here in the office. I have no idea how it got out on the Web."

"For heaven's sake, you know these clowns," I said. "Did you really think it wouldn't?"

"You could have a point," Jack said.

"Now you understand his motive," the chief said, leaning back and lacing his fingers across his stomach.

"Not really," I said. "What does Jack programming Nude Lawyers from Hell have to do with Ted's murder?"

Either Jack was a really good actor or he was looking forward to the answer, too.

"Mr. Corrigan was blackmailing him," the chief said.

"Ted tried blackmailing me," Jack admitted. "Back in April, when he found the Easter egg himself. I told him to go to hell, and he didn't try again."

"So you say," the chief said. "But Mr. Corrigan's blackmail log says differently. It says he approached you Sunday night — the night before the murder. And you struck the next day."

"You can't be serious," Jack said. "For

one thing, why would I pay blackmail to conceal something that anyone could stumble on if they pressed the right key combination?"

"And before you strangled him, you stunned him with a blow to the throat," the chief said, ignoring Jack's protest. "The kind of blow they teach you in those martial arts classes you've taken so many of."

"That's ridiculous," I said. "How can you possibly know from Ted's body that the person who hit him was a martial artist, instead of someone who just happened to hit the right place?"

"And then there's the location of Mr. Ransom's cube," the chief said. "Not many places along its route that the mail cart isn't visible to three or four people. But back here, no one but Mr. Ransom here can see the cart when it stops to give him his mail."

That was true, anyway, I realized as I thought back to my map.

"What kind of idiot would kill someone outside his own cube?" I asked aloud.

"An idiot who knows he can send the body rolling merrily on its way with the push of a button, and none the wiser," the chief said.

"And Jack would have to be crazy to kill

Ted here, when every few minutes, someone pops in to bother him about something," I said.

"He can tell all that to his lawyer," the chief said. "Haven't you found that damned card yet?"

He barked the last question to Sammy, who turned beet red and shook his head.

"Oh, for heaven's sake," the chief muttered. He unbuttoned his top left shirt pocket and pulled out a laminated card. He looked over his glasses, reproachfully, at Sammy, and then pushed them up on his nose and looked back at the card.

"You have the right to remain silent," he intoned, and then he gave the entire Miranda warning. Not that he seemed to need the card and he didn't rattle it off, either. He paced himself, savoring each word, with the rich, round delivery of a revival tent preacher or an old-fashioned small-town politician. By the time he finished you wanted to stand up and sing "God Bless America."

"You keep it in your uniform shirt pocket," he said, tucking the card away in Sammy's pocket. Sammy blushed again.

"I guess that means you're going to take me off to jail," Jack said.

The chief nodded. Sammy stepped forward, but the chief held up his hand and stopped him.

We watched as Jack exited the Nude Lawyers from Hell game, turned off his computer, put his glasses in a case, and stuck the case in his pocket. He pushed back his chair, stood up, and then reached over to grab an Affirmation Bear that was sitting on the counter of his cube.

"Here," he said, tossing the bear to me. "Little souvenir."

"Do you have a lawyer?" I asked.

"Not yet," he said. "Guess I should."

"I'll call and send somebody down," I said, remembering that I still had the names of the lawyers Michael had recommended.

"That'd be great," he said.

I watched as the chief and Sammy led Jack out; then I looked down at the bear.

"Damn," I said, and I punched the bear in the belly to take out my frustration.

"Here's looking at you, kid," the bear said, Bogart's voice sounding particularly incongruous coming from its smiling pink face.

I went back to my desk, fished out my notebook, flipped through till I found the names of the lawyers, and called one for Jack. The one Rob wasn't using. And then, when I was sure the lawyer was on his way down to the jail, I called Michael to vent.

"That's great," he said when I told him the news.

"Great? What do you mean 'great'?"

"Rob's off the hook, right?"

"Yes, but Jack's on the hook, and I'm not sure that's a big improvement."

"He's got a good attorney, right?" Michael asked.

"One of the ones you recommended," I said. "The one who isn't representing Rob."

"He'll be fine," Michael said. "You've managed to convince the police that Rob didn't do it — maybe you should back off."

"I can't," I said. "I just don't believe Jack did it, and I don't believe the chief is going to keep digging until he finds out who did."

"What's so important about this Jack character?" Michael said. Oh, dear. Was that a note of jealousy? I could have said that he was an attractive guy who'd been flirting with me, not to mention doing the kind of thoughtful, helpful things Michael would have been doing if he weren't three thousand miles away, and that maybe I felt just a little bit bad about not having discouraged him a little more firmly. But I didn't think that would go over too well. So I stuck to the business side of things.

"Apart from the fact that I've figured out he's the one who really runs the shop, and Rob desperately needs him to get Lawyers from Hell II finished on time and keep the company afloat, it bothers me that the chief used something I found for him to pin the murder on someone I think is innocent."

"Let his lawyer make a fuss, then," Michael said. "There's no reason for you to keep putting yourself in danger."

"I'm not going to put myself in danger," I said. "I'm just going to keep doing what I have been doing."

"Sneaking into the office by yourself in the middle of the night?"

"If you were paying attention, you'd remember that I've never managed to be by myself in the office in the middle of the night," I countered. "There's always at least one other person sneaking around."

"And what if the next time the person doing the sneaking is the murderer, and decides you're too close on his heels?"

"I'll be careful," I said. "I'm not incapable of taking care of myself. Besides, there's only one thing I need to sneak back into the office to do."

"There isn't anything you need to sneak back into the office to do."

"I need to finish studying the mail cart trail."

"I thought you said you'd done a complete map of the mail cart trail last night."

"Yes, but that only shows where the cart goes."

"And anyplace not on your map, the mail cart doesn't go," he said. "What's to find out?"

"I have the marked tiles that form the real trail mapped, and I know where there are loose tiles that show that Ted messed with its path sometime or other," I said. "But I haven't checked to see where there are loose unmarked tiles. That would let me figure out where the mail cart went that it wasn't supposed to go. The wrong paths."

"But what does that have to do with Ted's murder?" Michael said. "You don't know when the wrong paths were used; they could have been done for practical jokes days before the murder. Just tell the police about them."

"I already told you the police aren't listening."

We squabbled about it for a few minutes. We would probably have escalated to a full-scale argument, except his signal started fading slightly, and I decided it would be better for all concerned if I pretended we'd been cut off completely. When Michael tried to call back, I turned my cell phone off and left it off for an hour.

I fumed. And then something struck me. I pulled out the tote bag and extracted my copy of Ted's blackmail list.

"Of course," I muttered. Jack said he'd told Ted to go to hell. Which was exactly what Ted had written beside the name Professor Higgins on his sheet.

"*My Fair Lady*," I exclaimed, recalling the cover of the original Broadway album, with its pen-and-ink drawing of Eliza Doolittle dangling like a puppet from the strings held by Professor Higgins. I'd have bet that Ted, like me, had grown up with a copy of that around the house, and had remembered it when he saw Jack's Easter egg.

"And if Jack's Professor Higgins, he's not the Ninja."

But it would take more than a copy of the soundtrack of *My Fair Lady* to convince the chief. I'd need more evidence.

While I had the bag out, I fished out the legal documents that had been in the cache. As I now suspected, they were copies of the agreement the disgruntled Eugene Mason had signed on joining Mutant Wizards, and the yet-unsigned exit agreement. Had Ted stolen Mason's copy? Suspicious, but slim grounds for murder.

I was still fuming when Doc showed up again around lunchtime, bearing his black vet's bag and a bag of soy burger bribes.

"Come to see Katy?" I asked.

"Yes, please," he said.

Rico didn't answer when I called his office, so I flipped the phone into night mode and went looking for him.

"That's odd," Rico said when I finally tracked him down in Frankie's cube. "He didn't mention needing to see her again."

"You know Doc, always worrying about his patients," Frankie said, looking up from the computer he and Rico had been assembling. Or disassembling — it was hard to tell which. For all I knew, perhaps they were creating an abstract sculpture.

"Katy's down in the conference room," Rico said. "I'll bring her out."

When I got back to the reception room, I found that Doc had grabbed George's perch and had dragged it out into the middle of the room.

"Doc," I said. "What on Earth are you doing?"

Chapter 25

"I am liberating this poor downtrodden symbol of our country's national bird!" Doc shouted.

"You must have flunked your ornithology classes at veterinary school," I said. "Or maybe you're having a flashback to a previous animal liberation adventure. He's a buzzard, not an eagle."

Doc glanced at George, who hunched his neck and looked unmistakably buzzardish.

"This poor, downtrodden symbol of . . . of our society's callous insensitivity to the environment," Doc corrected. He took a deep breath, ready to continue orating, but he made the mistake of taking it too near George and began gagging.

"Just leave George alone," I said over the coughing. "I don't think he wants to be liberated."

"You'd be surprised how quickly wild animals learn to fend for themselves again," Doc wheezed. "His hunting skills will return to him when he returns to his native habitat."

"Buzzards don't hunt; they eat carrion," I pointed out. "Besides, George only has one —"

"He'll learn to find his own carrion, then," Doc said, beginning to sound a little irritated. He grabbed George's perch and began dragging it again. Now I realized that he was heading toward the window at the other side of the room.

"You're crazy," I said as I headed for the switchboard to call the police. Giving Doc and George a wide berth, of course.

"Here you go, George!" Doc shouted, flinging open the window and setting the perch upright again beside it. "Independence Day!"

George, who had been scrambling to keep his grip on the moving perch, greeted the outdoor air with as much enthusiasm as if Doc had tried to stick him in an oven. Which, considering that the temperature outside was again in the high nineties, wasn't too far from the truth. George gave an angry squawk and began sidling away from the window.

"You see, he doesn't want to return to nature," I said.

"He's been corrupted by civilization," Doc said. "We must push him out of the nest."

With that, he tipped the perch so it slanted rather steeply toward the window. George shrieked in terror.

"Stop that, this instant!" I ordered as I rushed over and tried to set the perch level again.

"Fly free, little bird!" Doc shouted, shaking the perch.

"He can't fly free, for heaven's sake," I exclaimed. "He's got only one wing."

Doc gaped at George, whose lopsided condition was now obvious — he was flapping his single wing wildly, trying to regain his balance, but unsuccessfully — he was sliding inexorably toward the open window.

"Oh, my God!" Doc exclaimed. After gaping for a few moments, he lunged out and grabbed George just as the buzzard's first foot slipped off the end of the perch. George, not surprisingly, interpreted Doc's lunge as an attack. He lashed out with beak and claws and then vomited on Doc. When the squawking died down and the blood, feathers, and other things stopped flying, George and Doc were sulking in separate corners, nursing their wounds and glowering at each other.

"Doc," I said. "If you really want to find George a better home, I'm all for it. He doesn't belong in a reception room. I'm sure there are places that take wounded birds of prey and try to help them lead the most normal lives possible. Come back and tell me you've gotten George a berth at one of those places, and I'll help you carry him out. But until then, leave him alone."

"Should I dress his wounds?" Doc asked.

We both looked at George, who fluffed his feathers out, bobbed his head, and shrieked.

"You can try, if you like," I said.

Doc limped out. I considered and discarded the idea of moving George back to his original corner. He was a little in the way, but I figured he wouldn't appreciate moving again right now. I cleaned up the reception room as well as I could, removed the old newspapers, and spread out a new set beneath George's stand.

By this time I calmed down and felt bad about hanging up on Michael. But now, of course, he wasn't answering his cell phone. Chill, I told myself. He's probably on the set, with it turned off. I'd catch up with him sooner or later, and make peace. And maybe it was better if I didn't until, say, tomorrow — when I would already have made my final late-night visit to the office and wouldn't be lying when I promised never to do it again.

About two o'clock, a call came through the switchboard that made me do a double take. A rather officious secretary asked to talk to Dr. Lorelei Gruber and, when I told her the doctor was out, left not only her boss's name and number but also their firm name. A law firm whose name sounded familiar, probably from when I was looking up numbers for the attorneys Rob recommended. I pulled out the yellow pages to check.

Yes, there it was. Savage and Associates, divorce attorneys. The wonderful aptness of the name for a lawyer specializing in divorces had made it stick in my mind.

Was Dr. Lorelei, the self-proclaimed expert on relationships, looking for a divorce?

Of course, there could be some perfectly innocent reason for a divorce attorney to call her. Perhaps he referred clients to her, clients who had some hope of reconciliation. Perhaps he was her client — even divorce lawyers must sometimes have troubled relationships. Perhaps he was her cousin.

Or maybe she was getting a divorce. Had she, perhaps, found out about her husband's secret life as Anna Floyd?

Normally, I pretended to be oblivious of the contents of the messages I gave people, but I couldn't resist. When Dr. Lorelei strode into the office after lunch, I looked her straight in the eye as I was handing this one over.

"Your lawyer called," I said.

She started visibly and looked around the reception room as if to see if anyone else had heard. "I hope you realize how inappropriate it would be for you to gossip about this," she said.

"I hope you realize how insulting it is for you to even say that," I replied.

She looked hurt, and I wondered if I'd been too sharp. Then she began fumbling in her purse, pulling out a half-shredded tissue, and I realized that she was blinking back tears.

"I'm sorry," she said. "This is very difficult for me."

"Here," I said, quickly pulling out several tissues from the box on the reception desk and handing them to her. If I were a better person, I thought, I'd go over to hug her, but I couldn't quite bring myself to try. She patted her eyes carefully, trying to soak up the tears before they hit her makeup, then blew her nose vigorously and held the used tissues back to me. I blinked at them, then picked up the wastebasket and held it up so she could deposit them.

"Sorry," she said.

"It's okay," I said.

"This is very embarrassing," she said. "In my situation."

"If you don't love the guy anymore, why keep beating your head against the wall," I said, shrugging.

"It's not that I don't love him," she said. "I do. But he doesn't meet my needs."

I was fishing for information, I admit, but this was way too much information.

She must have deduced my reaction from my face. "My emotional needs," she added.

"I see," I lied.

"He's just not romantic enough," she explained. "He's very intelligent and reliable. We have a very honest, healthy relationship. But he has . . . no imagination. No sense of play. Not a hint of romanticism."

I stifled the urge to giggle, remembering some of the more purple passages in Anna

Floyd's books. And wondered whether or not I should reveal her husband's secret. Would it rescue their marriage? Or was his lack of romanticism only an excuse she could replace in a heartbeat with being dishonest, impractical, and a male chauvinist pig.

What the hell. But she'd never believe me if I told her. I pulled open the drawer and snagged one of the Anna Floyd books. Under it lay the unfinished Anna Floyd manuscript. The first page had Anna Floyd's address — a post office box in a nearby town — and e-mail address: rosenkavalier3@yahoo.com. I grabbed a pen and jotted the e-mail address on the inside front cover of the book.

"Here," I said, holding out the book. "You should talk to the author."

Dr. Lorelei stiffened and backed away a step. "I really don't see what I would have to say to her," she began.

"It's a him, using a female pseudonym," I said. "I jotted his e-mail address inside."

"And why would I want to talk to him?" she said, backing up a few more steps.

"I think you'll find he has some useful insights on relationships," I said. "He might have some advice you'd find useful."

"I know you mean well," she said,

backing away. "But I really don't think you understand."

With that, she fled toward her office.

So much for trying to help the lovelorn, I thought. I dropped the book on the desk and answered a ringing line.

I tried to call Michael's cell phone several times before I left the office. No answer. I left a message at his hotel. Then I went home and repeated the process several times. Dammit, if he was going to sulk this long just because I resented his trying to order me around . . . I'd settle things with Michael tomorrow. After I finished skulking around the office one more time. I put on my skulking clothes, made sure the black light was in my purse, and then, realizing that 6:30 was a little early to reappear at the office, lay down on the sofa to kill an hour or so leafing through Mother's latest decorating tome.

It was past midnight before I woke up again. I just don't get this nap thing. I was sweaty from the stuffy air of the Cave, and more tired than before, thanks to nightmares of being chased down the halls of the office by bolts of flowered chintz. And while I knew the picturesque patterns ironed into my cheek by the tufted sofa fabric were unlikely to be permanent, I really hated having to go out of the Cave looking as if I'd gotten a Braille tattoo. Even if the only people likely to notice were any Mutant Wizard staff with nothing better to do than hang around the office after midnight.

As I strolled over to the office, I realized that I was getting rather used to prowling about Caerphilly in the wee small hours. I knew when to cross the street to avoid yards with overgrown shrubbery in which muggers or shoelace-hating cats might lurk. I knew that exactly in the middle of a particular block, a large fierce-sounding dog would begin barking when he heard my footsteps and persist until an irritated, sleepy voice called out, "Shut up, Groucho!" I knew that at some point along the route, a streetlight would buzz and go dark as I approached it, and even though I knew that it was probably due to a burned-out bulb or a malfunctioning photoelectric cell, I would, as usual, wonder if my body had undergone some strange mutation and now gave off streetlight-killing rays. And when a police car passed by the end of the block, I would make an extra effort to look relaxed and nonchalant, as if it were the most natural thing in the world to be strolling about town after midnight in dark pants, a dark shirt, and black Reeboks. Just another hardworking cat burglar on her daily commute.

By this time, I knew better than to barge into the office assuming the coast was clear. I skulked in the shrubbery at the edge of the parking lot until I was sure no one else was hiding there. Although come to think of it, all I could really be sure of was that anyone hiding there had more patience than I did. I waited inside the front door until my eyes had adjusted to the inside light level, which turned out to be useful. If I'd gone upstairs right away, I would probably still have noticed the suspicious shadow in the hall outside the Mutant Wizards office. But if my eyes hadn't been adjusted to the dark, I probably would have leaped out to neutralize the shadow's owner with a few swift kicks and punches, and I would have been very embarrassed when I realized I'd attacked an old-fashioned floor mop resting harmlessly in a pail outside the janitor's closet. I made a mental note to complain to the cleaners tomorrow.

I crept inside the office, easing the door shut so no one would hear me coming, and I skulked about from doorway to doorway, looking for signs of other skulkers.

And I spotted something. A flash of light. I paused, and peered in the direction of the light. There it was again. Someone was in one of the cubes, using a flashlight.

To be precise, someone was in Ted's old cube.

I slid silently through Cubeville until I was right outside the cube where the light had appeared. I readied my own flashlight and was about to leap out and confront the intruder when —

My pager went off.

Chapter 26

"Oh, hi, Meg."

Dad stuck his head out of the cube while I was struggling to silence the pager. Hell, struggling to find the pager, which had apparently migrated to the very bottom of my purse.

"You can turn on a light if you like," he added.

I sighed and pulled out the pager. Rob had called. What now?

"Hi, Meg," he said, when I called him. "Do you know where Dad is?"

"You're in luck; he's right here," I said. Of course, I didn't mention where here was. "Want to talk to him?"

"No, that's okay," Rob said. "I was just worried. He's usually home by now."

"I can send him home," I said.

"No, if you two are busy, that's okay," he said. "Just remind him he's supposed to take Spike when he gets home. Unless you'd like to —"

"I'll remind him," I said, hanging up. "Rob was worried," I added, to Dad.

"That's nice," Dad said. He was sitting cross-legged on the floor mat in Ted's cube, groping around to see if anything was hidden on the back of the file cabinet, on the underside of the desk surface, or inside the partitions.

"Having any luck?" I said after watching him for a minute.

"No," Dad said. "Ow."

He'd scratched himself on a sharp edge inside the partition. He sat for a few moments, sucking the cut and favoring the partition with the sort of disappointed look that suggested he was half expecting it to apologize.

"No, I don't think there's anything here to find," he said. "I can help you with whatever you're doing."

Normally, I'd have waffled. Dad helping with a task all too often escalated into Dad taking over and turning it into something larger, more complex, and completely different from what I intended.

Then on the other hand, considering what I wanted to accomplish . . .

"You're welcome to help if you like," I said. "I'm afraid it's not very exciting."

"You forget," Dad said, sounding hurt. "I've participated in investigations before. I know crime solving sometimes involves a level of patient, meticulous effort that would seem tedious to the uninitiated."

Yes, Dad probably did know that, but since patient, meticulous effort wasn't exactly his forte, he'd probably used the knowledge to make sure he was elsewhere when any such effort was going on.

"Right," I said. "Okay. What we need to do is test every floor tile in the place to see which ones are loose."

"Loose floor tiles?" Dad said. "Does this have something to do with the murder?"

Did he think I dropped by the office at midnight to catch up on maintenance work?

"Remember how you were riding around on the cart, trying to see where Ted could have been ambushed?" I reminded him.

"Yes," he said, shaking his head. "And I'm afraid the only place it seemed at all likely was right outside poor Jack Ransom's cube."

"And I don't happen to think Jack did it," I said.

Perhaps I said it a little too vehemently.

"I don't see why you're so upset about his arrest," Dad said, frowning. "I mean, at least the chief doesn't suspect your brother anymore."

"Oh, it's okay to arrest an innocent person as long as he's not family?"

"Well, what do we really know about Jack?" Dad said. He's a nice enough fellow; I can see why you might be worried about him, but —"

"I don't care if he's nice or the most obnoxious person left on staff now that Ted's gone," I said. "As far as I can figure out, he's an essential part of the Lawyers from Hell II development team, so if he's unjustly jailed or having to spend a lot of his time fighting a bogus murder charge, that's bad for the new release, bad for Mutant Wizards, and bad for people like you and me who have money in the company. So if there's a chance this very important staff member might actually be innocent, I think we should find out."

When I put it that way, Dad seemed reassured that I wasn't taking an inappropriate interest in Jack's welfare and reluctantly turned his attention to the floor tiles. At least, he was reluctant until we discovered that the best way to test whether they were glued down tight was to dance around on them in a sort of modified soft-shoe step.

Of course, this discovery drove any hope of stealth and secrecy out the window. Dad progressed from humming to singing as we skipped, stepped, shuffled, and moon-walked our way up and down the corridors.

"Singin' in the rain! I'm singin' in the rain!" Dad caroled, waving an imaginary umbrella and splashing through imaginary puddles. The next thing I knew, he had frolicked his way into the men's room, which had much better acoustics. Of course, it didn't happen to have any carpet tiles, but presumably the lengthy session of tap dancing Dad conducted on its ceramic tiled floors was essential to determine whether Ted had been interfering with the integrity of the grout.

I had less fun than Dad, since I interrupted my own pirouettes frequently to map any loose tiles the two of us dislodged. Gradually, a pattern of Ted's mail cart experiments emerged. Apparently he had tried to send them through the bathrooms — the women's room, anyway. I suspected that the ultraviolet dye didn't stick well enough to the tiles to make this scheme work; only in the grout could we detect any traces of it.

We'd been through the entire office once

already, but Dad had switched from Gene Kelly to Fred Astaire and had begun re-testing one of the large main hallways.

"You say tomayto, and I say tomahto," he was warbling. I went into the reception area, spread my map out on the reception desk, and frowned down at it.

At least half a dozen cubes showed signs that Ted had rigged the cart to chug in and ram the occupant, and if he hadn't actually detoured the cart through the lunchroom, the conference rooms, Rob's office, the library, and the computer lab, he'd been planning to do so. And as I was staring at the map, something started to take shape in my mind.

"Anyplace else we need to test?" Dad asked, sticking his head into the reception area. "The hallway outside, maybe?"

"No, we're finished," I said. "I've got all the loose tiles marked on my floor plan now."

"So what do you think it all means?" Dad asked. "Meg? Did you hear me? I said —"

"Right, right," I muttered. I heard him, but my mind was elsewhere. So completely elsewhere that I tripped over one of the loose tiles on my way back into the library.

"Meg?" Dad said, following me.

"Hang on a minute," I said.

I glanced around for the library steps, then pushed them back into place, where they'd been on Monday. Tucked the flashlight under my arm, climbed to the top, and sat where Liz had been sitting. Where she was in the habit of sitting. My shoulders were level with the top shelf of the bookcase, and if I looked to my left, I could see the reception area. I shone my flashlight down and to the right. With the beam, I followed a path outlined by the loose tiles — a path that, if you replaced the blank tiles with marked ones, would lead the mail cart right up to the base of the ladder. The spots that made the cart stop could have been where one of the tiles was loose at the base of the ladder.

"Have you found something?"

"Maybe," I said. This was crazy. It didn't necessarily have anything to do with the murder. Ted could have switched the tiles at any time since we'd moved in, to harass Liz.

Funny she hadn't mentioned it, though.

Maybe she had just been too exasperated to talk about it. This is Liz you're talking about, I told myself. We'd laughed together, commiserated together, become friends.

I stuck the flashlight back under my arm and turned to climb down. The beam hit the bookcase in front of me, and I saw something. One of the thick legal volumes had a small red stain on the spine. I plucked it off the shelf, examined it, and then climbed back down the ladder with it.

"What do you make of this?" I said, handing it to Dad. He trained his flashlight on it.

"It's not blood," he said, handing it back with a shake of his head. "Blood wouldn't stay red after it dried."

"No," I said. "It's stage blood. I've spent enough time with Michael and his drama department cronies to recognize the stuff when I see it."

"You think this is connected with the murder?" Dad asked, frowning.

"I suppose it's remotely possible that this book was already stained with stage blood before Monday," I said. "But I think you're looking at how the killer managed to stun Ted before strangling him."

"Instead of a karate chop?"

I set my flashlight on a shelf, where the beam would provide some general illumination, and climbed back up the ladder.

"Imagine you're Ted. You've switched tiles so the mail cart will cruise through here. And you're lying on the mail cart, with stage blood running down from your chest. Down your sides, your arms — and onto your throat."

"And I stop right beneath the ladder," Dad said, throwing himself into his role. He walked along my theoretical mail cart path, leaning back to become as horizontal as he could without actually falling on his back.

"From up here, I wouldn't need that much strength to hit someone hard," I said. "Gravity's on my side. So all I have to do is take a step or two down and wham!" I slammed the book down on an imaginary Ted's throat, with a violence that clearly startled Dad. Startled me, in fact. I was angry. Not at poor irritating Ted, but at the person who'd killed him. The person I'd considered a friend.

"And then," I went on, "if there happened to be a mouse cord on one of the pigeonholes of the mail cart — and there probably was since people were always sending each other stray bits of hardware on the mail cart — mice, disk drives, cables — all I'd have to do would be to pick it up and finish the job."

Dad and I stood, looking at each other for a few seconds. Then he reached out and patted me on the shoulder.

"Good job," he said. "Let's take this book to the chief and tell him —"

"I knew I was going to have to do something about you," came a voice from behind me.

Chapter 27

I turned to find Liz, standing in the library door, holding a gun.

"Liz, you —"

"Stay back," she said. "I'm a good shot with this."

"Yes, I remember," I said. "You took lessons, when you lived in a bad part of East Palo Alto. For self-defense. I don't think this counts as self-defense."

She shrugged. "Depends on your point of view," she said. "Here, catch!"

She threw something at us. Dad started and clutched his flashlight with both hands; I took a half-step forward and raised my good hand, out of reflex, to catch whatever it was before it hit him. I'd caught a roll of silver duct tape.

"You win the toss," she said. "Tie him up."

"Does it really count as tying up with duct tape?" Dad asked. "I think taping me up would be more accurate."

"I stand corrected," Liz said. "Tape him up. Just do it."

She kept the gun on us as I taped Dad's hands behind him, and then she ordered him to lie down, facedown, so I could tape his feet together. And roll Dad's flashlight over where she could pick it up. Which she did, very, very carefully, feeling the floor for the flashlight with her left hand without taking her eyes off me. Or, more important, without taking her gun off me.

"Okay," she said when she had the flashlight. "Now you sit down and —"

"What's going on here?"

A stocky form appeared in the other library door. Roger.

"I said what's going on here?" he repeated.

"Put your hands up," Liz ordered.

He blinked at her. She raised the gun a little higher. He raised his hands.

"Very good," she said. "Now lie down on the floor."

He started to do so, slowly. But when he was down on one knee, and no doubt thought her suspicions were somewhat lulled, he suddenly lunged to the left, trying to duck behind a shelf.

It might have worked if he hadn't been

standing on one of the loose tiles, which slipped out from under him as he lunged. He fell, hitting his head with an audible thud on the bookcase for which he'd been aiming.

And even so, his lunge might have given me a chance to escape and run for help. I threw the duct tape at Liz and made a leap for the door as soon as I saw him move.

Unfortunately, my throw went wide, and as I was trying to leap outward, I ran into someone else trying to leap inward. Luis. We cracked heads and both fell down in a heap in the doorway.

The grand escape attempt ended with the three of us lying on the floor, nursing our heads. At least Luis and I were. Roger seemed to be out cold. Liz stood looking down at us, still holding the gun.

Some people have far more luck than they deserve.

"Crawl back in here and lie on the floor," Liz ordered.

We crawled. Luis and I crawled, anyway. Roger only moaned softly.

"You were doing such a fine job," Liz said, kicking the fallen duct tape back toward me. "Carry on."

So I taped Luis's hands and feet, and then Roger's. Roger began drifting back to consciousness only when I was finishing off his feet.

"That'll do for him," Liz said. "Lie down."

I did — slowly — and then I steeled myself. She would have to get closer to tie my hands. And I had to make my move as soon as she got close. A move she'd be looking for, of course. But I was bigger than she was, and even with my injured hand, I could overpower her if I could just knock the gun away.

"Now —," she began, and we heard the office door open and close.

"Now what," she muttered, and slipped into the shadows to one side of the library door. I couldn't see if she was looking at me — was now a good time to make another escape attempt?

We heard soft footsteps approaching.

"Hello?" called a voice.

Dr. Lorelei.

Roger moaned softly.

"Is that you, Rosenkavalier?"

Rosenkavalier? Evidently Dr. Lorelei hadn't ignored my suggestion after all.

"Someone left the door open. . . . Did you come in here?"

Dr. Lorelei swayed into the room. Swayed, because she was wearing her four-inch heels again. I still found it hard to imagine someone her size wearing not only four-inch heels but also a low-cut, slinky black dress, but she was. And looking pretty damned good, if you ask me.

Of course, I might have been biased by the fact that another step or two would put her squarely between me and Liz. And more important, between me and Liz's gun. Come on, Lorelei, I silently pleaded. Just one more step and I can make a leap for the other door to fetch help.

Her foot moved. I braced myself for the leap. Then her eyes glazed over, her body stiffened, and she fell over, face first, revealing Liz standing behind her. Since the gun was now pointing straight at me again, I deduced Liz had beaned Lorelei with the flashlight she was holding in her left hand.

I followed Liz's glance from Dr. Lorelei to me and then back again. I did my best to look small and harmless. Normally it's hard for me to pull off, but compared with Dr. Lorelei in spike heels, even Godzilla would look harmless.

"Tie her up, too," Liz said, kicking the tape back to me.

"Tape, remember," Dad said helpfully.

"Meg, what's going on, anyway?" Luis asked.

"Wha's going on?" Roger slurred.

"Shut up, all of you," Liz said. "Tape her up."

"Liz killed Ted," I explained to Luis.

"I thought you said Roger killed Ted," Luis said.

"I thought he might have," I said. "Looks like I was wrong."

I taped Dr. Lorelei's hands and feet. I pretended to have trouble getting the tape off the roll, in the hope that she'd wake up while I was still half-finished. No such luck.

"This is getting very untidy," Liz said, frowning at the litter of bodies spread across the room. "Line them up."

"You've got to be kidding," I said.

"Line them up," she said, raising the gun slightly.

"One neatly aligned set of hostages, coming up," I said, grabbing Luis's feet.

"That's a little better," she said when I finished dragging everyone into a single neat line on the floor along one wall. With, alas, space left over for me. Space I didn't intend to occupy if I could help it.

"Now," Liz began.

"Lorelei?"

We glanced over to see Dr. Glass, the mousy therapist, standing in the doorway, holding a single red rose in his hand.

"Put your hands up," Liz ordered.

"Lorelei!" Dr. Glass exclaimed, seeing the lady herself trussed up with silver duct tape. He gave a great leap, and Liz jumped back, but instead of attacking her like one of the sane, sensible heroes in his books, he threw himself on top of his wife and began rather ineffectually trying to remove the tape from her mouth.

"I said put your hands up!" Liz shouted, and threw the flashlight at him.

He either fainted or pretended to go limp. I couldn't tell which, even while I was taping him up. So much for life imitating art.

"Now that we've taken care of that, lie down," Liz said.

I obeyed, as slowly as I thought I could without setting her off.

"Now —"

"Hey, what's going on in here?"

Frankie, Keisha, and Rico appeared in the door of the library, their hands full of paper, pencils, dice, and other role-playing paraphernalia.

"This is really starting to piss me off," Liz said through her teeth.

"Meg?" Frankie said, looking anxious. "Is something wrong here?"

"Liz is holding us hostage," I said.

"I have a gun," Liz said. That much was obvious; she was waving it rather erratically, and the three newcomers seemed transfixed by it.

"Meg?" Frankie bleated.

"She can't shoot all of us at once," I said.

"Put your hands up and drop to the floor," Liz said.

"Rush her. On three," I suggested.

"I mean it," Liz said.

"One."

"Meg," Frankie pleaded. "What are you — ?"

"Two."

"Hit the floor!" Liz shrieked.

"Three!" I said, but I didn't end up jumping — Frankie, Keisha, and Rico threw themselves on the floor, scattering dice, pencils, and papers everywhere.

"That's better," Liz said. "Now tie — tape them up."

I followed orders. I taped their arms and legs, and then, in deference to Liz's preference for order, I dragged them into a second neat row in front of the first.

I looked up to Liz for approval when I'd finished. I hoped she wouldn't tell me to even up the rows. The back row contained

Dad, Luis, Roger, Dr. Lorelei and Dr. Glass.

The front row, with Keisha, Frankie, and Rico, was two bodies shorter.

"Fine," she said.

That was a relief. I could have dragged Dr. Glass from the end of the first row to even them up, but he and Dr. Lorelei were staring soulfully into each other's eyes, oblivious of the rest of us. And rubbing noses. In retrospect, perhaps I'd find that touching. At the moment, I was just glad they were quiet.

The rest of the prisoners were staring hopefully at me.

Liz was looking up and down the ranks of prisoners with visibly mounting irritation. My spirits sank. Maybe she was going to have me even up the rows. Maybe even arrange them in height order.

"Dammit, why the hell are there so many people creeping around here in the middle of the night?" she finally snarled, stomping one foot.

Exactly the way I'd felt the previous two nights, when I was trying to skulk around an office that seemed suddenly more heavily populated than it was in the daytime.

But tonight, I was hoping a few more

people would show up, and that one of them would manage to get the drop on her.

Of course, to do that, he or she would have to be actually creeping, instead of thrashing around like a drunken giraffe. If you asked me, there weren't nearly enough people creeping around.

Perhaps I could get the drop on her myself. I had been so cooperative that perhaps she was beginning to take that for granted. I worked on trying to look apathetic and despondent, while actually keeping my body tense for a leap. And holding my bandage up in plain sight, to remind her that I was temporarily disabled.

"Come on, Ninja lady," Frankie said. "Fun's fun — why don't you let us go now."

"Ninja lady?" I echoed.

"Shut up," Liz said.

"That's what Ted always called her," Frankie said. "Cause she always wore black."

"Actually, he called her that because he'd seen her in action, negotiating a contract," Keisha said.

I sighed. If only I'd taken more people into my confidence, maybe I'd have found out Liz was the Ninja before the situation became quite this difficult.

Liz was digging in her purse. "Damn," she said. "I could have sworn I brought another clip. I'm not sure I have enough ammo for all these people."

"Don't you just hate that?" I said. "You plan a quiet little murder and all these freeloaders show up."

Liz just glared at me and continued rummaging through her purse — though, unfortunately, without quite taking her eyes off me.

"What kind of heartless cynic are you?" Rico exclaimed. "How can you make jokes at a time like this? This is serious!"

"Very serious," I said. "Or at least way too solemn."

Which seemed to baffle him. He stared at me, and looking back, I could see that I was doing so from the other side of a gap — in fact, an uncrossable chasm. The chasm between people who take life very seriously and those of us who laugh to keep from crying. The people who stand around lugubriously at funerals saying things like, "At least he didn't suffer" or "Doesn't she look lifelike?" and those of us who want to tell tall tales about what a wonderful old reprobate he was and imagine how she'd laugh if she could see the sideshow. The people who sob long-neglected prayers on the steps of the guillotine and those of us who know God will forgive us if we have to banter with the executioner to keep our courage up, as if laughter were a gauntlet we could throw in the face of death.

Or maybe I'm just a heartless cynic.

"Sorry," I said. "Just ignore me. It's how I cope."

"It's called displacement," Dr. Lorelei said. "Patients who —"

"Shut up!" Liz shouted. "All of you just shut up!"

They shut up. For about ten seconds. Then Frankie piped up.

"Can't we even — ?"

"That's it!" Liz shrieked. "I've had it. Gag them. Gag them all. I don't want to hear another peep out of them."

I've heard of Stockholm syndrome, when hostages start identifying with their captives and taking their side. I didn't think I was quite at that point, but I had to agree: things were a lot more peaceful when I'd put strips of silver duct tape over everyone's mouths. I felt a little guilty, but I could hear myself think again, and since I was the only one still able to do anything about rescuing us, if she ever gave me half a chance, I figured anything that helped me keep my wits about me was a good thing.

"That's better," Liz said. "I can hear myself think again."

Maybe it wasn't a good thing. It scared me that I was thinking the same thing Liz was thinking.

So use that, I told myself. If I were the one holding the gun, and my idea of what would be a nice, quiet way to dispose of inconvenient witnesses had gone to hell this badly, what would I be thinking?

No good. I'd be thinking how crazy it was, planning to shoot all these people. But for Liz, apparently, it was just another case of doing whatever needed to be done to take care of the problem. I could use that.

"Listen, I don't want to upset you or anything," I said, "but if I could make a practical suggestion . . ."

She gestured with her gun, in a way that I assumed meant for me to go ahead.

"With every person who barges in here, the odds of your getting out of this scot-free are shrinking," I said. "Why don't you just . . . well, you know . . . come clean. Turn yourself in. Everyone here knew Ted — I'm sure you could have a dozen witnesses to testify to what you had to put up with from Ted."

Around the room, silver-trimmed heads bobbed vigorously.

"With a good criminal attorney, you'd get off with probation or something," I went on. "Maybe even acquittal — the way the chief's been handling this, odds are he's made all kinds of errors that would help you get off — he probably has no chain of custody for the evidence. I'm sure there are procedural problems with the searches, or some of the people he's questioned."

"You've been playing Lawyers from Hell," she said. "I can tell. Everyone plays that damned game for an hour or two and thinks they know my job better than I do after three years of law school and four years of practice. Do you have any idea how hard law school was?"

"Yes, I heard all about it from Rob," I said. "He —"

"Rob!" she shouted. "He thinks he had it tough! Your parents paid his tuition, all his expenses. I had to work my way through college and law school. Do you think he has any idea what that was like? Any idea what I had to do?"

Something occurred to me — I remembered that on Ted's blackmail list, the Ninja's name had a note: "xxx pix."

"No, but Ted knew, didn't he?" I said. "The pornographic pictures, right?"

A long shot — but it hit home. Maybe a little too close to home.

"They were not pornographic pictures!" she shrieked. "I did an exotic dance act, period. They were publicity photos. Nothing more than that, no matter what Ted tried to insinuate."

"Still, it's not something you wanted people to find out about here on the East Coast, now that you're trying to make a name in your new profession," I said. "It's understandable that you'd resent him trying to drag all that up. Use that. I bet you could make it a feminist cause if you play your cards right."

"Oh, instead of the Twinkie Defense, we have the Pasty Defense?"

"The Twinkie Defense worked in the Dan White case," I reminded her. I refrained from mentioning that I knew this from playing Lawyers from Hell.

"Not entirely," she said. "He was still convicted. Of a lesser charge, but it was still a felony. You can't practice law if you've been convicted of a felony. I am not going to let this ruin my life. I worked too hard to get where I am."

"Your career means so much that you're willing to kill for it?" I asked.

"It wasn't just my career," Liz said. "It was for the good of the company. Ted was plotting something. Why do you think he was trying to blackmail people — not just me, but anyone he could manage. He was trying to get enough power to pull off something really big."

Maybe, I thought, but that sounded more like Liz thinking than Ted. I had a feeling the only thing Ted wanted to accomplish with his blackmail scheme was causing trouble. But I didn't think telling her that would be a good idea.

"Then use that," I suggested. "If you reveal what he was up to, I bet you can manage a plea bargain that doesn't even include a felony. But if you kill anyone else, you can't possibly get away with it."

"Just watch me," she said. "After I —"

"Police! Drop your weapon and put your hands up!"

Chapter 28

Liz froze — she didn't drop the gun, but she didn't do anything desperate, either, like whirl and begin blasting at the police. Which was a good thing. The voice had come from behind her back, but I could see that the figure standing in the library doorway wasn't the chief or any of his men. It was Michael. And my eyes were sufficiently adjusted to the low light that I could tell the object he was aiming at her wasn't a gun — it was his cell phone. I only hoped he'd turned it off before he drew it — even the most distraught homicidal maniac would be suspicious of a cop whose weapon began caroling Beethoven's "Ode to Joy" in the middle of a shootout.

"I said drop your weapon and —"

"Aaaaiieeeee!"

With a bloodcurdling shriek, a figure leaped out of the shadows and attacked Michael with a series of swift kicks and blows. Liz leaped out of the way as the two of them came sprawling into the library. Michael ended up flat on his stomach with the breath knocked out of him. But apparently he'd managed to land at least one well-aimed blow. His assailant was curled up in a fetal position with his hands between his legs. The cell phone landed a few feet from Michael's head and began tinkling out the "William Tell Overture."

"Oh," the assailant groaned. "I hate it when that happens."

"Rob?" I said, recognizing the voice. "Is that you, Rob?"

Michael couldn't speak yet, but he growled.

"Get your hands up," Liz ordered.

Rob put one hand up while the other continued to clutch his groin. Michael began raising his hands. Liz jumped to the conclusion that he was reaching for the cell phone.

"Don't touch that thing!" she shrieked.

Michael froze. Rob winced and quickly raised his other hand. The cell phone switched to "Auld Lang Syne," which I thought was an awfully tactless choice, under the circumstances. Apparently the fall had set off the feature that played all the tunes in the cell phone's memory, so you could decide which one you liked. I hated them all — what's wrong with a simple ring, anyway?

"Rob, why did you attack Michael?" I asked.

Rob raised his head, recognized Michael, and dropped back with a groan.

"I really blew it, didn't I?" he said.

"And Michael, what are you doing here?"

"I had a premonition that something bad was going to happen," he said. "So when you hung up on me this morning, I told the director I was having a family emergency and could we finish the big magical duel scene as quickly as possible so I could wrap up for the week. And then I caught the first flight I could get out of L.A."

"The white knight rides to the rescue," Liz said with a sneer. "Some rescue."

The phone chose this moment to switch to "Scotland the Brave." I pondered, momentarily, what would happen if you crossed a cell phone with an equally irritating Affirmation Bear and then stowed the idea away for future consideration.

"He tried to rescue us," I said. "He nearly succeeded. Rob, what the hell were you doing here?"

"When you said Dad was with you, I remembered that he was going down to the office to check something out, and I wondered what the two of you were doing," he said. "I figured you were detecting something. And then I saw someone sneaking up the fire escape and climbing through one of the back windows."

"That would be me," Michael said.

"Hey, at least I got that move right," Rob said, cheerfully. "Did you see how well I did it?"

"Fantastic," I said. Rob's face fell. Maybe I sounded too sarcastic. Ironic — it would be just Rob's luck that the one time in his life that he executed any kind of martial arts maneuver flawlessly it could very well cost him his life.

"I hate to break up the reunion," Liz said. "But you need to tie them up. Tape them up. I have some other work for you."

"I still don't understand how you think you're going to get away with this," I said, stalling for time as I fiddled with the roll of duct tape and the phone began playing "Für Elise."

"Don't worry about it," Liz said, gesturing with the gun. "I only hope I brought enough ammo for everyone. It would be so inconvenient if I had to go home to get more in the middle of this."

"You don't think the police will be a little suspicious when they find eleven bodies here in the office?" I asked. "You don't think maybe they'll look around pretty carefully to see who could be responsible?"

"The twelfth body will take care of that," she said.

"Twelfth body?" I repeated.

"Yes," she said. "Mr. Mason, our disgruntled ex-employee. Sadly, the police will find out tomorrow that he has gone postal, captured many of his former colleagues along with the boss who fired him, tied — taped them all up, shot them, and then turned his gun on himself. If I have enough ammo. I suppose I could just burn the place down, but I'd really rather not. Are you finished there?"

Alas, I was. Rob and Michael were taped up. As loosely as I could manage, but still, I didn't think much of their chances of getting loose. Unless she was serious about going home for more ammo, and lived pretty far out of town.

"Come with me," she said. She made a move to leave the library, and at that moment, the phone, now lying at her feet, broke into "Jingle Bells."

"Aargh!" she growled, and stomped

down on the phone. It took her half a dozen blows, but she finally damaged it enough that it gave up with a small, reproachful whir. Then she backed out of the library, gesturing for me to follow. I did, hands still in the air. She backed down the corridor, always keeping just out of reach, as I exited the library. Then she followed me down the corridor, barking orders when I was supposed to turn or stop or go through a door.

This is a good thing, I told myself. If I get a chance to make a move now, there's much less danger of hurting anyone else.

But she wasn't giving me a chance. Normally I admire efficiency in anyone. But I hadn't found a chance by the time we ended up outside the janitor's closet in the hallway.

"Open the door," Liz ordered.

I hesitated. I suspected she had Mason inside, and I wasn't sure whether he was still a live prisoner or whether she'd already turned him into the twelfth body. I'm not as squeamish as Rob, but I still wasn't all that keen on making the acquaintance of another corpse —

"I said open it," she snapped.

I braced myself and followed orders.

A duct-tape-trimmed face snapped up

when the door opened, squinting through a pair of oversize glasses that had been knocked askew. He was lying in the space previously occupied by the mop and pail that had been in the corridor. If only I'd taken the time to put them away, I thought, mentally canceling my plans to give the cleaners a tongue-lashing.

"This is Eugene Mason?" I asked.

"Drag him out," Liz ordered.

I examined Mason's face as I did so. He didn't look at all familiar for someone who had supposedly been hanging around the office for weeks.

He wasn't easy to drag, partly because he was a big guy — maybe 250 pounds. And partly because he was squirming as hard as he could.

I realized I could use that. He'd obviously been rubbing his mouth against something, trying to loosen the duct tape. I managed to turn him so his face was on the floor, and then stepped on the duct tape, ripping it more than half off.

"Help!" he shouted. "She's going to kill me! You've got to do something."

"I would if she didn't have that gun," I said. "Why do you think she's going to kill you?"

"Oh, nothing in particular," he said with

heavy sarcasm. "Except maybe the fact that she knocked me out, tied me up, and now she's waving a gun at me?"

"Let me rephrase that: Why does she want to kill you? Why you?"

"Look, you don't even have to give me the last check," he said, looking up at me. "I'll sign anything you want. Just let me go!"

"That's her call," I said, indicating Liz.

"Keep dragging," Liz said.

"Sorry," I said. "Just out of curiosity, have you been hanging around, watching the office?"

"Hanging around here? No," he said. "I got a job up in D.C., just after they fired me here. I don't have time to hang around in Caerphilly."

"Then what are you doing here tonight?"

"She called and told me Rob had changed his mind and they were going to give me my final paycheck after all. And I didn't have to sign their stupid agreement, just a receipt for the check. I was supposed to meet her here at the office after hours."

"Clever," I said to Liz. "And I bet the threatening phone calls were phony, too."

"Threatening phone calls?" Mason repeated.

"Absolutely brilliant," I said, not trying to hide the bitterness in my voice. "You had this planned all along."

"Actually, the original plan was to lure both him and Ted here at night, and make it look as if Ted had surprised him trying to break in," she said. "But when the mail cart suddenly appeared with Ted just lying on there . . ."

She shrugged.

"Irresistible temptation, I suppose," I said. "And you could still use your disgruntled employee as one of the suspects. Everyone believes in the stalking and the threatening phone calls, of course, because it wasn't just you reporting them. I mentioned them to the chief, and I bet you got other people to do the same thing. Rob, for example."

"Most people are so easily manipulated," she said with a smile that I would once have called sly. Now I was trying to decide between sadistic and just plain crazy.

"Keep dragging," she said.

So I kept dragging until we had Mason inside the reception room. By the time we got him there, I was panting from exertion. I was faking it, a little; I do have more upper body strength than that, but I figured if she thought I was overcome from the exertion, I'd have a better chance of getting the drop on her. I feigned exhaustion and let Mason fall to the floor with a thud by the reception desk — about where the mail cart stopped, I thought.

"Pick him up again," Liz said. "Or I'll get someone else."

"Right," I panted. "Just give me a second."

The door opened.

"Do you realize you left your dog in the car?" Doc said as he walked in, leading Spike. "It may be nighttime, but it's still in the eighties out there. Do you want the poor thing to — ?"

"Put your hands up!" Liz snapped. "Stop that immediately. Get back there!"

The last order was to me. When I realized that Doc's entry had distracted Liz, I made a wild leap for the reception desk, intending to vault over it and grab something — anything — that could be used as a weapon. I wasn't quite so tired as I'd been pretending, but I guess I was more tired than I realized. Instead of clearing the top of the reception desk, I landed on it and slid across. My foot caught on the upright pole of George's stand as I passed. The stand tilted way back and then righted itself with a snap as I fell off the desktop and landed on its base. George, though half-asleep, managed to keep his grip on the perch during the initial tilt, but then lost it when the stand snapped back, propelling him across the room like a misshapen cannonball.

Straight at Doc, whose hands had shot into the air on Liz's command. He was still holding Spike's leash, and Spike, to keep from choking, was standing on his hind feet. And not happy about it, from the sound of his barking.

When Doc saw George flying toward him, he dropped the leash and put his hands in front of him, either to catch George or fend him off; it was hard to tell which.

And when Spike realized he was free, he lunged at the nearest object. Which, bless his evil little heart, was Liz. He buried his teeth in her ankle.

"Get that thing away from me!" Liz shrieked. She was shaking her ankle, but Spike was doing his best pit bull imitation and refused to be shaken off.

I saw this from behind the reception desk, where I was frantically scrabbling to find something I could use as a weapon. But when I saw Liz aiming her gun at Spike, I decided I had to act, weapon or no weapon. Although she was probably as likely to hit her own ankle as Spike, the odds were better that she'd miss both of them and plug poor Doc, who was struggling with a very angry George. So I vaulted back over the reception desk, grabbed Liz's wrist with my right hand, and began smacking her in the face with my bandaged left hand.

We teetered back and forth a few times until I managed to bang her wrist hard against the edge of the desk. I must have hit a nerve or something; her right hand went limp and the gun fell to the floor. She shrieked and tried to claw at my face with her nails, so I hit her in the stomach, hard. She half staggered and half fell backwards, into the closet.

She landed in the box that held the Affirmation Bears, several dozen of which squeaked various encouraging affirmations as she landed. At least most of them squeaked affirmations. Obviously the box contained a few that the guys had been tinkering with. As I grabbed the gun and pointed it toward Liz, one of the bears produced a prolonged belch, and another squeaked "Hehehehehe . . . wipeout!" followed by a familiar riff of surf music.

"Don't move!" I said. "Doc, are you all right?"

"That was wonderful," he said. "Risking your life to save your beloved dog!"

"Yeah, right," I said.

I risked a glance to where Doc was half sitting, half lying. George had found a new perch, on Doc's head. The excitement had obviously made George sick to his stomach again. And from the many small claw and beak wounds on Doc's face I deduced that George had been fairly insistent about reaching his new perch, and Doc seemed eager not to move any more than he could help.

"Nyuk-nyuk-nyuk!" trilled a bear, alerting me to the possibility that Liz was on the move.

"Stay where you are!" I said. "I have the gun, and I know how to use it, too."

Which wasn't a lie. I may not have taken lessons, as Liz had, but I'd already figured out which end to point in her direction. If this species of gun had a safety latch of some sort, logically she'd already have taken it off while guarding me, so presumably if I pulled the trigger, bullets would emerge. Where they'd go was anybody's guess, of course. Unfortunately the odds were low that any of them would end up where I wanted them — in Liz's black, treacherous heart. Which was probably just as well; I might feel less bloodthirsty when the last hour or so was further in my past.

"Never put off till tomorrow what you can do today," a bear chirped.

"I'm not moving. They're just settling or something," Liz said hastily.

"Still, it's good advice," I said, stepping over Doc to get to the switchboard. Using my bandaged left hand, I managed to knock the receiver off the hook, snag the cord with my arm, and drop it down where Doc could grab it.

"I'll dial 911," I said. "You talk to them."

Once I was sure the police were on the way, I gave Doc the gun and told him to guard Liz for a couple of minutes. I left him sitting on the floor, clutching the gun with both hands and telling George, who was still perched on his head, what a good, brave buzzard he was. I went back to the library. Everyone looked up anxiously when I came in.

"Relax, folks," I said. "George and Spike saved the day, I've called the police, and Doc is keeping Liz out of mischief until they get here."

I could tell if they hadn't all been gagged I'd have heard a collective sigh of relief.

They all began squirming, each obviously hoping to catch my attention and get untied first. The room looked like my fifth-grade science project the day all the cocoons began hatching at once.

I played favorites and untied Michael first. He reacted the way you want the love of your life to react after a close brush with the grim reaper, and we briefly ignored the restless wiggling of the others.

"One of these days I will manage to rescue you, you know," he said finally, in a shaky voice.

"The way my life keeps going, I have no doubt of it," I said. "Go help Doc keep an eye on Liz."

"Oh, God," Rob moaned when I took off his gag. "This is terrible."

"Relax," I said. "The danger's over."

"Yes, but think of the bad publicity we're going to get," he said.

I was momentarily stunned into silence. When had my happy-go-lucky brother begun worrying about publicity? But he looked so miserable that I took pity on him.

"Don't worry," I said. "It was a lawyer gone bad. Can't you see the headlines already: Real Life Lawyer from Hell Attacks Mutant Wizards CEO. Hit Game Comes to Life in Hostage Crisis. You couldn't buy better publicity if you spent millions."

"You think?" Rob asked, rubbing his wrists.

"Sales will go through the roof," I said. "Go untie Dad."

I headed back to the reception room. Not that I didn't trust Michael to keep Liz neutralized. But Chief Burke had a very big "I told you so," coming, and the way I wanted to deliver it was to have him walk in to find me holding a gun on the real killer.

I never claimed to be subtle.

It was several more hours before Michael and I finally got back to the Cave.

"I could sleep for a week," I said, gazing fondly at the lumpy sofa bed and thinking how wonderful it was that I'd been too busy that morning to transform it into its sofa incarnation.

"We could fly back to California in the morning," Michael said. "Give me one good reason why we can't do that. In fact, give me one good reason why we can't just get back in the car and drive up to Dulles right now."

"I'll give you three," I said. "One, I'm too tired to pack right now."

"I could pack for you."

"Two, I don't plan to wake up till to-morrow afternoon."

"Yes; but what about tonight?"

"Three, we have better things to do to-night," I said, hitting the light switch.

"You're right," Michael said, a little later. "Tomorrow afternoon."

Chapter 29

"You've finished everything you need to do at Mutant Wizards," Michael said, finishing the last of his morning coffee.

"Just sit on the suitcase so I can close it."

"Here, let me do it. You've proved Rob's suspicions were right, there was something fishy going on, and you've exposed the perpetrator, not to mention solving Ted's murder. I don't see why you need to go back there."

"I just need to pick up a few things and delegate a few things," I said. "It won't take more than an hour, and we've got plenty of time. You booked the three p.m. flight, right?"

"Yes, but I was hoping we could drive by and take a look at our house before we left," he said.

"Our house?"

"Yes . . . I've got the house," Michael said.

"House? What house? Not the one with the five-and-a-half-foot ceilings?"

"No — Ted's house. Edwina Sprocket's house. Home of the attack moose. I was going to surprise you — after you told me about going there, I put in a bid on it — and I got a message yesterday afternoon that Mrs. Sprocket's heirs accepted."

He was grinning from ear to ear, obviously waiting for me to shout with joy. All I could think of was the long string of zeroes at the end of the sale price.

"Michael, we can't afford Mrs. Sprocket's house," I said. "I know what they're asking, remember?"

"I got them to knock the price down," he said.

"Knock the price down? Every house that's been sold in Caerphilly over the last year has gone for fifty to one hundred percent over the original asking price, and you got them to knock the price down? How?"

"I agreed to take the house as is," he said.

"As is?" My jaw dropped. For some reason, I kept seeing tiles raining down from the roof, although there were probably other areas of the house equally in need of complete replacement. Like the plumbing and wiring. And possibly the supporting beams.

"Yes. Oh, and we give them ten percent of anything we make selling the contents."

"Selling the contents? 'As is' includes taking the contents?"

"Yes — apparently they didn't want to take the trouble of having them appraised and sold."

"Michael, were you listening when I told you what the place was like? How run-down it was? How completely packed with clutter?"

"Your dad says the family will all pitch in to help fix it up."

Yes, I was sure they would, but I'd have a hard time thinking of any relatives I'd trust to hammer a nail in straight, much less do the kind of work Mrs. Sprocket's house would require.

"And who knows?" Michael continued. "Maybe we'll find some valuable antiques in the clutter. Apparently, your mother knows all kinds of appraisers and antiques dealers."

Yes, she did, though her experience with them was almost entirely connected with buying hideously expensive objects, not selling household junk.

"She says she'll come up and help."

Come up and see if she could abscond with anything that struck her fancy, more likely. Never mind; she could have every antimacassar in the house as long as she took them away. And helped clear out the rest.

"You don't seem happy," Michael observed.

"I'm overwhelmed," I said. "It's going to be a lot of work."

"It will still take weeks and weeks to clean up all the red tape," he said. "Time for us to rest up in California."

Yes, and possibly time for me to find someone we could hire to do some of the worst of the renovations and junk removal. If we could still afford to hire anyone after buying the damned thing.

"Okay," I said. "I'll make it as quick as I can at Mutant Wizards, and we'll go by the house on our way to the airport."

Actually, I wanted to talk to Rob — I felt bad about just leaving him without formally resigning.

Of course, the first person I ran into was Doc.

"Great news!" he exclaimed when he saw me. "I've found George a place to live. It's a raptor sanctuary — they have special facilities for injured or elderly birds. He

434

can live out his life with dignity in much more natural surroundings."

"That's great," I said. "You can take him anytime."

"Small problem," Doc said, looking sheepish. "He doesn't seem to like me."

Yes, George definitely didn't like Doc. He shrieked whenever Doc tried to go near him. I couldn't blame George. I think I'd dislike anyone who tried to throw me out of a second-story window, and for that matter, George had no way of knowing that Doc wasn't responsible for the short, involuntary flight that had propelled him into Doc's arms the night before. Doc looked crushed; he obviously wasn't used to rejection by nonhumans.

"Feed him a mouse," I advised. "He always warms to anyone who feeds him."

I explained where to find the mice and the microwave, and Doc loped off, looking hopeful.

Meanwhile, I did a turn through the office, saying good-bye and good luck to various people. Rob wasn't there, though. In fact, a lot of people were missing, probably inspired by the cooler weather to play hooky.

I left a note for Rob and headed back to the reception area.

Doc had returned with George's dinner. I could see that George was already feeling friendlier toward the vet. He started doing the hunching act when he saw his dinner.

I left them to it. Jack and Luis were arriving in the reception room, visibly exuberant about something.

"Morning," Jack said while Luis went over to the window.

"Yes, that's him," Luis said. "He'll be up in a few minutes."

"Who?" I asked.

Luis and Jack exchanged a grin.

"So, do you want to know what's in store for Roger?" Jack said.

"Something mildly unpleasant, I hope," I said.

"What do you have against this Roger guy?" Michael asked.

"Wait and see," I said.

"More than mildly unpleasant, if you ask me," Jack said. "And I doubt if the legal authorities will allow us to avail ourselves of Roger's talents for much longer."

"I assume you've got something on him for the porn operation," I said. "Since he had nothing to do with the murder."

"Since Ted was blackmailing him, too, it's not completely unrelated to the murder," Jack said. "But yes, it's about the porn site."

"It would have taken us half the time to figure out what he was up to if we'd been working together," Luis grumbled.

"Less than half," Jack said. "Not only did we each have to do all the same steps to figure out what Roger was up to, we also had to eliminate each other as suspects when we figured out someone else was trying to hack the same site."

"Sorry, but when I asked, I hadn't exactly eliminated either of you as suspects. In the murder."

"True," Jack said. "Okay . . . Roger has definitely been running a number of porn sites."

"Can we have him arrested?"

"Not for the sites, no," Jack said. "Pornography isn't actually illegal, you know."

"Unless it's child pornography," Luis put in.

"Yes, if we'd found any child pornography, we could have the FBI all over him," Jack agreed.

"But apparently even Roger has some standards," Luis said.

"Or maybe just a well-developed sense of self-preservation," Michael suggested.

"Any chance he's just hidden the illegal

stuff better and you'd find it if you kept looking?" I asked.

"We've looked," Jack said.

"Brother, have we looked," Luis said, rolling his eyes.

"Oh, come on," I said. "It wasn't that unpleasant, was it?"

They exchanged a glance.

"Oddly enough, it was," Jack said.

"After the first few thousand pictures . . . ," Luis said, and shrugged.

"Do you feel a strange compulsion to go watch one of those period movies where everyone gets all hot and bothered when the heroine unbuttons her glove?" Michael asked.

"Yeah," Jack said, laughing. "Right now, that's about my speed."

"Maybe I should try that," Luis said. "I couldn't even get into Disney cartoons last night. Cinderella's got this whole foot fetish thing going, and the Little Mermaid's costume shows way too much skin."

"Are you telling me that Roger's site is so perverse you're both considering vows of celibacy and there's nothing we can do about it?"

"Not the pornography," Jack said. "But he is using hardware, bandwidth, and IP addresses that belong to Mutant Wizards."

"That's illegal, right?"

"Very illegal," Jack said. "He's history as soon as Chief Burke shows up to arrest him, which should be —"

"Right about now," I said as the office door opened to reveal the chief, followed by several uniformed officers.

"Glad to see you, Chief," Jack said, holding out his hand.

"A lot more glad than you were yesterday, I expect," the chief said, shaking the offered hand. "So where's this evidence you want to show me?"

"Right this way," Jack said, leading the chief out of the reception area.

"So we show Chief Burke the evidence, and he arrests Roger?" I said.

"I think he's going to get fired before he's arrested," Luis said.

"Fired? Who's going to do that?" The last several times Mutant Wizards had fired anyone, I recalled, they'd dumped the job on Liz, due to Rob's complete inability to say a harsh word to anyone.

"Some people thought maybe you could do it," Luis said. "But Rob says the chairman of the board will take care of it."

"The chairman of the board?" I repeated.

Luis nodded.

"I'd better go see if they need me," he said, and ducked out of the room.

"Who's the chairman of the board?" Michael asked.

"Mother, of course," I said. "She came up this morning, armed with all her decorating supplies. Lucky for us last night's excitement has distracted her from measuring the Cave for drapes."

"Your mother's going to fire Roger?" he mused. "That should be worth seeing. Not that we're going to stay to see it."

"Of course not," I said.

"Come take a look," Luis said, sticking his head back into the room. "Roger found out what we did to his site."

"You mean you didn't just shut it down," Michael asked.

"That would be too easy," Luis said.

"So what did you do?" Michael asked.

"It was Meg's idea."

"My idea?" I exclaimed. "You mean you really did that?"

"Did what?" Michael asked.

"We took down his site this morning," Luis said. "After backing up everything to turn over to the cops, of course — and replaced all the pictures."

"With screen shots from Nude Lawyers from Hell," I explained. "I suspect that after the initial surprise, traffic on his site is going to drop way off pretty soon. Did you get his backup CDs?"

"Oh, we got everything," Luis said, chuckling.

We followed Luis out into Cubeville. Roger was standing in an open space in the middle, holding a CD in each hand. A dozen or so CDs were lying on the floor around his feet.

"Dammit!" he yelled, shaking the CDs over his head. "I want my files!"

Smothered laughter rippled through the room, and then, from behind him, a CD arrived, rolling on its edge like a hoop, until it hit his foot and plinked to the ground with the others. Roger whirled as if attacked.

"I want my files!" he bellowed again.

"Roger, dear, we need to talk to you."

Roger whirled again to face Mother, who had come up behind him, a bland smile on her face. Roger froze, like a mouse that suddenly spots a snake. If it had been anyone but Roger, I'd have felt sorry for him. Mother gestured, and Roger followed her into the conference room. I could see through the room's glass walls that Rob, the chief financial officer, the human resources person, Jack, and Chief Burke were already waiting inside.

"I'd better see if they need me," Luis said. "You want to get in on this?"

"You'll manage without me," I said, and he scurried off.

"Meg?"

I turned to see Doc peering out from the reception room.

"Do you want to say good-bye?" he asked.

"Oh, right," I said, grabbing his hand and shaking it. "It's been great meeting you."

"Thanks," he said. "Actually, I mean to George and Spike. I'm ready to leave now."

"Spike?" Michael said. "You're giving him Spike?"

"Not giving," I said. "He's going to take Spike for training."

"Aggression-reduction therapy," Doc added.

"I cleared it with your mother," I said. "She was very pleased to learn that Spike would be spending a rejuvenating few weeks in the Caerphilly Canine Rest Spa."

"I really owe you one for that name, by the way," Doc said. "That's going to double my business; I can tell already."

We followed Doc to the reception area and bade farewell to George and Spike.

Neither of them seemed upset at the idea of parting from us, and unlike Michael and me, they weren't particularly good at faking it.

"Here, let me help," Michael said, taking Spike's leash so Doc would have both hands to hold George's cage.

"I'll meet you down at the car in a minute," I said. "I just need to get a few things from the reception desk."

"You're not going to take all that to California?" Michael said, looking dubiously at the copier-paper box I was packing.

"No, but I don't want to have to come in here to get any of it when we get back in town," I said. "Way too dangerous — before you know it, I'd agree to help out just for a little while."

"Good thinking," he said. "See you down at the car."

As I was finishing up my packing, Chief Burke strolled up.

"I guess I have to thank you," he said, offering his hand. "Not that we wouldn't have figured out who the Ninja really was sooner or later."

"Might have taken you a while," I said. "Up until she pulled a gun on us, I thought she was the Iron Maiden."

"Oh, no," he said, chuckling. "You were

the Iron Maiden. We found several earlier versions of that blackmail file on his hard drive, and the first time the Iron Maiden appeared was a day or two after you came on board here."

"That's the last mystery solved, then," I said. "I can leave with a clear conscience."

"You're leaving?" he said.

"Not leaving Caerphilly, except for a vacation," I said. "But yes, my days at Mutant Wizards are over, thank God."

"That's a pity," he said. "I guess you won't get to work on that new game your brother talked me into helping him with."

"Let me guess: he's doing Cops from Hell."

"Please," the chief said with a frown. "Police from Hell."

"Sounds like a winner," I said. "Good luck with it."

"Ah," he said. "Here they are."

Several uniformed officers appeared, escorting Roger. The chief watched with satisfaction as they herded him out the door, then tipped his hat and followed them out of the office.

"So you're leaving us."

I turned to see Jack Ransom leaning against the entrance wall.

"I've done what I set out to do," I said.

"And running an office really isn't my line."

"That's a pity," he said. "You're good at it. Only a couple of weeks, and already things are light-years better."

"That's because all the real problem cases have been killed off or arrested," I said.

"And just when I thought things were going better for me, too," he said. "Did you hear about my promotion?"

"No — what to?"

"Head of all development," Jack said. "Apparently Rob was waffling on who to choose — wasn't sure I had the necessary daring and creativity, he said. But when he found out I was responsible for the Nude Lawyers from Hell version, that clinched it."

"So all's well that ends well," I said.

"Almost all," Jack said. "I was hoping the absent boyfriend would turn out to be . . . well . . ."

"Permanently absent?" I suggested.

"Or maybe a myth to scare away people like Roger," he said.

"Sorry," I said.

And I was. Sorry, that is. Not that it changed anything. But with Michael waiting for me in the next room, I felt safe admitting, at least to myself, that the chemistry worked both ways. I was attracted to Jack, and if things had been different, it would have been fun finding out if it was more than a passing fancy. And he was right — I was good at this office stuff. Not managing the switchboard, but organizing things, keeping them moving. Running things, so Rob and the programmers and artists could do their job. All the stuff I'd been doing the past few weeks — and all the stuff Liz had been doing, too. Rob needed someone to do all that. If I didn't have my blacksmithing career, I might find I could be very happy working at Mutant Wizards, and if I didn't have Michael . . .

I allowed myself, just for a moment, to imagine that there was another Meg. A Meg who, instead of falling in love with wrought iron at twenty was still, in her thirties, looking for her place in life. A Meg who hadn't ever walked into a dressmaker's shop to be fitted for a bridesmaid's gown and met the most drop-dead gorgeous man she'd ever seen. I could see that other Meg very clearly. I could see her staying on at Mutant Wizards, gradually taking over the practical side of running things, getting to know Jack better. It wasn't a bad life she'd lead. Maybe even a better one in some ways. Or maybe it only seemed better because I didn't know the complications it would bring, while I knew all too well the complications of the life I had — the financial instability of blacksmithing, the chaotic juggling act that would probably always be part of Michael's and my life together. Yes, probably a good life. But it wasn't my life. Not the life I'd chosen and was choosing again.

"If I had two lives," I said aloud. "I could see spending one of them here. But I don't; and I need to get back to my real life."

Jack nodded with a wry smile, saluted me, and strolled out of the reception room.

I wrote my name on the box, left it by the reception desk where, surely, someone would eventually remember to pick it up and drop it off at the Cave, and headed for the parking lot.

So now I knew where everybody had gone.

To my left, I saw Dr. Lorelei and the burly anger-management therapist talking intensely with Keisha and Rico. I drifted over to where I could eavesdrop.

"I love it!" Rico was saying. "Shrinks from Hell!"

"It could be a very important thera-peutic tool," Dr. Lorelei said.

"Yes," Keisha said, nodding. "It's got to be authentic and genuine."

"And a hell of a lot of fun," the burly therapist said. "That's more important, if you ask me. Make it fun, so people will want to play."

Wonder of wonders, I thought. The Hatfield therapists and the McCoy program-mers were learning to coexist.

In another corner, I saw Dr. Brown talking to two programmers. They seemed to be discussing an Affirmation Bear that one of the programmers was holding. Oh, dear, I thought. I hoped my allowing the guys to play with the bears wasn't still causing trouble.

As I strolled over to intervene and take the blame, I saw the programmer put the bear down on the asphalt. Surprisingly, it stood up, instead of flopping over the way the bears usually did. Then the pro-grammer took out a small gizmo, like a television remote, and began pressing but-tons.

I heard a loud "urp!" and saw, to my sur-prise, that the bear's mouth moved when it belched.

"Excuse me," the bear said, and then

giggled. He didn't sound particularly penitent to me, but maybe there were limits to how much emotion you could expect from a plush toy.

The programmer pushed a few more buttons, and the bear began walking toward the therapist.

"Oh, my goodness!" she exclaimed as the bear reached out and hugged her ankle.

"Hiya, babe! How's tricks?" the bear said. And winked.

"Oh, that's wonderful!" Dr. Brown exclaimed, jumping up and down and clapping her hands. "That's absolutely wonderful!"

"How about another brewski?" the bear asked.

I didn't stay to see if they'd taught him how to drink.

I could see that most of the parking lot was filled with people doing some sort of vigorous leaping exercise. I strolled up to where Michael was watching them, with a bemused expression on his face.

"So what are they doing now?" I asked as two programmers and a therapist passed by, doing an involved step that looked as if they were trying to pedal miniature tricycles.

"Don't you recognize it?" Michael asked. The dancers had changed to some leaps that Baryshnikov might have executed, if he'd been born with more than the usual number of left feet.

"Am I supposed to?" I asked.

"Your father said you'd taught him this kata," Michael said.

"Kata?"

Most of the crowd in the parking lot now appeared to be imitating a gorilla lifting barbells while ridding itself of a hairball. As I watched, they returned to pedaling tiny tricycles while flapping their arms up and down as if they hoped to achieve liftoff.

"It's called The Buzzard Celebrates, according to your Dad," Michael said.

Rob whirled by, doing a step obviously inspired by the cancan, and waved cheerfully.

"It's certainly aerobic," I said.

"I told Rob we were taking off now," Michael added. "He said thanks, and see you in a few weeks."

We watched for a few more minutes as the programmers and therapists leaped and cavorted together — if not in unison, then certainly in unprecedented harmony.

"Ready to take off?" Michael asked.

"Way past ready," I said, heading for the car.

As we drove carefully through the throng of Celebrating Buzzards to the road, I caught sight of Dad, whirling by with the rest, executing a particularly ridiculous maneuver that seemed to combine a standing broad jump with the hokeypokey. He paused for a moment, winked at us, and then threw himself back into the fray.

"I think Dad's got everything under control," I said. "Step on it. We have a plane to catch."

About the Author

DONNA ANDREWS is the author of three previous books featuring Meg Langslow. She lives in Reston, Virginia, near Washington, D.C.

The employees of Thorndike Press hope you have enjoyed this Large Print book. All our Thorndike and Wheeler Large Print titles are designed for easy reading, and all our books are made to last. Other Thorndike Press Large Print books are available at your library, through selected bookstores, or directly from us.

For information about titles, please call:

(800) 223-1244

or visit our Web site at:

www.gale.com/thorndike
www.gale.com/wheeler

To share your comments, please write:

Publisher
Thorndike Press
295 Kennedy Memorial Drive
Waterville, ME   04901